MW01171183

Kidnapped Killer

Nina R Schluntz

This is a work of fiction. The characters depicted in this story are completely fictitious, and any similarities to actual events, locations or people, living or dead, are entirely coincidental.

No part of this publication may be reproduced, in whole or in part, without written permission from the publisher, except for the brief quotations in reviews.

Kidnapped Killer
Copyright © 2022 Nina R Schluntz
All rights reserved
ISBN: 9798838244437

Cover Design by Mary K. Wright

Issued 2022

Kidnapped Killer

CHAPTER one

Kidnapper

I stood in front of him, my palms sweaty as I gripped the baseball bat in my hands. I held it as if it could protect me from him, though he was the one needing protection from me.

Old habits die hard. I choked down the thought and concentrated on the present. I shifted the bat to my right hand and gently brushed the tip of it across his cheek. He jerked away from it, unable to see what the object was that had touched him.

He kneeled with his hands cuffed behind him. A dirty blood-streaked cloth tied around his face to acted as a blindfold.

"Who are you? Where am I?"

I wanted to speak, but if I did, he would know who I was, and the fear I heard in his voice would vanish. If he knew the man who had taken him was half his weight, he would laugh in mockery, regardless of the upper hand I held.

So, instead of a response, I swung the bat into his chest, hoping I broke a few ribs in the process. He sagged forward and coughed. The cough repeated over and over as if someone was clearing their throat to get my attention.

My eyes burst open, and I sat up, my eyes briefly locking with my classmate who held his hand in front of his mouth, posed in the common stance one took when coughing. He now changed from coughing to chuckling and turned his attention back to the front of the classroom.

"Why did you wake him?" the student next to him asked.

"His snoring was annoying," my awakener responded.

I tugged on the edges of my hoodie so it concealed more of my face and slumped back in my chair. I glanced to the other side of the room at the desks where my attention was better placed. The boy I'd imagined chained and passive in my basement sat three rows ahead of me and two rows over.

His blond hair was perfectly spiked, his pale skin untouched, no traces of the blood and grime I'd been imagining. He still upheld his position of power, but if my plans went as I wanted, he would not hold that status for long.

The frizzy-haired man seated next to him, who looked far too much like a hippie to truly be worthy of my muse's friendship, elbowed him as he glanced at me.

His lips moved, and although I couldn't hear the words spoken, I knew he was alerting Nic to my watchful eye, because Nic then turned his head so he could look over his shoulder. His brown eyes, a light chestnut color like an almond, glanced past me as if I were invisible to him. My stomach churned at the lack of attention and fueled whatever doubts I'd had.

He *would* notice me. He'd have no choice when chained before me, begging me to provide the necessities to keep him alive. His head turned back to his papers, uninterested in whatever he had been looking at behind me.

"Time's up," the professor said. "Hand in your essays as you leave, and I'll see you tomorrow."

On the board was whatever writing prompt we had been given. We were supposed to diligently write a two-page response to the question, but not only had I neglected to pay attention to the question, I hadn't read any of the assigned material. My presence in the class had little to do with learning or getting a few college credits.

"See you at Kenny's Pub," the throat-clearer said.

"Yeah, for sure. You'll be there too, right Nic?" throat-clearer's friend asked as Nic walked by them. Nic didn't stop. These insects weren't worth his time any more than mine was, but his hippie friend glanced their way and smiled.

"We will be. Around seven, right?" hippie asked, tucking his overgrown hair behind his ear.

Several people uttered confirmations, and nearly everyone was looking now and taking quick notes of where this gathering would occur. I wasn't the only one drawn to Nic. And I wasn't ashamed to admit that if Nic was going, I would go, just as everyone else in class would be adjusting their lives accordingly.

Kidnapper

At seven-thirty, because I did not want to be early and dawdle around waiting for him to arrive, I stood in front of the bar. I shoved my hand in my front pocket and felt the small round pill there. The internet promised the tiny capsule would take effect fifteen minutes after consumption and last for eight hours. It would weaken the person and make them more susceptible to manipulation.

Nic was bigger than me, so this was the easiest way to get him into my home. All I had to do was slip the tasteless pill into his drink. Then make sure he entrusted me to take him home and not one of the other vultures lurking near him.

I stepped into the bar, my black hoodie and jeans not matching the décor of the place at all but still, no eyes raised to look at me. I was as invisible as ever. I weaved through the crowded bar, bumping into a few people as I edged past full tables. I spotted Nic sitting at a table surrounded by his fan club of eight, with a smattering of more at nearby tables.

I reached the bar and wiggled my way between two seats. I waved to get the bartender's attention. He was a man that didn't look much older than me. His two-day scruff of a beard sent a trickle of excitement through me as I imagined it rubbing against the tender skin of my inner thigh.

"ID?" he asked. I hesitated, not because of his request, but because he was actually looking at me. "I can't take your order unless…"

I jolted out of my trance and presented the card for him to see that I was five years past the legal age limit for purchasing alcohol.

"What can I get you?"

"Two Negronis, please." I put my cash on the table with a generous tip. It was Nic's favorite drink, and I was confident it was the best beverage to entice him to consume. I noticed a bit of an eye roll from the bartender, but he poured the simple three ingredient cocktail and put both glasses in front of me.

I retrieved my pill and tucked it in my palm. I hugged the drinks close to me and as discreetly dropped the pill in one of them. I swirled both drinks around a bit, making it seem as if I was stirring them.

"One of those for me?" Nic asked, standing next to me. A jagged bolt of fear ran down my spine.

"Huh?" I managed to utter.

"Whenever I hear someone ordering a Negroni, my ears tingle. You can call it a spider sense if you will." He didn't wait for me to confirm if the drink was for him or not. He reached over and dunked his index finger in the liquid and used his partially submerged digit to slide the glass over to him. "If it's not for me, I'll order you another."

He gave the drink another stir with his finger, then raised it to his lips and swallowed it in one gulp. I stared at his Adam's apple as it bobbed. The glass clunked back on the table, and he licked the final droplets off his finger with a flick of his tongue.

"The bartender always ignores me," Nic said. "Thanks for saving me some time. I think he has a personal grievance against me."

"Why?"

He shrugged. "You'd have to ask him." He eyed my remaining glass. "You going to drink that one?"

"I can order another if you want to drink it," I said, by far the longest chain of words I'd ever spoken to him. He smiled, and my knees trembled. Nicodemus Greene had just smiled at me. Not past me, not through me, but directly at me, full eye contact and everything.

"I can't wait to see where this is going," Nic said. He took the second drink, and I watched him slowly sip it. This felt too easy, almost like he was the one entrapping me.

Kidnapped

There was a slight pulse of pain right between my eyes as if someone had flicked their fingers on my forehead in a playful manner. I fluttered my eyelashes, but they didn't want to open just yet. I reached a hand toward my face, hoping I could rub the ache away.

That's when I noticed the extra weight around my wrist and the gentle clink of metal. Interesting. I shifted my other hand and found it also had a brace of some sort on it. Distracted by this oddness, I shrugged off the sleepiness, opened my eyes, and sat up.

I stared at my hands laying in my lap. I was wearing chains. Not cheap shit either, these were good solid cuffs, and the brackets were thick, meant to tie up a bull or larger creature. I raised my arms and turned them around, analyzing the restrains from all angles. I was a bit impressed. Even if I broke every bone in my hands it would be difficult to slip myself free of the metal cuffs.

My eyes followed the chain and found them looped around a support beam for a house, it was a good foot thick, but wooden. Well, if I really wanted, I could slowly chew away at that wood, so it was a moderate flaw in my imprisonment. My feet were also unhindered, another disappointment. I was torn between my captor being a professional or amateur. I surveyed further and confirmed my location. I was in someone's unfinished basement.

"Ah, a bit cliché," I said to myself.

I tried to recall how I'd ended up in this situation. All I could remember was that stupid bartender at Kenny's Pub smirking at me while I was… The memory shrank away as floorboards creaked above me.

Light filled the room from overhead as the basement door opened. I bent my legs and rested my elbows on my thighs as I watched my captor descend the steps.

It was hard to see their face at first, since the light was behind them. Their silhouette defined them as a slender man. They reached the bottom of the steps and flicked on the main light for the basement, a dangling bulb that hung out of reach above us.

"You're awake already?" The man gaped at me, a four-foot-long iron pipe gripped in one hand and resting on his shoulder. Ah, so that was why my feet weren't chained. He was going to break my ankles with that pipe.

Now that the light was on, I could see my captor clearly. His name didn't come to mind immediately, but I had seen him before. Was he in one of my college classes? The kid who always sat in the back row with a hoodie on? This had to be the best view I'd ever had of his face and possibly the first time I'd ever seen his hair. He always had that hoodie on.

"You'll have to forgive me," I said. "Your name is escaping me. Can you refresh my memory? We have American Literature together, right?"

He stood there, not more than two feet from the staircase; his eyes locked on me. I wondered which part puzzled him more: my quick recovery from his drugs or the fact I didn't seem to mind my current situation.

"Eh, if you don't want to tell me, I'll just ask around tomorrow," I said. I pointed at his hair. "I like the haircut. You should show it off more." He had dark black hair cut very short, likely done himself. It was a stark contrast to my own spiked hair with frosted tips.

He narrowed his eyes and crouched so he was on my eye level. "I think you might just miss class tomorrow."

I grinned. Oh, I was going to enjoy this.

"Is that so? Education is important. I would prefer to not miss any school."

"That's going to be a bit of a problem since you're never leaving this basement."

"Never?" My senses were clearing, the last bits of his drugs fading away. I sniffed the stank air. "It doesn't smell like I'm your first guest to visit this place. Are the others still here?"

"What?"

I saw a glimpse of doubt cross his face.

"At least I will not be alone."

"You think corpses make good company?"

"Do you not? Why else would you have so many under your house?" I tilted my head and looked at the pipe. "Is that for me?"

"Aren't you going to ask why you're here?"

I shrugged. "If we're simply going to talk, are the restraints needed?"

He smiled, his grin quite wicked on his face. "What are you willing to do for me in exchange?"

"Do you mean to imply I can earn my freedom?"

"You just got here," he said. "I think we should start smaller." He lowered the pipe and twirled it around playfully. "Are you hungry?"

"I must earn my food?"

"Oh, yes, ask me to feed you."

I leaned back against the support beam. "Alright, feed me."

His expression darkened. "I have a nice heaping serving of—" He didn't finish. Instead, he let his actions complete his thought. He swung the pipe, slamming it into my left ankle with bone-shattering strength.

Kidnapper

My awareness came back in a quick rush. I looked up at the single bulb above me, idly resting on its long string. Is this what my victims did? Did they lay here and stare at that bulb? Wait, what was I doing? I sat up and scanned the basement. Where the fuck was he?

The chains were on the floor, coiled loosely around the beam my human captive was previously attached to.

Had I hallucinated it? Had I *not* kidnapped him?

But my arms were still sore from the strain of moving his unconscious body. He'd been heavier than I'd expected. And why did the base of my neck hurt? Had I fallen down the steps? Or had he attacked me and freed himself? But how? I hadn't brought the keys with me. I grabbed one of the cuffs, it was still locked. There was no blood. No sign that he'd forced himself free.

There was no sign of him ever having been here.

I backed away from the spot where he'd lain, my eyes glancing worriedly over at the steel pipe I'd been carrying that was now under a shelf in the corner.

I must have fallen down the stairs and knocked myself out. Then I'd dreamt that I'd kidnapped Nic. That's how badly I wanted him, so much that I was dreaming about the day I would finally have him in my grasp. Yes, that was the only thing that made sense. It had been a dream. How else would he have said the things he had?

Still. My hands kept shaking. I'd never had such a vivid dream. The shaking only got worse when I went to class—the one I had with smooth-talking Nic, the kid with outrageously good looks who treated everyone like scum but who people still adored because he was that suave. I hated him and wanted him at the same time. Which was why he needed to be mine and only mine.

I put on my red hoodie and hunched my shoulders as I walked into the classroom. Last night I'd had my lucid dream, and today, I'd awoken alone in my basement. Had I drugged myself? It was the only explanation.

The afternoon class was at a community college, and I was only taking one class. I paid out of pocket and didn't do any of the homework. I would fail it, but that was fine. I was here for Nic. The guy I'd met randomly one day at a gas station and begun stalking. I'd found out he was a full-time student at the local college, and I'd signed up for a class he was taking so I could get closer to him. I'd been enjoying my hunt for a full six months now, and we were two months into the semester.

Hippie-friend was sitting behind Nic today. In his place was a girl with locks as blond as Nic's. Suzie. I knew her name because people were constantly talking about her, and she'd spent not one but at least eight nights in Nic's apartment over the past six months.

Nic's eyes moved away from Suzie and her trilling laughter and locked with mine. He followed me with his eyes as I walked past his third-row desk and went to the very rear of the classroom. That was weird. He'd never looked at me. I was invisible to him. Scum not worthy of his attention.

I sat and folded my body into as small of a ball as possible, going into observation mode. The chair screeched as Nic got up. He limped slightly and kept his intense gaze on me until he was standing in front of the two-seat desk I'd chosen. He grabbed a chair from the desk in front of mine and sat backwards on it. His face lowered to mine, which hovered near the table's surface since I'd slouched so low. My arms were crossed in front of me, only my eyes visible between them and the hoodie I wore.

"Hi, Jimena," Nic said. "I didn't believe our classmates at first when they said that was your name. It sounds too much like a girl's name. But then I thought maybe the misgendered name is part of what made you into a psychopath."

He kept a straight face as he said it. I wasn't sure which shocked me more. The words he was saying or the fact he was saying them *to me.* I glanced at the group he'd been speaking with. They were all staring, looking as shocked as I was.

"What did you say to me?" I asked.

The darkness I saw in his eyes suddenly lifted, and the smile that I now recognized as a mask fell upon his face.

"Sorry, you said some weird shit last night. I guess you're just a bit different when drunk, but then, who isn't, right?" He dropped two crumpled bills on my desk. "For the drinks."

I stared at the twenties in front of me.

"I went to the bar?" *That part had happened?*

The dark cloud crept over his face. "Am I that forgettable?"

"Good morning, class. Everyone, take your seats," the professor said, clicking the projector on.

Nic relented and took a few steps away from me. "I'll see you tonight, Jimena."

"Why?" I croaked the words too softly to actually be heard.

He aimed that movie star smile at me before he turned around and took his seat.

Kidnapper

I raced home with more speed than I'd ever had before. But once I arrived, I couldn't bring myself to go in the basement. I hovered by the door and listened, hoping to hear him down there. Or not hear him.

I busied myself with supper by boiling some spaghetti noodles and covering them with sauce. I stirred it all together and portioned it into two bowls. Then sat at my dining room table and stared at them. Because if

Nic was in my basement, I should feed him. But if he'd freed himself and then returned, did I need to feed him?

"That's not possible, he can't come and go as he pleases. He's either down there or he's not." I had either imagined him in class today or imagined him in my basement. Although both versions of him had said crazy things, so maybe he wasn't in either place. Maybe I'd killed him and now his angry spirit was haunting me.

"Or I've lost my mind."

I picked up the bowls and moved to stand in front of the basement door. I stood there for a solid ten minutes.

"What the hell is wrong with me?" I stomped back to the kitchen and put the bowls on the counter. "I'll go down there and see if he's there. And depending on his behavior, I'll decide if I should feed him."

I resigned myself to it and went to the basement door before I could change my mind. I yanked the door open and strode down the steps, being careful because I did not want a repeat accident where I may or may not have fallen down these stairs.

Sitting next to the wooden support beam in the center of the room was Nic. His wrists in chains, his knees pulled to his chest. His hair still stunning and perfect. He didn't look at all like he'd spent the night confined in my basement.

His almond eyes looked at me, and he smiled. "Finally. I know I said corpses make for good company, but if you're going to kidnap someone, you could at least have the decency to spend some time with them."

Why did he keep saying weird shit like that?

"Were you in class today?" It was impossible, but I wanted to hear his answer.

"I told you education is important. I do not intend to let this situation keep me from maintaining my perfect attendance."

I scoffed. "You make it sound like you have a choice. You aren't my new roommate. You are my hostage. You don't get to leave."

"Are you going to break my ankle again?" He slid his foot out. His shoes were removed like they had been last night, and I could see the dark bruise on his left ankle. "You keep hurting me like that, I'll be inclined to hurt you back."

"You need to stop saying fucked up shit like that." I went to the shelf in the corner where I'd left the pipe. I bent to grab it, and when I straightened, he was standing next to me.

"What the fuck?" I jumped back and slammed into the shelf, knocking several items from it, and filling the small room with the sounds of shattering objects.

I staggered away from him, the shelf and fallen items between us. The cuffs were gone, and he stood before me completely unrestrained. He crossed his arms but didn't approach. I held the pipe between us.

"You should put the pipe down," he said.

I tightened my grip and held it between us.

"This is my last warning," Nic said. "Put it down."

"Why?" Maybe he was good at slipping out of cuffs, but from how I saw it, I still had the upper hand. I was armed, and he wasn't.

"Because you kidnapped someone who is more of a monster than you are, and if you strike me with that again, I may no longer find your antics amusing."

Kidnapper

I'd still swung, and now I was staring at the ceiling in my basement again. An odd sense of déjà vu crept through me. Every time I swung at him with that pipe, I passed out, and woke up sprawled on the floor, alone with an ache at the base of my neck.

I sat up and rubbed my neck. I scanned the basement, but like before, I was alone. I walked upstairs a bit more sluggish than I had the day before. Whatever he was doing that made me pass out was not something I could endure many more times.

Luckily, our class only met three times a week, so I had a one-day reprieve before I would see him in class again. Was I really believing that? Was I accepting that he was both here in my basement and in class?

What other options did I have? I went to bed and slept the deep slumber of the dead. My alarm blared, and I went through the routine of life, all of it meaningless. Only Nic mattered and whether my interaction with him was real or all in my head.

CHAPTER two

Kidnapper

I worked part time at a mall in one of the department stores. I mostly stood at a register that no one ever came to because who actually still shops at the mall anymore? To mix it up, I sometimes folded clothes. Normally, I would be scanning the crowds for someone who might be a good fit to spend a few days screaming in my basement. I'd daydream about how they'd squeal and what color their bruised flesh would become under the bite of my belt. But since the occupancy of my basement was currently uncertain, such ideals were absent today.

I folded new dress shirts in the women's department, preparing us for the spring clothing line, when a familiar voice spoke to me, his breath so close it tickled my neck.

"This is where you work, huh?"

I jerked and stumbled into the display, undoing several piles of hard work. I held myself upright with both hands sprawled on the table, preparing to toss handfuls of clothing at him in defense.

"I didn't mean to startle you," Nic said. "Would you prefer to keep our interaction strictly to the classroom and your basement?"

"What? What is with you?" I hissed the words at him in barely a whisper. I scrambled to collect the fallen garments, noting that the few customers near us were staring.

"I thought you liked me, Jimena? Isn't that why you kidnapped me?"

"You can't be at my work," I said, refusing to look at him. "I'll get in trouble."

"Oh, and we wouldn't want that, would we?" He snaked a hand over mine and squeezed. I couldn't tell if it was meant to be romantic or a threat. "Are you gay, Jimena?"

"Get the fuck off me!" I flailed wildly, and he let go at just the right moment to mess up my balance, resulting in me falling hard to the ground. I landed on my rear, tears of frustration blurring my vision, and when it cleared, it wasn't Nic standing above me but my balding boss. I swiped at my heated cheeks and erased the tears.

"What are you doing? Are you okay?" His face looked concerned, but whether for me or the possibly damaged shirts, I couldn't tell.

"Sorry," I said. I got to my feet, grabbing shirts as I did. "A jerk from the college I'm attending startled me."

He surveyed the area, as if preparing to take on the bully himself. "I don't see anyone."

"He probably ran when I screamed. I'll get this cleaned up."

"I'll do it. Go work in the back for the rest of your shift." He had a keener eye than I expected. My arms were trembling and some wayward customers were still peering. He lowered his voice. "Are you sure he didn't hurt you?"

"I'm fine."

I sorted boxes we'd received and tidied the returns area until my shift ended. I stood in front of the timecard machine and realized I didn't want to go home. At work, there was the hope someone would show up and chase the phantom away. At home? I should invite someone over. I was losing my grip on reality and experience told me isolation would only make it worse.

But what if he was there? I couldn't have my cousin chilling on the couch with me asking, "Who is that screaming in your basement?"

Twenty minutes later, I stood in my driveway and found myself dreading entering my own home. I couldn't move. I considered checking into a hotel. He wouldn't be able to find me, would he?

"What the hell am I saying?" I clasped my forehead and shook my head. Was I really afraid to go home because I was concerned the guy I kidnapped would be there?

I pushed my doubts aside and went inside the house. I refused to look at the basement door. In fact, I would ignore my basement completely. Fuck Nic! He could rot down there. I ate supper, showered, and settled in the living room to watch some television.

That's when the shouting started. The only words I could understand were my name. The basement was pretty sound proof, otherwise it would make for a shitty place to put captives. The fact I could hear him at all, meant he was standing right on the other side of the door, shouting at the top of his lungs.

I had two locks on the basement door: the door handle and a bolt. I turned around on my couch, peering over the back of it, and watched the door and its locks shaking as Nic pounded relentlessly on it.

If he could magically get out of the chains, why could he not enter the rest of my house? He was in class and at the mall, but somehow the first floor of my house was off limits? The lack of sense behind it only supported that this was all in my head.

But which parts were real and which were fake?

I crept toward the door and pressed my ear against it.

"Jimena!" He repeated my name over and over, then I heard him run his fingernails across the grain of the door. I jumped back and stared at it. How could this simple door entrap him when the chains didn't?

I slammed my palms on the door. "Stop it!"

He fell silent. I heaved, my heart thumping loudly. I would get no sleep if he kept this up.

"I'll come down if you promise to be chained and you promise to keep the chains on. Okay?" I'd become fully delusional, but at this point, there was little sense pretending he didn't have the ability to remove the chains at will. Still, knowing he had them on brought me comfort.

I yanked the door open, fully expecting him to be standing there, prepared to murder me. The entryway was empty. I rushed down the steps and flicked on the lights as I reached the bottom.

He was there, sitting on the floor, chains on his wrists, wearing the same designer sweater and torn jeans that he'd had on at the mall. They were not the clothes I'd kidnapped him in.

"Do you normally ignore your victims like this?" he asked. "Do you realize I've been down here several days, and you haven't offered me water?"

"What difference does it make? You keep leaving!" Whether I understood how or not, I'd accepted it as my current altered reality.

"Perhaps if the treatment in this establishment was better, I wouldn't need to."

"Treatment? This isn't a day spa!"

"Feed me."

"No!"

He stood and jerked his hands, rattling the chains. I couldn't help but flinch when he did it. I couldn't take this anymore. I'd brought the key with me this time. I unclipped it from my belt loop and shoved it in the lock on the cuffs.

"I'm freeing you, okay? You can leave."

"I don't want to leave."

"What?" I stepped back and watched in horror as he put the cuffs back on. "Stop that." I grabbed his wrist and tried to jam the key back in but he pushed me away. "You can't imprison yourself in my basement. Let me free you."

"Or what? Are you going to call the police? Do you think they'll believe I chained myself?"

"Why are you doing this?"

He shrugged. "I like your basement. The rent is very affordable."

"You aren't paying me any rent!"

"That's why I said it's affordable."

"Let me get this straight. I kidnapped you, and now you're refusing to leave?"

"That's correct."

Well, he did leave when I threatened him with that pipe, but I wasn't a big fan of how I felt afterwards. My eyes unconsciously went to the pipe that lay where I'd last dropped it.

"Don't." His tone was icy. *Did the pipe hurt him?*

"The only way to get you out of my house seems to be threatening you with that pipe, so if you don't want me to take another swing, you should leave."

He sunk to the floor, looking defeated. "Why did you bring me here?"

"Whatever my reasons were, they don't matter now. I want you out."

"This must be very odd for you."

"What?"

He moved only his eyes to look at me. "Your victims likely begged for their release until they lost their voices, and now, you are begging your victim to leave. How ironic. Tell me, did you ever let one of them go? Did you ever take pity on them?"

There was no real way for him to know if others had been where he was. I refused to admit anything.

"Or did you merely play games with them and give them false hope? You said I could earn my freedom. Are you still willing to play those games, Jimena, in the hope that you might be rid of me if you win?"

I didn't answer him. There was no reason to. I had no choice.

"Bring me food," he repeated.

I turned around and stomped up the stairs, not believing what was happening. Had I just become a servant to my own prisoner?

I cooked up some instant noodles, glad he hadn't made a request regarding what he wanted to eat. My stomach flopped as I wondered if his requests would grow more difficult over time. Mine always had, so why shouldn't his?

He was trying to groom me, but it was me that was supposed to be grooming him. But what could I do? Kill him? He kept doing weird shit when I turned violent so… I stared at the bubbling broth in the microwave. What if I poisoned him?

The flunitrazepam had worked in the bar. He'd become a staggering idiot, willing to do anything I'd suggested.

I'd wondered if the driver of the cab would remember us. Or would we become yet another drunken couple he drove home? We had to be one of several if not dozens he dealt with every night. The car parked in front of my house, and I paid in cash. I stepped out and told Nic to follow.

"I'm too tired, my body is heavy, help me." He managed to get out of the car but swung his arm around me and slumped against me.

"I've got you," I said. It seemed to take forever to progress up my walkway to the front door. He was barely helping us move. I unlocked the door and pushed it open.

"You need to invite me in," Nic said.

"Sure, sure, come in," I said. I didn't turn on any lights. I led us across the foyer to the basement door. I fumbled to open it, wondering if he would be able to stand well enough to go down the narrow steps. "Come down here. I want you to stay here."

"Huh?" He took a few disjointed steps forward, then stiffened. "Your house. I need you to invite me into your entire house."

"Later. I want you to see my basement first. We'll have fun down here."

The microwave beeped, breaking me from the memory. There was no way he was that good of an actor. The drugs had affected him, I had no doubt. I left the soup in the microwave and went to my bathroom medicine cabinet. If the flunitrazepam had worked on him, other drugs would too. And once I had him sedated, I'd cut off his damn feet. Let's see him come and go as he pleased then.

I grabbed various pills from the cabinet and dumped them in the soup. They were all downers, enough to put a fucking horse to sleep. I'd done a few stints as a cleaner in a nursing home, skimming various drugs from the patients until they'd caught me and fired my ass.

I added a ton of spices so the taste would be completely masked. Then, grinning like the proud fucker I was, I proceeded to the basement, holding the bowl with both hands.

He was sitting on the floor, one leg straight, the other bent so he could rest his chin on it.

"What took so long?"

"Perfection takes time," I said. I held the bowl out for him, spoon already in it.

"Feed me."

I furrowed my brow. "What?"

"How many times do I need to repeat myself? Feed me. I've been chained up down here for days. I'm too weak to feed myself."

"You left every day! Are you honestly telling me you didn't eat anything when you were out?"

"You wouldn't have to hand-feed me if you'd taken better care of me from the start. You're the one who kidnapped me."

Was it possible I'd kidnapped someone more mentally unstable than I was? I took several deep, angry breaths, then spooned up the soup and fed it to him like he was a damn baby. He swallowed the first spoonful and smacked his lips for a bit.

"You call this perfection? Did you put every spice you own in it?"

"You're my hostage. You have to eat what I give you." I shoved another spoonful in his mouth. The quicker he ate it, the faster I could cut his damn tongue out.

He managed to eat half of it before he pulled away, a hand on his stomach.

"You're cooking isn't agreeing with me. I don't want anymore."

I'd been stirring it between scoops, to make sure the drugs didn't settle on the bottom, so I was confident he'd gotten a good dose.

"You should rest then," I said. I sat a glass of water near him and a bucket. "For you to use as a toilet." Or for throwing up, which was highly likely.

He blinked his eyes a bit but wasn't asleep yet.

"So, what happens next?"

"You get some rest," I said. "I'll check on you in the morning."

"No, I mean…" He waved his hand around the basement. "Why did you take me? Is it just to lock me down here? What's next? What are you getting out of this?" His eyes went to my crotch. "Do we have sex? Do you rape your victims?"

I looked at him, my expression serious so he would understand I wasn't joking.

"We will have sex, but you won't be around to enjoy it."

I placed the bowl on the fourth step and sat on the third, intending to watch him until he passed out. I couldn't risk him vanishing on me like he tended to do. Keeping his eyes open seemed to be a struggle, so I didn't figure it would be much longer.

"What does that mean? Necrophilia?"

I nodded, only familiar with the word because I'd searched for it on the internet. I'd wanted to know if I had it in common with other people.

"You want to kill me and have sex with my corpse?" He leaned back, not appearing nearly as alarmed by this as he should. I dismissed it as a side effect from the drugs that had to be making him groggy.

"Incapacitated works too," I said.

"Huh. That…" His eyes closed and it took him nearly a full minute before he could open them again. "How long… do… you…" He slumped, slowly falling onto his side. I stared at him, uncertain if he were truly asleep or merely faking it.

I covered my mouth to quiet my own breathing so I could listen to his. I watched for any sign that he was still aware. I didn't think he would die. A normal person, for sure, but he had proved resilient.

I glanced at my watch and waited a full ten minutes before I moved. I approached him, worried he would have some final fit of strength and grab at me in a rage for being poisoned. I gave his thigh a kick, and he did nothing. I lifted one of his arms and dropped it. He seemed completely unconscious.

"Nic? Can you hear me, Nic?" I flicked a finger on his cheek. Nothing.

I grabbed some scissors and cut off his clothes. It was easier than trying to undress him. I added cuffs to his ankles as well. I needed to think of a better way to secure him so he would stop escaping. Maybe something around his neck.

I rolled him onto his back, his entire body exposed to me. I straddled him and put a hand over his neck, pressing into his esophagus and stopping his breathing.

"I could kill you now. Wouldn't that be unexpected?" And he would completely deserve it. His body didn't struggle as he suffocated. He was too sedated for his natural instincts to kick in. "Maybe, I will fuck you while you're still alive."

The thought of him waking up to find his ass sore and my cum splattered on him was already getting me hard.

"You want to live the life of my prisoners? I'll give you a taste." I grabbed a blanket from the far shelf and rolled it so I could use it to lift his hips. I wedged it under him and spat into my hand. I didn't like sex to be well lubricated. I preferred the rough grating feel of a dry hole, so a little spit on my dick was more than enough.

"If you hadn't brought it up, I wouldn't have thought of doing this," I told him. It didn't take much effort to get his body to open up for me. That was the perk of having an unconscious partner; no struggle and no worry of refusal.

I'd imagined doing this to him so many times it was hard not to come early. I wanted to savor this and fuck him long enough that he would feel sore when he woke up. I'd always imagined his body to be toned and perfect, but now that I was seeing it, I was annoyed by how correct I had been. He didn't seem to have any fat on him. Not a single part of his body jiggled as I thrust into him because it was all firm muscle.

"Why do you have to be so perfect, huh? If you weren't so perfect, you wouldn't be here. So perfect, so popular... Do you know how much that kills someone like me? Someone you never bother to even look at? I'm a fucking insect to you. But look at you now? Who's the insect now?"

I spread my palms across his pecs and felt his chest barely rising and falling with his shallow breathing.

"You are completely at my mercy." I shifted my weight to one hand and placed the other over his throat, my thumb digging into his Adam's apple. I licked the other side of his neck, tasting the cold sweat on his skin. I grazed my teeth across his collar bone and pushed up, letting go of his throat as I rose.

I froze mid-thrust. His eyes were open. But that wasn't the worst part. His eyes were this weird golden color, with a narrow sliver of black in the middle. His pupil wasn't round, it looked like the eyes of a cat and—and weren't they a different color before? What had happened to the almond eyes I loved?

"Nic?"

My world became a blur as my head crashed into the cold cement of the basement floor. I closed my eyes to fight the dizziness and figured this was when our fun would end. I would open my eyes and he would be gone, leaving me to once again doubt if this was real or all a hallucination. Maybe I had drank the soup and was fantasizing about this while my body struggled against the sedation cocktail.

"What did you do to me?" Nic rasped, his voice a bit raw from how much I'd choked him.

I opened my eyes and saw him on top of me, still naked, eyes still golden, chains still on, and… I twitched my hips to verify that, yup, my dick was still in him. He had flipped us over, so he was on top, but he'd kept us together.

"My stomach, what the fuck?" His weight dug into me as he struggled to stay awake. He put a hand on either side of my head and leaned forward, his face inches from mine. "What the hell did you use?"

I stared at him, unable to grasp what was happening. Only thirty minutes had passed, if that. How was he awake already? And out of everything that was happening, why was he only concerned about the cramps from the food poisoning?

He blinked his eyes a few times, and I hoped they would change back to normal, but they didn't. He leered closer, the level of intimacy making me uncomfortable. I didn't do close contact like this, not when a person was awake. I tried to turn my head to look away but he dropped his forehead onto mine, preventing all head movement with the weight of his skull that felt like a twenty-pound dumbbell.

"Did you think I was dead? Jumped on me a bit early, didn't you?" He moved his hips a bit and actually slipped my dick in and out. It was a weird and horrible sensation, like he was now the one raping me.

"Stop it." I put my hands on his chest and tried to push, but he weighed so damn much.

"Don't you want to finish?"

"Get off me."

"No."

I managed to turn my head so his stale breath was out of my face. I squirmed, but he kept on thrusting, and my dick wasn't listening to my objections. If I could just get it to go limp, this whole charade would end.

Our new position put his face dangerously near my ear, and he lowered his voice to whisper in it.

"Scream for me."

"What?"

"You get off on fucking someone who is unconscious. I prefer my partners alive and screaming. So, the sooner you start, the sooner I'll let you go."

"I'm not screaming. I'm not a damsel in distress."

His teeth bit into my neck, right below my jawline.

I screamed, more from the shock of what he'd done than from actual pain.

"Get the fuck off!" I swung my arm, and he sat up, dodging the blow and grabbing my wrist.

"Will you scream louder if we change positions and I put my dick in you?"

"No! Augh!"

"I think you will."

"No. Fuck. I'm screaming, okay?" But screaming on cue wasn't exactly easy, and it was more an odd assortment of wails, whimpers, and moans. I was finally saved when he grimaced and grabbed for the bucket. He had to get off me to reach it.

I scooted out of his grasp as he vomited. I went to the safety of the stairs and remembered how he'd freed himself from the restraints so many times before. With a tremble, I sprinted up the stairs and slammed the door, bolting it shut. I sank to the floor, my entire body shaking.

He'd raped me.

I was raping him, but somehow, he'd twisted it and… I glanced down and saw ejaculate on my shirt that was not mine. I wailed again.

Kidnapper

I was determined to kill him but also terrified to go back in the basement. He'd made me scared to go into a prison I owned. It was my house. He was my prisoner, but somehow, I'd become the victim.

I'd showered and scrubbed my skin raw to get the scent of him off me. I laid in my bed but couldn't sleep. Knowing he was down there plotting, waiting, had me on edge.

What if he came upstairs? I had no idea why he hadn't before, and now he was probably pissed. What if he killed me before I killed him? I squeezed my eyes shut and tried to dismiss the irrational thoughts.

Morning came, but I'd barely slept. I paced back and forth in front of the basement door. I needed to go down there and check on him. If he was asleep, I would kill him. If he was missing… Well, what then?

If he was missing, I would need to find him and drag him back here. He knew too much. He needed to die. His weird eyes flashed in my memory. That had to be my imagination or a really strange side effect from the drugs.

At five minutes until noon, I finally mustered my courage and unlocked the basement door. I pushed it open and waited, half expecting him to charge at me.

"Nic?" I edged toward the entrance and flicked on the light. I looked downstairs. From my vantage point I should be able to see him.

The cuffs were there, but no Nic. The place smelled of vomit. I slowly made my way down the steps, my eyes searching every hiding spot for him.

"Nic?" He was gone. Only a bucket full of barf remained.

I spent the next few hours cleaning the place up and getting rid of the smell. We had class today, so I didn't have to worry about when I would see him next. Kidnapping him at school wasn't an option though.

I considered skipping because I feared seeing a completely recovered and rageful Nic. But going to class was my best way to get information on where he was. If he hadn't recovered, he would be in a hospital. And if he'd gone to any form of authority, I needed to know.

His poisoning was enough proof to get police to come to my house. Maybe not enough to convince them to search my grounds for previous crimes but enough for them to get a warrant to search for evidence of Nic having been here.

I had to get rid of that evidence.

I barely took care of it all before class. I had to run across the campus to make it in time. I was huffing when I pushed the door open, the entire class pausing in their chatter to stare at me. Even the professor stopped writing on the board and glanced at me.

"S-sorry," I said. I pulled my hood over my head since it had slipped off during my sprint. My eyes went to Nic's empty seat. He wasn't there?

My foot tapped nervously the entire hour and a half of class. Nic never showed. As soon as we were dismissed, I went to the group of people Nic always hung out with.

"W-where's Nic?"

They ignored me.

"H-hey." I tapped Suzie on the shoulder, and she stepped away from me with a disgusted look on her face. "Where's Nic?"

"Sick, I guess?" She shrugged.

"At home or a hospital?"

All three of them stared at me as if the question was the oddest thing they'd ever heard.

"It's like a stomach bug or something," the hippie said. "So, home, I guess?"

I nodded and scampered away from them. I knew where Nic lived so going there wasn't a problem. I'd observed his house for several months. He lived with his brother in a third-floor apartment. They'd gone on a weekend trip once, and I'd snuck in while they were gone. I'd even spent the night there. I'd tasted their food and slept in Nic's bed. I had memorized the layout, and I knew exactly the kind of lock he had on his bedroom window.

Breaking in would be easy. Drugging him for a third time and convincing him to return to my house might not be as easy.

CHAPTER three

Kidnapper

I slipped in the window quietly, not turning on a light. I had memorized the layout of the room. There would be a single mattress on the floor and a lamp to my right. I let my eyes adjust to the darkness, and I could see his clothes arranged in various piles that were itemized in stages of cleanliness. There was no bulb in the fixture on the ceiling. His bedsheets weren't on properly, his pillow had no case, and the rod holding up the curtain was lopsided.

I pulled the rope from my duffle and reached to tie his hands. He was laying there, his hair slick from excess sweat. He moaned softly as if having a bad dream.

"Are you dreaming of being back in my basement?" I asked. I put the rope down and instead touched his forehead. He was warmer than he should be.

His eyes managed to flutter open.

"Jimena?"

"You weren't in class," I said. "And you didn't come back to my house."

"Your cooking made me sick."

"I'm here to take you back," I said. "I need you to get up."

"I'm staying here."

"You're in no condition to contest me. I could just drug you again." I didn't think that was needed, though. He seemed unable to fight back. He'd dressed in shorts and a shirt but had kicked his sole blanket to the side.

"If you're so keen on being near me, you're welcome to stay."

"Stay?"

"Yes, you can stay here."

"Like a sleepover?"

"Sure." He closed his eyes. He was inviting me to stay at his place? In his bed? My heart raced.

"This isn't a trick? I can stay? I can… I can sleep in your bed?"

"Wherever you want."

I laid next to him on my side, staring at him. My mind wondered if I had hallucinated his mutterings. Would he wake and refuse me? Have no memory of his invitation?

No. This was real. He had invited me into his bed, just has he had accepted a drink from me in the bar and gone home with me. I would not allow myself to believe otherwise. I was beyond giddy. This was all I'd ever wanted. I was being allowed into his life. I would never have needed to kidnap him if he'd simply done this from the start.

He'd shifted around while sleeping and was now facing me. His too perfect face started to annoy me. He was too attractive to actually want to be with me. People would mock us. I was too ugly to be with someone as handsome as him. He needed a blemish to mark him as an equally untouchable person.

I reached into my pocket and pulled out my Swiss Army Knife. I ran the blunt side of the blade across his skin. He didn't stir. His illness was so intense that he was in a feverish slumber. If his face wasn't so perfect, we would be more compatible. And if he wasn't going to stay in my basement all the time, it would be good for him to bear a mark that let others know he belonged to me.

I kept my blade sharp, so it took little effort to lance his flesh with it. I cut him, from an inch above his left eye, over his eyelid, down his cheek and stopped about half an inch from his mouth. His eyes popped open. They had that same oval iris of a cat from before.

"What the hell are you doing?" He hit me in the chest with both of his hands, knocking me off the mattress and onto the floor. He sat up and inspected his face. "What did you do?"

"I marked you." I folded my knife and put it back in my pocket, securing it in case he tried to take it from me.

"What? Wh—" He kept one hand over his injured eye. With his good eye, he stared at me, but the expression on his face, aside from pain, wasn't anger. He seemed… perplexed? Annoyed? He growled the kind of frustrated sound a parent makes at a child who'd spilled their drink by accident. He got up, stumbling from both the lack of depth perception and the fever he still endured.

"It's not deep, you'll be fine," I said. He yanked open his bedroom door and went into the hall. He turned back as I moved to follow him.

"Stay here." He pulled the door shut with a slam. I stared at it for a moment, wondering what he was doing. Getting his own knife so he could come back and butcher me? He hadn't hurt me yet, but something about those eyes told me he was more than capable.

I wasn't about to just wait here for him to come back and seek his revenge. I turned the knob and found no resistance. I slowly opened it and peeked out. The hall was dark but unoccupied. Light came from under one of the doors. Down the hall, in the living room, I saw more faint light and heard a conversation. The brother?

I stepped into the hall and went to the living room, wondering if Nic was reciting to his brother what had happened. What if they ganged up on me? Perhaps, I hadn't thought things through as well as I should have before coming here. I could just walk right by, give the brother some random excuse regarding why I had been here, and excuse myself out the front door. If Nic hadn't told him everything already.

I rounded the corner, my mouth open with a prepared story, and the words died in my throat. I'd seen the brother before but always from a distance. He was tall and lanky with long hair that went past his shoulders. He sat on the couch with a woman's head in his lap, her body stretched out on the couch. Her eyes looked right at me but were unseeing. Kneeling next to the couple was another woman, she had long hair like the brother, her back to me.

Both had their faces hovering over the prone woman and inhaled deeply, as if breathing in the scent from the base of her neck. I subconsciously touched the nape of my own neck, right where the ache always was when I woke up after Nic knocked me out.

The living room was dimly lit. The very air seemed grungy and filled with incense smoke. For a moment, I thought they might not notice me, then a light came down the hall from behind me. Nic had opened the bathroom door and not turned the light off. My shadow was cast directly upon the brother, and he looked up at me. His eyes were golden like Nic's. The woman turned her head and looked at me, hers also catlike. The stone-faced, possibly dead woman remained unchanged.

The group looked a bit like they'd come from a Rock concert, their clothes black and littered with holes. Their skin was adorned with metal, and the woman's midriff was exposed. I didn't think it was possible, but they actually looked cooler than Nic.

"Who are you?" the brother asked, his voice rough like he'd smoked cigarettes for more years than possible for how young he looked.

My mouth failed to move. A hand gripped my forearm and pushed me to the side. Nic stood in front of me.

"He's with me. Fuck off." He shoved me again, guiding me back to his bedroom.

"What happened to your face?" his brother asked.

"What happened to yours?" Nic quipped back. We reached the bedroom, and he pushed me in first. He sagged against the door after closing it. "I told you not to leave my room."

I blinked a few times as my senses returned. He'd put six butterfly bandages on his face to hold the cut shut.

"What is your brother doing to that woman?" I asked.

He looked a bit angry at me. Of all the things I'd done, this was what flared his temper the most? Me stepping out of his bedroom?

"That's not your business, is it?" He touched his stomach like it still hurt.

"You sure found some energy, pushing me around like that. You must feel up to going to my place now?"

"No. You barely let me get any rest at all. Can I trust you to not go out there again?"

I sat on the mattress and smirked. "Probably not. You know how I get around unconscious people."

He stared at me for a long time, as if hoping he could figure out a way to read my mind.

"Are you saying you want to fuck her?"

I tapped my foot nervously. "Well, you're in no state to have sex, so… it would be a way to keep me off you."

"Are you saying you cut my face as a means to distract yourself from raping me?"

"No, of course not, but I'm saying I'll be tempted to if I'm really sleeping over." Damn, I should have phrased it differently. I'd given him an opening to retract his previous offer. He was definitely going to kick me out of the apartment.

He gave that annoyed groan again and pulled the door open.

"Marcanian," Nic said. "Can we barrow your fo-friend?"

"For what?"

"My friend wants to fuck her."

My skin prickled as he said it. I hadn't thought he would actually let me. What kind of person would help me fuck someone who was unconscious?

Kidnapped

At least if he was busy molesting Marcanian's victim, Jimena would leave me alone. Was it selfish of me? Absolutely, but the throbbing cut across my face was proof that shy of shutting Jimena in a closet, this was my best chance of getting rest.

I laid on the bed and closed my eyes, letting my body relax as Jimena's attention focused on the unconscious woman.

"Aren't you curious why I prefer my partners to be asleep?" Jimena asked.

Any other time I might have amused him with an audience, but right now, I just wanted to be left alone. Still, I opened my eyes and looked in his direction. I was on my back, the woman next to me on the mattress.

Jimena had undressed her, so now she lay naked. Jimena licked her nipple and squeezed her breasts while staring at me.

"See this?" He flicked the perky nipple with his fingers. "See how her body reacts to me? If she was awake and knew who I was, she would never let me touch her. But right now, her body doesn't know any different. Her body wants me." He pulled his other hand up from between her legs and showed me the fluid coating his fingers.

My stomach grumbled and new cramps arced across my belly. I should really toss this fucker out of my room and tell my brother to do whatever he wanted to him. Why was I enduring his abuse? It had been amusing at first, but now it was becoming insufferable.

"Just like you," Jimena said. "You never would have paid attention to me or let me fuck you, but when you were passed out, your body wanted me as much as hers does."

My eyes stayed closed for long periods between blinks, so it was like watching a flip show with several pages missing between. He was suckling her nipples and fingering her, then her body was moving in a jarring beat as he thrust against her. His sexual skills were rather lacking, probably because he'd never had a conscious partner. He was pawing at her like she was a bag of meat and thrusting his hips against her in jabs at random directions.

Watching it and being jostled along with her on the mattress was almost as painful as the stomach pain I was enduring.

He was panting from his effort, his eyes filled with a crazed lustful look of a hungry predator. I should have been repulsed by what he was doing, but instead I found myself getting hard. And dare I say it… I was jealous. I knew my body was in no condition to take the abuse from him, but that didn't stop me from reaching out for him.

My initial intent was to pull him over to be on top of me, but somehow, we rolled and I ended up on top. His damp and erect dick pressed against my clothed body.

"Did that get you turned on?" Jimena asked. He made a show of glancing down at my crotch. "I thought it might make you jealous."

"I'm not jealous. Watching you is embarrassing."

He lunged up. I tensed, expecting him to bite me, but instead his lips pressed against mine. That was one thing I hadn't seen him do. He hadn't kissed her on the mouth. I pushed him back down.

"Stop that."

"Go on then." He wriggled his hips and poked my stomach with his dick. "Fuck me."

"What?"

He undid my fly as I held myself above him.

"It's what you want to do, right? Go on. I want you to."

"It's no fun if you want it," I snapped. There was very little in it for me if it was consensual. And after seeing his display, the last thing I wanted to do was give him what he wanted.

He slid his hands up my shirt, exposing my belly that was still gurgling with agony. He lifted his hips and poked at me again with his erection.

"Show me how much you want me. How pissed you are that I was inside her instead of you." He tried to pull his face up to me again, but I held him down. Had he fucked her to intentionally make me jealous?

"You really—" I paused then, my hand about to grip him tight enough on the shoulder to make him squeal. Because his expression had softened, and I could sense the most unthinkable thing from him.

Love.

Not infatuation. Not the rush of feeling good from an orgasm, but the pure love a mother felt for their newborn child. The shit you took vows for and would risk your life over.

I hadn't even felt this from my own mother, let alone a sexual partner. How could this demented man below me be full of such a sincere emotion… toward me? A person he only knew from a distance?

"Come on." Jimena squirmed under me, noticing my extended hesitation. I dropped my body to press against his and took him in a deep kiss.

Kidnapped

I'd made love before, at least to start. It was easier to lure someone into isolation if you were playing the game they wanted and promising them a good time. So, I knew what humans liked, where they wanted to be touched to feel pleasure. I'd just never pleasured them all the way through to the end.

I wasn't even sure I could climax if I didn't torture him.

Keeping my lips on his, I reached down and slicked my hand with the juices coating his dick. I spread it onto my own hardened dick and began teasing his entrance, which made him moan and jerk about. He was so sloppy when it came to sex. I broke our kiss, and he bit my bottom lip harder than was comfortable.

So, I rammed inside him rougher than I would have if he'd been a real person I was trying to seduce. He yelped and let go. I shifted until I was rubbing against his prostate. He arched his back and cussed. I could see his soul exposed and floating around him like a fine mist. I slipped a hand under his shirt and rubbed his nipple while leaning down and kissing his neck. I inhaled and the sweet fragrance of his love-flavored soul filled me.

The cramps in my stomach lessened, the throb of my headache eased, and even the cut across my face mended. Without the anguish distracting me, I was able to give him my full attention. I absorbed more of his soul but not enough that he would feel any ill effects. He would regenerate the amount in a few days with no problem.

"S-slower," Jimena said. I did as he wanted, completely enthralled by him and the embrace of his affection. I'd never been inside the warm cocoon of someone's love before. I would do this for as long as he wanted if it meant I got to continue basking in his waves of adoration.

I found a new rhythm that he seemed to prefer, one where I slowly pulled myself out an inch before pushing back inside. I lost all track of time as I made love to him, touching him in all the places that prompted a response from his body.

"I love you," Jimena said, his voice thick from the endorphins flooding his system. My body trembled at the words. He repeated them over and over as he climaxed, ejaculating all over my stomach. I stifled my own cry as I came with him.

I dropped my head to his forehead and breathed heavily onto his face as he did likewise. His fingers trailed down the side of my cheek, and I lifted slightly off him.

"How did? Your cut is? Healed?" He stared at my face as his fingers picked at the butterfly stickers.

How would he react if he knew he had healed me? Would he still display love for me if he knew it was beneficial to me? He seemed to only want to cause me pain, and I suspected the reason he had wanted to make love was because I'd expressed a desire for violent sex.

"Yeah, it is." I hoped he didn't pry for more of an answer. I moved inside him again, not wanting things to end. He pushed at my shoulders and looked away.

"Come on, get off. We're dirty."

I pulled out of him but couldn't resist suckling his neck again. I wanted to stay like this, as close to his body as possible. He was now my most prized possession, and I did not want to let go.

"Get off." His words were harder now, and I relented. "Can I use your shower?"

"Yeah, sure." I got up and watched him as he assessed the various body fluids on him. He collected his discarded garments while I endured the torture of not touching him.

I followed him into the hall and pointed to the bathroom. I tried to follow him in, but he glared and shut the door. I resolved to keeping watch from the hall.

"You guys done with her?"

I stifled a snarl as I turned to my brother. I reminded myself that he didn't want Jimena. He wanted the woman back.

"Y-yes," I said.

My brother stared for a moment and sniffed the air. Was he smelling the sex or could he also sense…? I shoved the thought from my mind, worried if I even thought about it in front of Marcanian, he would hear it.

Marc pushed open the bedroom door and looked at the woman.

"Wow, he really did fuck her. What kind of freak is he?"

I bit my lip to keep from responding.

Marcanian pointed to my face. "You better have used your human to heal that instead of mine."

"I didn't touch your human," I snapped. He narrowed his eyes at my response and stepped closer.

"Exactly what is your relationship with that guy?"

"He's my stalker," I said. "He came here to kidnap me for a second time."

He quirked an eyebrow and looked at the door like he could see Jimena on the other side.

"Should I be worried?" Marcanian asked.

"You're not his type," I said, hoping he didn't rephrase the question, because if he was concerned about my wellbeing while around Jimena, it wasn't misplaced.

"Alright, but if I think it's getting weird, I'm gonna tell Dad." He went into my room to retrieve the woman as I wondered what exactly would qualify as weird if none of what he'd currently seen did.

Marcanian and his girlfriend were dressing their woman on the couch when Jimena opened the bathroom door, his hair damp and smelling of my shampoo. He probably loved that, getting to use my toiletries. Instead of being repulsed by the idea, I found myself turned on, my body already zinging for another round of being smothered against his body. His body that now smelled like me.

"You look hot wet," I said. I thrust my hands into his hair and pushed him back into the bathroom. I blacked out for a moment, not even realizing I was kissing him and grinding my crotch against him while pinning him against the bathroom counter. Maybe this was why demons avoided feeding on someone's love. It was more addicting than any other kind of soul.

"Are you making fun of me?" Jimena asked, wriggling free of me.

"Huh? Why would you say that?"

I let him push me away and distance himself even though my body screamed at me for it.

"If you expect me to believe that all this time all I had to do was wet my hair to get you to notice me, you must think I'm retarded." He crossed his arms protectively.

"Did you ever try to talk to me? Before you kidnapped me? Did you ever approach me? Ask me out?"

He gave me an odd, one-lifted-eyebrow look.

"Do you realize how insulting it is that you have to ask that? You're admitting how you don't know the answer."

"No, I'm not. I know you didn't."

He looked at the floor and shook his head like he would have if disappointed in a pet.

"Are you feeling better? Can we go to my place now?"

"Yeah, sure, just let me wash up first." I glanced at him before I got in the shower. "And can you stay in here? So my brother doesn't bother you."

He nodded. I stripped, doing it intentionally in front of him. He kept the same indifferent, impatient expression on his face during my tease. I tried not to let it bother me and quickly showered, then dressed with less vigor. He was a necrophiliac, so I shouldn't be surprised. He would likely get more turned on watching me sleep than watching me waggle my dick around.

CHAPTER four

Kidnapped

He collected his things from my bedroom, and I followed him through the apartment, giving my brother a polite nod as we passed. They'd finished dressing the woman and had positioned her in a comfortable pose on the couch so she wouldn't be alarmed when she woke.

Outside, we walked down the dimly lit street.

"Where did you park? Or did you walk here?"

"I parked five blocks away. I couldn't be seen near your place."

"Why?"

"I can't do anything that would implicate me when you go missing."

He was still on that? My brother had seen him, so weren't we past that? I opted to not mention it, in case he got it in his head that he needed to kill my brother.

"I guess that means we can't stop somewhere for food before we go back to your place?"

"No, we cannot."

"I would really like to pick up food instead of eating at your place. Your cooking makes me sick."

"You can watch me prepare it so you'll know I didn't put anything bad in it."

"Or we can go on a proper date and get some food. My treat."

"No."

"Come on, has that really never been a fantasy of yours? To go on a real date with me?"

"If people see us together, then they'll suspect me when you go missing. If you are going to insist on leaving my basement—"

"Which I am."

"Then you have to pretend to not know me. Understand?"

"So, we can only talk and interact when we're in your house? Otherwise, we are indifferent strangers?"

"Yes."

I didn't like that one bit. But I didn't see a means to change his mind, not yet. I tried to think of various ways to convince him to open this up into a more full-time relationship where I could be around him all the time, both in and out of his house. But I still had no feasible ideas by the time we'd reached his car.

"What about a drive thru?" Baby steps.

"No. It's four in the morning anyway. Nothing is open.

"Several places are open."

"No."

I groaned and bit my tongue to stay silent. The drive to his place wasn't long, and soon, I was following him up to his front door. I stopped at the threshold and waited. He went inside several steps before stopping to look at me.

"Aren't you going to invite me in?" I asked.

"You asked me to invite you in the night I brought you here after the bar too. Doesn't that still count?"

If that was true then why could I only go in his basement?

"You can't come in unless I invite you, can you?"

"I'm not a vampire," I said. "It's called manners, Jimena. I'd like an invitation."

"You've only been in my basement, even though I know you wanted in the rest of my house. I think you need my permission."

"Then invite me." I didn't want to confirm or deny his assumption. I didn't want to give him more power over me than he already had.

"I grant you permission to go directly to my basement and stay there."

Is that what he had said last time?

"Fuck you. You said I could watch you cook."

He rolled his tongue around in his mouth for a minute. "Fine. Come in." He gestured past himself to the darkened house. "You are welcome inside my *entire* home."

I stepped inside, my restrictions finally lifted. I expected his house to either be painfully clean or severely dirty. He was obsessive, so I figured it applied to all aspects of his life. There wasn't much furniture, but the place had a lived-in appearance, not overly tidy or untidy. I wiped my finger across a table with a lamp as we passed it and left a smear in the dust. The house was large for one person, so it wasn't surprising he failed to keep it dusted.

While he led me to the kitchen with his back to me, I dissipated into black smoke and infiltrated every nook and cranny of his habitat.

Five bedrooms, three bathrooms, ranch style, surprisingly small kitchen, two living rooms, a sun room, patio, deck in the back with a garden, a dining room that looked untouched, and another table in the center of the kitchen, an old folding table. He resided in the master bedroom, but the other bedrooms were fully furnished with beds and dressers. This place had once contained a full family, with kids and everything, judging by the items in the rooms. Each one was basically an untouched shrine to the former occupant. Where were they all now? A family didn't move and leave *all* their things behind.

He'd reached the kitchen. I reassembled myself seconds before he turned to look at me. I plastered on a smile as he narrowed his eyes almost like he knew what I'd done.

"You can sit here while I cook."

The folding table had four folding chairs around it. I moved to the closest, and he smacked his palm on the table, shaking it and nearly making it collapse.

"No. On the floor. You'll sit on the floor, like a dog."

"Like a—"

"Yes. Down." He pointed firmly.

It was one thing to attempt dating someone who wanted to murder me and keep our relationship a secret, but now he wanted to delve into some sort of dominance shit with me pretending to be an animal?

He went to a drawer and pulled out a dog's choke collar and chain leash.

"When you aren't in the basement, you'll wear this and behave like a dog. That way my neighbors won't see you through the windows or anything. And I can make sure you aren't snooping."

"Close the damn blinds," I said. "And if I'm next to you, how can I be snooping? We've established restraints don't work on me, so this is pointless."

"Then you shouldn't mind doing it. You can free yourself if you really need too." He stepped up to me and put the collar around my neck, looking into my eyes as he did it. He clipped on the leash and gave it a tug, effectively choking me.

"Now, get on the floor and be quiet. Remember, dogs don't speak."

"Does that mean I can bark?"

He yanked on the leash again, digging the chain into my skin. I growled but sank to my knees.

"Good boy." He stroked my face and patted my head like I was a damn dog. I clenched my teeth. He tied the leash to one of the table legs, which was stupid, because all I had to do was lift it, and I could slip the leash off. This was all a show of dominance. We both knew I wasn't truly restrained at all.

"Have you done this with other people?"

He whirled so quickly I felt the sting from his slap before I saw it.

"I told you no more speaking!"

I dropped to my hands, huffing for air and half expecting to spit out blood from how hard he'd hit me. I kept my eyes on the floor, abandoning my original intent of watching him cook. The worst part was the fact my dick was getting hard. I was half tempted to talk again and rape him when he lunged to attack me.

I chanced a glance up and saw him put a pot of water on the stove. He took out pasta noodles and a cheap tomato sauce. I watched him in silence with my legs folded under me, palms spread on the floor, and my dick throbbing for attention. It had never taken water this long to boil in my entire life.

He finally turned and faced me, holding a bowl of noodles covered in sauce and shredded cheese.

"I didn't put poison or drugs in it. I promise."

I didn't trust that statement at all, but I would still eat it. He dropped the plastic bowl onto the floor, making some of it splatter out. He expected me to eat on the floor? I stared at him for a moment, wondering what he wanted. There was no fork.

"Eat it like a dog would," he said. "Or I can drag you into the basement, and you can eat it like a human down there, chained to the wall, where I will leave you all night."

And if I ate it here? Wouldn't I end up down there after I ate anyway?

"Don't you want to eat with me?" He put his own bowl on the table and sat. He began eating, watching me as he did so.

Fine. If this is what he wanted and doing this would bring me closer to feeding on his love-flavored soul again, then I'd do it. I put my hands on either side of the bowl and shoved my face into it. A good portion of it went up my nose, reminding me why humans did not eat like this. Still, I managed to eat a good portion of it while coating my entire face in sauce.

I sat back up, coughing a bit and snorting to get the food out of my nostrils. He rose from the table, his pants tented with arousal. That had turned him on? He liked it when I was submissive. I could work with that.

"Good boy," he said. He undid his fly and pulled his cock out. "Since you were so good, I'll let you play with your favorite toy. No hands. You're still a dog."

Did he want me to only lick it? And he wasn't even going to wipe the food off my face? Whatever. I did want to make him come so he would give me the food I really wanted. I shuffled toward him on my knees and took his length in my mouth. I completely swallowed him, which may have sounded impressive, but he actually had a small dick. I suspected it was part of why he avoided having sex with awake people. He didn't want to be mocked for it. For me, it meant giving him a blow job was easier. It also meant it was easier for my ass to take it when he raped me. All wins in my book.

"You really like that don't you? You dirty dog. Look at how dirty you are." He used his finger to wipe some of the sauce off my face. "You're a horny little bitch in heat, aren't you?"

I rolled my tongue around the tip, and his body shuddered. Was I the first person to ever blow him? Or had he done this with someone else? And why did the idea of him doing this with someone else bother me so much?

"Want me to fuck you like a dog? Do you?" He pushed me off of him and slammed his arm into my head. My temple arced in pain as I heard his next command. "Take your pants off."

I did as he asked, staying on my hands and knees.

"You really want it don't you? You really want me to fuck you?"

I gave a supportive woof. I didn't even care if he used lube. I was pretty sure I could come if he was fucking me, even if it hurt.

"Yeah, I have exactly what a bitch like you needs. Put your head down."

I dropped to my elbows and kept my eyes on the floor. I heard a drawer open and close. I assumed it was to retrieve lube. His fingers touched my ass cheeks. Then he pressed something into my hole. It was colder than a dick should be. He shoved it in hard and fast.

"What the fuck?" I jerked away, nearly falling to the ground as the leash pulled me back. I reached around to my butt and touched the object lodged in it. I didn't want to put too much thought into it before I removed it, so I gave it a firm yank, hoping it didn't cause more damage on the exit.

In my hand was a rubber dog toy in the shape of a bone. It was a used chew toy that was marked with teeth marks. It had likely belonged to the same dog whose collar I now wore.

Jimena doubled over as he laughed, his face quickly turning red.

"That was great. You're really something. I can't believe you did all that." He laughed more and eventually sat in one of the folding chairs and calmed himself.

I put my pants back on, deciding to be grateful he hadn't shoved something sharp in my ass. I needed to be more careful with him.

"Alright, back in the basement." He untied the leash from the table leg.

"But I did want you wanted," I said.

"I said no talking." He clenched his fist but didn't swing.

"You would really keep a dog tied up in your basement? I want a dog bed next to your bedroom."

His arm trembled from the restraint it took for him to not hit me.

"Or maybe I should put you in a kennel in the backyard after I hose you down. You're covered in filth from being on the floor. I'm not letting you in my bedroom." He jerked on the chain and half dragged me across the floor. We reached the basement door, and he opened it. He unclipped the leash. "Your reward for playing along is that I won't tie you up, but you are still staying down there."

He gave me a firm push, nearly knocking me down the steps.

"Stay in the basement." He slammed the door.

I'd done all of that, and this was what I got? Fucker.

I stomped down the steps and rummaged around, eventually finding a sink in the corner that had running water. Combined with some rags I found on a supply shelf, I managed to clean myself in the sink.

I sat on the bottom step and stared at the cuffs that had originally held me here. Was I really going to play along and stay here?

Kidnapped

I sat in class, my three friends all chattering to themselves, oblivious to the fact I was remaining silent. In the end, I had left Jimena's basement after fifteen minutes. I had checked on him upstairs before I'd departed, and he'd been sound asleep. He had gone to bed and intended for me to rot in the basement all day. I knew I shouldn't have expected better, but it still stung.

My eyes darted to the classroom entrance as Jimena walked in. As usual, he had a hoodie pulled over his head, and his shoulders slumped. His typical submissive outcast appearance. I forced my eyes away from him but noticed his shadow looming over the desk I shared with Suzie.

"N-Nic," Jimena managed to stutter. My body suddenly felt heavy as I turned my head to look at him. I'd left his basement a mere six hours ago, and neither of us had likely gotten much sleep. Suzie stared at him. Alex and Jake ceased their exchange as well.

"You left," Jimena managed to finish.

"What the hell are you talking about?" Alex asked. Jimena's eyes darted to Alex for a brief moment before they returned to me. I tapped my pen on the table as the awkward seconds passed.

"We're working on a group project together for a different class," I said. "I left before we finished."

"What project? I have every class with you. Jimena isn't in any of them."

"You're not part of every aspect of my life, Alex. Fuck off." I tossed my pen at him for emphasis. "I'll come by tonight, alright, Jimena?"

He lingered at the edge of the desk like my response might not be good enough, but he wasn't able to muster the courage to extend our confrontation, so he retreated to his desk in the back of the room.

"What the hell was that?" Alex asked.

"Nothing. He asked me to help him with a project he has for another class. One we already took, and I'm helping him, okay? Is that a problem?"

"He's creepy, okay? Just be careful."

Kidnapped

Be careful. If my friends only knew. I wanted to go to his door and knock as a normal person would, but I knew that wasn't what he wanted. He wanted to find me in his basement, tied up down there as he'd left me. No, he hadn't tied me this last time.

I materialized in his basement as dusk hit and found the choke collar where I'd left it. I slipped it on. The cool metal burned against my skin, reminding me of where it had bruised me a mere twelve hours ago.

Now, what? Should I make noise so he would know I was here? Bark? Pound on the door? I needed a rulebook that explained what actions would result in his dick in my ass rather than a dog's chew toy.

I went up the stairs to the door and debated between knocking or seeing if it was unlocked. He had said I could access all parts of his house so long as I was in dog mode. But a dog couldn't open a door, regardless of if it was locked.

There was really no winning in his games, and I had a feeling he had intentionally made them that way. I tried the handle, and it twisted, no resistance. I turned it all the way and gave it a pull. I walked into the hallway and only had to make one turn before I found him in the kitchen pacing frantically.

He froze when he saw me, and I had no idea what his reaction would be to seeing me there. So, we both stood there a moment, neither of us moving.

"Is that how a dog stands?"

Finally, some fucking guidance. I dropped to my hands and knees.

"You should have stayed. Why didn't you stay? Why do you keep leaving?" He put a hand under my chin and tilted my head so I would look at him. He tightened his grip until it hurt. "I don't like it when you leave."

"Then let me stay here as a person," I said. His hand smacked the back of my head.

"Just when I thought you'd understood how this works, you go and talk. Did you learn nothing? You don't talk." He grabbed the loose bit on my chain and pulled. I followed on my hands and knees, barely with enough slack in the chain for me to keep breathing. He led me down a narrow hallway to the master bedroom. He released his grip and pointed to a dog bed that he'd put in the corner of the room.

It looked new. Had he gone out and bought that? At best, I'd expected him to dig some old, used, flea-covered blanket out of a shed and tell me to use that.

"You wanted a dog bed in my room, so now you have it. So, no more running away, right? You'll stay here? With me? When I sleep?"

Was he realizing he couldn't keep me here by force, and he was now trying to bribe me? How quickly he'd forgotten a few days ago when I'd refused to leave and he'd begged me to.

I nodded. If we'd made this much progress in a day, I was pretty sure I would be sleeping in that bed next to him within a week.

"Good." He smiled. It might have been his first non-sinister smile I'd seen. He was truly proud of what he'd accomplished. He walked up to me and removed the collar. "As a reward, you can eat at the table with me tonight and speak."

Kidnapper

My hands kept shaking as I prepared the food. He was sitting on a chair at the folding table, staring at me. I was allowing us to be equals for the moment, and it was terrifying. I kept thinking of how his hands and body had felt against mine. He'd actually made love to me last night. I had no doubt that's what we'd done, and I had no idea why.

I'd dared him to do it because I thought it would irritate him, but now I feared he had actually enjoyed it. That we'd both enjoyed it. Or worse, that only I had enjoyed it, and he was setting me up so he could hurt me more. Like it was some cruel joke.

In my mind, I imagined him telling his friends how he'd convinced me I had a chance to actually be with him. They'd all laugh about it when he publicly humiliated me.

How would he do it? Lure me into attending some event with him and then pretend he didn't know me? Have me confess my love on a stage and then they'd all laugh?

I wanted to punish him for the potential pain he would cause me in my imagined scenarios.

I'd taken the gamble and given him what he'd wanted: the dog bed and speaking to him in public. He'd made up a lie for why I'd wanted him to come over, so perhaps he didn't want to be as public as I'd thought.

I sat the freshly stove-grilled hamburger and toasted bun on a plate and put it before him. I'd already arranged an array of condiments and garnishes for him. I'd known exactly which ones he preferred. And I, of course, would only eat what he did. If he noticed the lack of mustard and onions present, he opted to not say it. When I produced the spicy hot chips, he did raise an eyebrow.

"My favorite," he said. "You like them too?"

He really had no idea how long I'd been stalking him. He had no recollection of our encounters prior to my kidnapping him. That fact still stung, no matter how unsurprising it was.

"I got them because I know they're your favorite," I said.

He smiled slightly and took a bite. I'd expected him to wait for me to eat first, to make sure I hadn't drugged or poisoned the food. He chewed and swallowed, then I realized I was staring and proceeded to also eat mine.

"So, you want to talk about our firsts?" Nic asked.

"Our first what?"

"The first person you killed. You've never been able to talk about it with someone before, have you? Wouldn't it be nice to?"

"You want a confession out of me?" Is that what this was? Some ploy to get me charged with murder?

"Do you want to hear about my first?"

"Your first what?"

"The first person I murdered."

Was he messing with me? Did he really expect me to believe he had murdered someone?

"It was my little brother," Nic said. "I was six, and my mother had married a man that wasn't my father. They had a baby together, and I could tell both of them loved my new baby brother more than they loved me. I was going to be discarded, neglected, and ignored. I suppose most siblings feel that way when their life is disturbed upon the arrival of a needy infant." He paused like he expected me to agree with him. "But as the weeks passed, I knew this child was evil. It would never bring myself or my family the joy they all expected. I tried to tell my mother this, and it only angered her. They said the baby had colic, which is just a fancy word for saying it cried all the time for no reason. My stepfather started drinking, and my mother cried all the time. Yet, neither of them realized the child was to blame. They say sudden infant death syndrome is common in babies and unexplainable. When the baby slept through the night, my mother thought it was a blessing, until she went to feed it and found it dead." His choice of words, to call the baby it instead of he, did not go unnoticed by me.

"She looked at me differently after that. Like she always suspected I'd done it but couldn't bring herself to say it. The baby had rolled onto his stomach and suffocated. My stepfather left shortly after the funeral, and I went to live with my real father a few years later. My mother never touched me again after my brother died. She looked at me as though every dead animal found in the yard was killed by me. I couldn't squish a bug without her judging me for it."

He'd finished his burger and paused in his story, waiting for me to respond. If I hadn't already researched his family, I might have thought his story was bogus. But my obsessive dive into his past had uncovered facts that matched his tale.

"You're saying you did it? You rolled your brother onto his stomach?"

"I covered his mouth with his baby blanket and stared into his eyes as I…" He paused, the first indication he'd shown of altering the story for my benefit. "As I watched his soul leave him. But we all do shit things when we're kids, and we don't know better, right? I thought I was doing the world a favor, ridding it of one more asshole before he grew up."

His words left no inclination of regret, like maybe he still thought he had done the right thing.

"So, tell me about the first person you killed."

He'd already had plenty of chances to go to the police. There was a slim chance he was wearing a wire and trying to get me to confess to something. I could meet him halfway, though, and tell him *something*.

"I was sixteen," I said. "This house, it's the one I grew up in. Well, kind of. I was adopted, and this was their house." I paused, wondering if he would interrupt me and make some conjecture regarding what I was going to say. He simply waited. "The family was prettier than me, fit in better, they were all better. Their son, he was close in age to me, he threw this party when we were sixteen. Our parents were out of town, so he was breaking all the rules and had even gotten alcohol. All the popular kids came, and I was this socially awkward thing loitering in the house because I lived here, not because I was invited or had any right to be here.

"I mostly hid and listened to people make comments about me. When the party died off and most people had left, I started cleaning up. I found this girl in the basement. We had a couch and some chairs down there. She was passed out from drinking or whatever. She was a bigger girl and not all that pretty, but she'd still treated me like scum. Never glanced at me or even said hello. But here she was, passed out in my house like she owned the place.

"No one was around. My brother was with some other girl in his room, and everyone else had left. So, I touched her. She was right there, open and available for me to do whatever I wanted. She started to wake up when I was fucking her, so I covered her mouth to keep her quiet. She must have vomited a bit from her hangover, and she ended up choking on it. I didn't stop. I was worried if I let go of her mouth, she would scream and tell my brother what I was doing. And I didn't want to stop fucking her. I didn't climax until her skin was cold to the touch."

Even talking about it, remembering how it had felt to feel her body slowly changing as she'd gone from being alive to being a corpse, made me aroused. I adjusted my pants to conceal it and looked at my half-eaten burger.

"I'd worn a condom because they'd taught us that in school, and I didn't want to get any diseases from her. My brother had this whole jar full of them for anyone at the party to use. I made sure to clean up any evidence of my touching her. When my brother finally found her in the basement and tried to get her to wake up and leave, I'd already restaged her to look like she'd thrown up and drowned without my involvement. The ambulance came, then the police. They drilled my brother, asked for the names of everyone at the party. They could tell she'd had sex, possibly rape. I heard them talking about it, but they didn't suspect me. Not me, the weird social outcast brother. They still took DNA samples from us all, but mine was dismissed because I lived here. Of course, my DNA was all over the crime scene. Other people had had sex in the basement during the party, and it turned out she'd even had sex with other boys that night. It was impossible to figure out what had happened.

"In the end, they dismissed it as an accidental death. I wasn't even included in the list of men she'd fucked that night."

"And that's when you learned you could get away with things no one else could," Nic said. "Because no one notices you."

"And that's why I don't want people to see me with you. It will ruin my anonymity."

"Wouldn't it be nice, though? To actually be in the spotlight for once? To show all the naysayers that you—"

"Can what? Get a guy like you? If I hadn't kidnapped you, you'd still be ignoring me. Don't try to act like this is something it isn't." I dumped my burger into the trash.

"Am I the first person you told all this to?"

"The first that's still breathing, but—"

"It aroused you talking about it, didn't it? Remembering the thrill of taking your first life. Controlling her last breath. You liked the power it gave you." He stood up and edged around the counter. "Do you want to use my body to satisfy the hunger you have now? You can. I won't stop you."

"You interrupted me."

"You did the same to me."

"This isn't an equal relationship. This is a momentary lapse in my judgement." I stopped because he'd dropped to his knees now, and I could see the tent in his own jeans. And his eyes, it actually looked like he was lusting for me. It was impossible. Why would he be so cruel and tease me like this? Pretend like this?

"You can punish me however you want, but right now, you need to let me please you."

"Let you please me?" I unzipped my fly. "Is this what you want?"

"Your first time was with a drunk whore in a basement. Someone's filthy leftovers. I want to show you what your first time should have been. Let me make love to you in your bed."

"Why?"

"You love me. So much that you want to keep me to yourself forever. Why would you not want me to make our time together as pleasurable as possible?"

"Or I could kick you down the stairs for trying to make a fool of me."

"Why not get something out of me first? Then… you can abuse me all you want."

It felt like a game of chicken. Which of us would back down first? Which would admit what they really wanted? There was no way Nic actually wanted me, but I was willing to see how far he would take his gambit.

"If you mean that, then do it. Bed me."

He hesitated as though perhaps he thought it was a trick.

"Don't make me tell you again. If you mean your words then—"

He lunged and his lips crashed into mine with a hunger I couldn't fathom. Something inside me broke, a longing to be touched and desired by someone overwhelmed my instinct to stay in power and never be vulnerable.

I'd seen people in movies do this, watched plenty of it poorly acted out in pornography, but never had someone done it to me. I'd considered paying a prostitute, but I didn't want to see the judgment in their eyes.

He lifted me. I was smaller than him, but the ease in which he did it was startling.

"Tell me if you're uncomfortable with any of this," Nic said, his lips muttering the words between kisses against my neck. He carried me down the hall and laid me on the bed. I stripped off both my clothes and his, doing it in a manner that allowed him to never break contact for more than a few seconds.

Kidnapper

I laid in the bed and stared at him. I'd wrestled free of his grasp after he'd fallen asleep. I wanted to demand he go lay in the dog bed where he belonged. He was a mongrel unworthy of being in my bed.

But he had also spent the last few hours driving me to a level of ecstasy I had never imagined possible. My body was exhausted from it, every nerve ending still tingled. We had been inside each other in every way possible, and I flinched and closed my eyes, not wanting to think about it. Because it wouldn't last. Whatever enjoyment he was getting from this would end, and he would be off pleasuring someone else.

Someone like Suzie.

"How many people have you pleasured?" I asked his unconscious body. I didn't want him to ever touch someone else. I wanted to murder anyone who had ever orgasmed from his touch. He was mine and mine alone. But he would keep slipping away from me, and I couldn't allow that.

I had to end this. I had to end him.

It was the only way.

CHAPTER five

Kidnapped

I woke to find him staring at me in that demented manner only a true psychopath could pull off. And here I thought we'd had a breakthrough. He'd actually let me make love to him like a normal couple. He hadn't even cut me when I'd slept.

It made me dread even more what he might be planning now. What punishments did he have in mind to make up for how kind he had been?

"It's the weekend," Jimena said. "Do you have plans or can you spend the day with me?"

"I'm all yours." I was still naked, half covered by bedsheets. He was fully dressed and sipping a cup of coffee.

"Where's your cellphone?"

"I don't bring it with me when I come over."

He smiled a devilish grin. "I like that."

Did he think I did that so no one could trace my location? If my brother wanted to find me, he could. And I knew if I split my attention between my phone and Jimena, there would be anger. Besides, the bastard would probably steal my phone and go through it. So, why bother bringing it?

"I want to play a game. Will you play?"

"Sure."

He let me dress and eat. He'd actually prepared me an egg burrito. I ate it, hoping someday I could eat his food with less worry about whether I would feel sick afterward.

He took me outside to the backyard, and I noticed the choke collar in his hands. Damn, I had hoped we'd moved past that.

A wooden privacy fence bordered the yard. Other than grass and some neglected flower beds here and there, the yard was nothing spectacular. There was no sign of the potential dog that might have lived here. Which made me wonder if he'd ever owned a dog. What if that collar and chew toy came from a dog he'd snatched off the street?

Would being with him mean an onslaught of finding tortured and dead animals mixed with the occasional human tied up in the basement?

Jimena stopped at the far back corner of the yard where the soil looked recently disturbed, as if it was being prepared for a flowerbed.

"I want you to dig," Jimena said. He held the collar out to me. "Put this on and dig like a dog."

The ground looked soft enough, so it wouldn't be too horrible. And I'd absorbed enough of his soul energy last night, I could easily recover from whatever this was leading toward.

"Is there a goal? Size or shape?"

"Just dig. And once this goes on, remember, you can't talk."

I wanted to point out that this would look more bizarre to any neighbors who happened to see than if I simply dug a hole with a shovel, but whatever. He'd said this was a game, and if it's what he wanted… I let him slip the collar on, and I dropped to my hands and knees.

I dug at the ground, fearing what I might unearth in the soft soil.

"Keep digging until I tell you to stop." He walked off. I figured he would only be gone a short while, but he stayed away. I saw him go from the garage to the shed and back to the house, making multiple trips.

I kept digging, moving the ground around and unsure exactly what my goal should be. One small deep hole? A large wide one?

I paused and looked at my soot-covered hands. I didn't know why I was pretending this was anything other than the obvious. He was having me dig my own grave.

With this in mind, I dug a hole big enough for my body to lay in. I went about a foot and a half deep. It was shallow enough that I could get out. If he expected me to dig a six-foot-deep grave, he would need to give me a shovel and several days.

He came over with a snorkel, shovel, and garden hose around noon. He twisted the control knob and held the flow of water in front of me. I *was* thirsty. I swallowed a bit more pride and lapped at the stream like a dog.

After I drank, he turned the hose off and removed the collar. Because, of course, we couldn't have done that in reverse so I could actually drink like a human.

"Put on the snorkel and get in the hole."

"Does this game have a name?" I asked, as I moved into the grave and put the snorkel on my head. I laid on my back and put the snorkel tube in my mouth.

"We're pretending we are on a beach. I'm going to bury you in the dirt like you'd bury someone in the sand. Just breathe through the snorkel, and you'll be fine. Once you're buried, I'll let you out. It won't be long."

He shoveled the dirt on top of me, starting at my feet and working his way up until my world was covered in darkness. This—this couldn't be how he normally did it. Bury them alive?

I shifted, dematerializing into mist, leaving behind the snorkel so it would still look like I was in the ground. He'd piled enough dirt on me that the lack of my body wasn't overly noticeable. I watched, invisible to him, as he used the shovel to stack up more dirt, and even more, then he held the shovel over my head. This would be when he would say I could come out. Right? He crouched, and his fingers hovered over the snorkel hose. Was he going to plug it? I wasn't that deep. I could get out if I sensed danger. He had to know that. Was that going to be the joke? He plugs the hole, and as I start coughing and digging myself free, he laughs and gets some thrill from it?

He moved quickly, suddenly making up his mind and solidifying his resolve. He rose and held the shovel above me, directly where my head— no—where my neck was. He slammed it down, hard, aiming to cut my neck in some beheading move. He lifted the shovel and slammed it down again and again in a frenzy.

If I had still been in the ground… Well, I didn't think I would have actually died, but it would have been painful, messy, and… I *might* have died. His intent was unmistakable. He wasn't done. He was still thrusting, this time driving the shovel into more areas, chopping me up or at least stabbing me. He was doing it in such a fervor that he hadn't noticed there was nobody under the dirt.

I swirled away, solidifying in the front yard, and threw up. Not because I'd inhaled dirt, which I might have slightly, but because seeing him like that was disgusting. I didn't care how good he tasted. His sickness to murder was too great for me to risk being with him.

Even as I thought it, part of me doubted my resolve. Because his soul *was* addicting, and the moments when he showed me affection even more so.

Kidnapper

I regretted it. As soon as I stopped, and my brain realized what I'd done. A terror rushed through me. What if he hadn't done his magical whatever? What if I'd killed him?

I threw the shovel to the side and started digging at the dirt where his body had been. Minutes ago, I was determined to kill him so no one else could ever be with him.

But my heart already ached because… Because I did love him. I wanted him. I didn't want him gone.

"Nic, Nic, Nic." I clawed at the ground but only found the snorkel. That meant I'd either had another manic episode and none of this was real—Nic wasn't here, never had been, and our night of lovemaking was simply a hallucination. Or, Nic had pulled his magical disappearing act before I'd attacked his buried body.

I wasn't sure which was worse, but no matter how much I dug, his body was not there. Not even a single trace of his clothing.

"No, no, it was real. He was here. He was here." I pawed at the dirt until the sun was down and my knuckles bled.

He would come back. He had to. He wanted me. I wasn't crazy.

I forced myself to go in the house. I checked the basement. Empty. I paced. I searched the house, and I eventually fell asleep cradling the dog collar as I sobbed.

The next day, I repeated my search of the house and yard. Should I go to his brother's house and look for him again? I had commitments. I had a job I needed to bother with, and I didn't feel like begging Nic to come back. Because what if I was wrong? What if I was crazy? What if I was now sane, and he would have no idea what I was talking about?

I worked my Sunday shift at the mall. I'd slept decently Sunday night, but I was dragging a bit as I went to class on Monday after my shift at work. I'd considered skipping class, unsure how he'd react when he saw me.

I stepped into class with my gray hoodie pulled over my head. I peeked out and glanced at the desks he and his friends sat at.

He was there, looking as normal as ever. I took a route to an empty desk that avoided him and put me behind him. Far behind him.

It was like we'd gone back in time to before I'd kidnapped him. I was invisible to him. And I did not have the courage to approach him.

Kidnapped

Jimena had glanced at me a few times when he'd entered class, but that was it. So, was it officially over? By burying and murdering me, had he concluded his obsession with me?

I went with my group of friends to the food court in the mall and sat, distracted in my own thoughts as they excitedly muttered about things I no longer cared about. I needed to decide if I would visit Jimena tonight. Or did I let things end?

He was no good for me. Risking my life just for some amazingly flavored soul wasn't worth it. *It wasn't.* And if I kept saying that to myself enough times, I might eventually believe it.

And then I saw him. He must have worked a shift tonight. I should have objected when Alex had suggested we come to this mall.

I watched as he walked through the food court. He wasn't wearing a hoodie. He had to slip out of that skin when he was at work and plaster on a different image to show the world. He walked up to another man and *hugged him!*

My vision blurred for a moment in a silent rage. Who the hell was that? Even from across the food court, I could tell the man was handsome. He had groomed hair and clean clothes. He could be a model for cologne or some other cheap shit. No way would I give him credit for being worth more than a toss-away model in a magazine. But still, he was too attractive to be with Jimena. Was he the new suitor? Had Jimena already moved on to a new victim? *In two days!* He did target attractive men. I was proof of that since he'd come after me.

"Nic? Hey, Nic?" Alex waved a hand in front of my face, pulling my attention away from Jimena. "What are you staring at?"

"He's here with someone."

My three friends all turned their heads to look at Jimena.

"Who?" Suzie asked as if Jimena was invisible. Shit, was he really that unnoticeable of a person?

"Jimena, from our class," I snarled. "Do none of you recognize him over there?"

They looked again but only regarded me with more confusion. Alex leaned forward and spoke slowly as if I was the confused one.

"Jimena wears a hoodie. No one here is wearing that or looks even remotely like him," Alex said.

"I'm pretty sure Jimena never leaves his room other than to attend class," Jake said, chuckling a bit at his joke. "And he only does that so he can stare at you."

"You're all retarded and blind." We were seated in a booth, and to get out, I needed Jake to get out. Instead of asking him politely, I stood and stepped over him, nearly kicking his head in the process.

"Dude, no good can come from you going over there," Jake said. "It's not him, and you're going to embarrass yourself."

With my back to them, I put my hand above my shoulder and gave them the rude gesture of my middle finger. I reached Jimena's booth and slammed my palm against their wobbly table, which sent their fries shaking. They both paused to gape at me.

"Who the hell is he?" I asked, pointing my free hand at the model and aiming eye daggers at Jimena.

He didn't speak. The color drained from his skin, and he seemed unable to move.

"You buried our relationship and moved on, is that it? He's your new boyfriend? It's been two days, and you're already with someone else?"

"Whoa, hey, uh, excuse me," the model said, his tone soft and gentle as he tried not to increase my anger. I aimed my gaze at him. He flinched but managed to continue. "I think there's been a misunderstanding."

"You were intimately hugging Jimena. There's nothing to misinterpret."

"He's my brother," Jimena said. "The one I told you about. That's my age." With my gaze no longer on him, he'd recovered enough to speak.

"And who is he?" the so-called brother asked.

"A classmate from college. He's been helping me study for a project."

"Is that all I am?" I nearly growled the words. "Do you let all your classmates stick their dicks in your ass?"

I heard the brother gasp, but I didn't look in his direction.

"What are you doing?" Jimena asked, this time his tone unfriendly.

"You either tell your bother I'm your boyfriend or—"

"Or what? Let you continue looking like a lunatic? Why are you screaming at me in the mall? I barely know you!"

I staggered back. That was really how he felt then. My friends came into view a few tables away, possibly approaching in an effort to stop me.

I turned away from them all. I resisted the desire to flee by mist—that would be dumb with so many people now staring at me. I went to the nearest public restroom and turned the faucet on. I splashed the water on my face and tried to settle my temper.

I wasn't sure how long I had stood there, scrubbing my face in an angry fury before I noticed Jimena's reflection in the mirror as he stood behind me.

"What was that?" Jimena asked.

"You hugged him."

"He's my brother. Why would you say all of those things in front of him?"

"Why shouldn't I? Will your treatment of me become worse than burying me alive and bludgeoning me to death with a shovel?" I didn't turn around. I looked only at his reflection.

"We had an agreement. You're supposed to pretend you don't know me. Not scream at me like some jealous lover in the mall I work at."

I whirled then and faced him, sending a splatter of water onto him from my face and hands.

"I need more."

"No."

"Why? Why can't you agree to *not* kill me?" I shouted it so harshly a man attempting to enter quickly spun on his heel and left the bathroom. "When you're ready to be more, you know what you need to do. Until then, fuck off."

Kidnapper

"'Until then, fuck off.' Can you believe he said that? He was giving me an ultimatum. Me!"

The woman in front of me whined, the gag in her mouth keeping her from properly responding. I'd tied her hands behind her back and chained her left ankle to the support beam in my basement.

I'd grabbed her on my way home, a pure wrong-place-wrong-time situation. She'd been out for a walk or running an errand perhaps. I'd pulled my car up, slammed the car door into her, hit her a few more times, and thrown her into my trunk.

Now, she kneeled on my floor sobbing, her face smeared with mascara. I'd needed to prove I didn't need Nic. I would not relent and do what he wanted. This woman would fill the void he'd left.

Nabbing a random stranger was not something I normally did. If a profiler was working on me, he would probably not categorize her murder with me. The idea frightened me a bit because it meant Nic *had* changed me.

"You would never say that to me, would you?" I stroked her chin and considered keeping her alive for a few days. But what if Nic came back and found her here? This had to be quick. "I shouldn't have brought you here."

I picked up the pipe I'd used on Nic, the one that had always backfired and resulted in him vanishing. I swung and felt the satisfying impact as it struck the side of her head. Her neck crunched, and she crumpled.

"Sorry, we couldn't have played a few more games first," I said. I went about stripping her and dragged her onto a tarp so clean up would be easier. Her bowels expelled their contents, which I'd feared would happen since I'd just nabbed her and didn't have time to make her fast for a few days. "So gross." By the time I had cleaned up, her blood was starting to pool on her underside. I positioned myself above her, but... I wasn't hard. Maybe it was because I had just dealt with all the urine and fecal matter.

Or it was because I had no emotional connection to her since she was a stranger.

"Just do it. Pretend she is someone else." I took my clothes off and rubbed my groin against her, but try as I might, I couldn't get hard.

Kidnapped

Was Jimena going to come to class anymore? I suspected the only reason he came was because of me. So, if he'd moved on, he wouldn't bother attending anymore.

He darted into the classroom just as the professor rose to begin the lecture. I refused to look at him, because I did not want him to see my eyes flash with the excitement I'd had upon seeing him.

I hadn't seen him since our fight in the mall. The figurative ball was in his court. I'd told him what I wanted, and now I had to wait for him to do something. Considering how obsessed he was with me, I didn't think I would need to wait long.

"Jimena, since you are the last to join us, why don't you go first today," the professor said. I didn't look, but I heard the screech of the chair as Jimena got up. "You have prepared a poem for today, haven't you?"

"Yes, sir," Jimena said. He walked to the front of the room, and I allowed myself to look at him since all the students were also watching him.

He had his red hoodie fully up as though it was a protective shield to keep him safe. He pulled a crumpled paper from his pocket.

"I wrote a modified ghazel," Jimena said. "It's called *You and Me*."

He kept his eyes on the paper as he began to read.

"I see only you,

You see all but me.

I am loved by no one,

You are loved by everyone.

I rejoice and praise you,

You scoff and admonish me.

I pray for your success,

You laugh at my excess.

I hear only you,

You hear all but me.

You are adored,

I am ignored.

I am weakened by you,

You are strengthened by me.

I must endure,

You are pure.

My gaze abhors you,

Your gaze astounds me.

You flinch at my sight,

I shudder at your might.

I exist only for you,

You exist for all but me.

You are my only brightness,

I am your only darkness.

I wish only to pleasure you,

You wish to pleasure all but me.

You dream of greatness,

I dream of loneliness.

I cast the sun upon you,

You doom the rain upon me.

I await a single glance,

You avoid my every nuance.

I will always love you,

You will never love me.

I will forever wait,

You confirm my fate.

My love empowers you,

Your neglect disembowels me.

I live for your gain,

You live for my pain.

I will wink at you,

You will confirm it true.

I will our love to be,

You will forever love me."

He finished and everyone was silent. My skin prickled from a fresh chill in the air. All I could think was, was that poem about me?

Had I ever winked at him? I didn't think I had but the rest; the gloom, the admiration? Did he really feel that ignored by me?

Alex was sitting next to me today, and he leaned close to whisper. "Was that about you?"

I shot him a glare to silence him.

The professor seemed to realize the poem was over. He cleared his throat and sat up. Had he even been listening? It *had* been an incredibly long poem.

"Very good, Jimena. You may take your seat. Uh, who wants to go next?"

I didn't pay attention to the rest of the poems. When it was my turn, I read my Haiku about sunflowers, which I'd put about ten minutes of effort into.

The class was over once the last person read their poem, and since most of us had written short ones, it ended early. Jimena bolted for the exit when the professor released us, as he always did. I jumped from my seat and took chase, managing to catch up to him before he left the building.

"Jimena!" I shouted his name and grabbed his shoulder to turn him around. He jerked away and glared at me. "Was that poem about me?"

"Don't flatter yourself. It's about all the people who have dicked me over."

"I'm sorry if I ever made you feel invisible or insignificant."

"You don't have to lie, and I told you not to speak to me in public."

"Come here then." I went to the nearest restroom and was grateful when I turned around to find that he had followed. "Have you thought about what I said?"

"I'm not telling people you're my boyfriend."

Kidnapper

What was the point of this? I'd written the poem months ago, and when the teacher had put me on the spot, I pulled it out and read it.

"I haven't changed my mind about anything, so what happened to the whole fuck off statement? I didn't think we were talking to each other." And I needed to get home and deal with the topsoil on the not-nearly-buried-deep-enough, freshly rotting corpse in my yard. I'd put her in the hole that had been meant for Nic.

"I miss you," Nic said. "I'm willing to give you… humor you with—"

"Just say what you want. I have things to do."

"I want you to fuck me in the bathroom stall."

I'd never had someone say that to me. And the way he was looking at me made it seem he truly meant it.

"My poem got you all hot and heavy?"

"Will you do it or not?"

Why was I already getting hard thinking about it when I'd been limp as a noodle when I'd tried to fuck my nameless corpse? *Stop. Changing. Me.* What if sleeping with the dead had lost its appeal? What if my victims needed to be alive from now on?

"Get in the stall and take your pants off, and you'll find out," I said. He didn't hesitate to go directly to the first stall. I followed slowly, not sure I truly believed he was obeying me so easily. I peered in the stall, and sure enough, his pants and underwear were around his ankles.

I stepped inside with him and pulled the door shut. I locked it and ran my fingers over his presented ass. I wanted to cut it. Carve up the perfectly shaped melons until they were so covered in scars that no one would ever—"

"Are you just going to stare or are you going to do something?"

I undid my fly and spat into my hand. I fingered his opening, and he groaned.

"Don't make any noise," I said. "If I do this, you have to be completely silent." He nodded and looked away from me.

I was annoyed at how aroused I was. But rather than dwell on it, I shoved my cock into him so hard and rough that I knew it had to hurt. Yet, he managed to stay silent. I only felt the tremor of surprise in his body. I didn't hold back. I hadn't lubricated us enough, so every thrust abrased me as much as it did him. But I wanted the pain. I wanted this to be punishment.

And despite it all, he stayed silent and impossibly still. I climaxed in less than a minute. Did that qualify me with erectile dysfunction? I looked down, horrified at my performance because this... this kind of embarrassment was exactly why I wanted my partners to be dead and unable to comment. Because no matter what words he offered, it was simply unthinkable to let someone witness me in such a situation.

I pulled out, unnerved and unsure how to reclaim control. He spun, impossibly fast and put his face against my neck. He inhaled deeply, then made a sharp huff, as if he'd smelled something bad. He jerked back and glared at me.

"Did you not like it? What's wrong?" he asked.

What's wrong? Was that his way of inquiring about my premature ejaculation?

"You're the one who asked me to fuck you, so I did. Beggars don't get to be picky," I quipped, trying to put up a good front. That's right, I had come that quickly on purpose. "I didn't want my dick in you any longer than necessary. I came, so it counts as fucking you, which is what you asked me to do."

He leaned closer. His eyes were so close to mine I couldn't focus on his face.

"You've never been scared of me before. Why are you now?"

"What? I am not. What the fuck? Get out of my face." I raised my hands to push him away and heard the restroom door open. He put his hand over my mouth and put a finger on his own lips to gesture for me to be silent.

"Nic, hurry up. What's the problem? We're going to be late for our meeting with the professor," Alex said.

Nic removed his hand and gestured again for me to be quiet. Then… his body vanished. I blinked my eyes, unable to grasp what I had just seen. There had been Nic's body in front of me, then an instant of black mist where his body had been, which then dispersed like someone had blown it with a fan.

And now Nic was gone from the stall I stood in.

A door two stalls away slammed open noisily.

"Can't a guy take a dump in peace?" Nic asked.

"You want me to say that to the professor?" Alex asked. "Oh, sorry, Nic couldn't make it. He thought taking a dump was more important than—"

"I'm coming. Stop being an ass."

I heard the sink run, then some paper towels were grabbed, followed by two sets of footsteps exiting the room. I exhaled a breath I hadn't realized I had been holding.

What the hell had just happened?

I cautiously opened the stall door and peered out. No one present. I cleaned myself in the sink, feeling a great need to wash my dick off because I had no idea what I'd just been sticking it in.

I walked stiffly to the campus library. I didn't work tonight, and the idea of… being alone wasn't something my brain could process at the moment. I was in shock. A new level of delirium, and I needed to sit somewhere and decide if I should check myself into a clinic.

I flashed my student ID as I passed the librarian and logged onto a computer. I pulled up the archives and stared at the search box.

If I sat here and did nothing, someone might notice my odd behavior. Slowly, with one finger, I typed "black mist meaning." Maybe it would tell me that seeing black mist clouds that aren't really there is a warning sign for brain cancer. That would give me a good opening comment to tell my doctor.

The urban dictionary was the first result. It said, "A sexual predator who is bisexual that has also been charged with rape."

"I mean literal black smoke," I muttered at the computer. I ignored the games and products that had the name black mist and reached the articles written about actual black smoke.

> *Black mist may be a spiritual being, good or evil. Black is often associated with evil.*

> *Paranormal activity? Black mist captured in hotel surveillance video.*

> *Most demonic hauntings, the occupants often claim to be followed by black mist or black fog.*

"It's in my head. It has to be." I deleted the search and typed another. Things demons don't like. I skimmed over the religious bullshit that I didn't think for a moment would work. Different metals came up along with references to salt. Metals. I stared at the screen for a moment as I recalled my pipe. He had vanished every time I'd swung it at him.

I typed lead into the search.

Certain metals, such as lead, have been proven effective against demons. The metal is toxic to their skin and can be used to weaken them to the point where normal means to kill them can be achieved. This means—

"Hey, Jimena."

I jumped, clattering the keyboard and quickly closing the windows. In the seat next to me sat Suzie.

"I've never seen you in the library before. Is this research about the project Nic is helping you with?"

I shook my head.

"You know, I've taken the same classes he has. So, if you ever need help, you can ask me."

"Th-thanks." Why was she here? Why was she talking to me?

She glanced around as if worried someone might be watching. Normally, I'd take offense and assume she was concerned to be seen talking to someone as disgusting as myself, but something told me this was not the case.

She leaned closer and lowered her voice.

"Nic seems like he's lost interest in you, so, I don't mean this the wrong way, but you should get out while you can. He's not the kind of person you think he is. So, whatever it is that he's helping you with, I can help you, instead, okay?"

I stared at her, not sure how to take her kind words. Was she a vying demon wanting to take me from him?

"I-I don't understand."

I'd never paid her all that much attention other than what was needed to observe Nic. She reached up with her fingers and pulled on her collar.

Beneath it was a dark bruise, a fresh one, possibly days old. Once she knew I'd seen it, she released the material and covered it.

"Jimena—" Her voice wavered a bit as she spoke. She found some internal strength as she said the next words. "Take his lapse in interest as a blessing and *get out*."

I was wrong.

She wasn't a demon wanting to snatch me away from Nic.

And she wasn't Nic's friend.

I'd glossed over a part in the articles that had said some demons would keep a collection of humans near them for regular feedings. They would do things to manipulate the humans into staying near them, a bunch of passive aggressive shit that I was sure any psychiatrist would have a field day researching. I doubted Suzie or the others knew Nic was a demon. He was their charismatic friend who occasionally turned violent on them. Maybe they just thought he had a bad temper.

"Thank you," I said. "Suzie, do you think you could not tell Nic you saw me here? Can we keep it a secret that we spoke?"

"I-I'd like to do that for you, Jimena. I would, but Nic is the one who told me to come here and find you. He wanted me to give you this." She put a piece of paper on the desk next to the keyboard. "I have to give it to you, but you don't have to look at it."

She stood up quickly and rushed out of the library so brashly that people probably thought I'd said something rude to her.

I picked up the paper and flipped it open.

On it was a scribbled phone number and the words, *Call me*.

I scrunched up the paper and stuffed it in my pocket. I deleted all traces of what I'd been researching and restarted the computer. For whatever good it did.

Nic knew I was in the library, so it was a given that he knew what I'd been doing.

I wasn't an idiot. It wasn't in Nic's best interest for me to stay alive now that I knew what he was. But it wasn't in my best interest to let him keep living since he knew what I was. There was the potential for a mutual agreement of silence.

He had to know he wasn't in immediate danger. If I told people he was demon, it would only mark me as a lunatic. Even I was questioning the theory.

"It doesn't matter," I muttered as I got up. "If he was going to do something, he would have done it already."

I still had a shallow grave in my yard to deal with. Fuck whatever Nic was. And so, I went as planned to the local hardware store to buy cement so that I could make a nice patio above the grave. And I bought all the lead items I could find, because those could come in handy.

As I shoved the receipt into my pocket, I touched the paper with Nic's number.

"I think we're past pretending to not know each other," I said to the empty parking lot. And at this point, people knowing I knew him was as much a safety net for me as it was for him. I stood next to my car and grinned as I typed his number into my phone.

"Which of us will kill the other first, I wonder."

I texted a to-the-point message of *I'm busy, what do you want?*

I opened my trunk and hefted the first bag of cement into it, and my phone chimed.

I need to know you are okay. Why were you scared?

What the hell? Was he still hung up on that? Why did he think—? My mind jumped back to the moment we were in the bathroom together.

When he'd inhaled near my neck, I had been afraid… afraid he would judge my sexual failure. Had he… sensed that? But misunderstood it as… something else? And why would that matter?

Another text came, this time in all capital letters. *WHY*

My pulse quickened as I stared at my phone, suddenly regretting giving him this new avenue to speak to me.

I wasn't about to tell him the truth, but if I didn't tell him something, he would assume the worse—that I was afraid of him as a demon. And if I was afraid of him, I was likely to do something rash, like kill him.

He had the same kind of phone as me, so he'd already been sent a notification that I'd read his message. I started typing, hoping it would appease his impatience.

It was public sex. Why would I not be terrified? I thought someone would catch us. And you know I don't want anyone to know about us.

I sent it and waited. The read notification came through immediately.

The phone rang, and I tossed it into the car as though it were a hot coal. A couple walking past gawked at my odd behavior, and I tried to offer them a smile. I retrieved the phone and answered.

"I'm sorry," Nic said before I could even say hello. "I shouldn't have pressured you like that. Can I come over tonight and make it up to you? I'll do whatever you want. You can punish me for—"

"I can't tonight." I gritted my teeth. I really did have a valid reason for why. Not that I could say it over the phone.

"Jimena—"

"Your punishment is that you aren't allowed to come over or talk to me until Friday when I see you in class. Understand?"

Silence.

"You're allowed to tell me you understand."

"I understand."

"Good." I disconnected the call. Did I believe he would actually stay away? No. But at least if he did come looking, he would find I was simply dealing with a dead body, not plotting his murder. Or at least I would make it look like I wasn't doing both.

CHAPTER six

Kidnapper

Time to put my plan into action, sort of. I walked into class ten minutes early, but I knew Nic would already be there with his gaggle of friends. They were always early. I kept my hands in the front pockets of my white hoodie as I approached the desks they sat at.

"Hi, Nic," I said, but the words came out so softly even I didn't hear them. Suzie glanced in my direction, not because she'd heard me but perhaps out of pity or surprise that I hadn't heeded her warning. I cleared my throat and tried again.

"Nic, I think Jimena is trying to get your attention," Alex said. The four of them went silent and stared at me, putting me in the spotlight at maximum peer pressure.

"Nic, w-would you go on a date with me?" I asked. That wasn't bad, only one stutter. And when you considered how this was the first time I'd asked someone out in my entire life, I thought I had done pretty damn good.

"What was that?" Nic asked, even though I knew darn well I'd spoken perfectly clear. The professor walked in, along with a few more classmates.

"I was wondering if you'd go on a date with me," I repeated, louder this time, in the hopes he wouldn't ask for another attempt. I didn't dare check, but I was certain every set of eyes in the room were now staring at me.

"What kind of date?" Nic asked. He rested his chin on his hand and peered at me curiously.

Jake chuckled as he misread what Nic was doing.

"Yeah, what kind of date?" Alex the hippie asked. "Shouldn't you have brought some flowers and chocolates so you can ask him properly?"

"At least he didn't bring a ring and ask for his hand," Jake said. I couldn't recall ever hearing Jake speak before.

"He has to save something for next week," Alex said. The two of them high-fived as they fed off each other's glee. No sooner had their hands touched, then both of their chairs flipped, knocking them both to the ground. I saw Nic's foot move away from where the legs of their chairs had been.

"I was asking a serious question," Nic said.

"What's going on over there?" the professor asked. Jake and Alex quickly apologized as they put their chairs back in order.

"Suzie, move seats. Let Jimena sit next to me," Nic ordered. She quickly grabbed her books and moved to the row in front of us. "Sit."

I obediently plopped down, and Nic draped an arm around my shoulders.

"So, what kind of date, Jimena?" Nic asked again.

"Um, the classic kind."

"One in public?"

"D-dinner and a movie, maybe."

He was too close. I could feel his breath on me, and I swear he leaned in and sniffed my neck. He must not have liked what he smelled because he gave a short growl and detached himself, moving back to his own seat.

"What?" I turned to face him since the hoodie kept my peripheral vision limited. He had the same expression on his face that he'd had in the bathroom.

"You're still afraid of me," Nic said, like it was the worst possible thing imaginable.

"But... I'm not."

"You're lying."

"I'm nervous because you haven't answered me yet. Don't interpret my emotions however you want. If I'm scared it's because I'm scared you're going to reject me because I've never put myself out there like this before. Fuck!" I pulled my hoodie over more of my face, wishing I'd brought a notebook to busy myself with.

He didn't press me any further. The professor had started the lecture, and true to Nic's word, he took his education seriously, so of course, he wasn't going to talk when the teacher was. My mind raced through various levels of panic because Nic had still not answered me.

Had he done that on purpose? Just to torment me? The amount of adrenaline rushing through me should have given me a heart attack right there. I was not built for this kind of stress.

It was weird being next to him instead of in the back of the class where I could watch him. If I turned my head to view him, it would be too obvious. I sat so stiffly that every muscle in my body ached from the tension.

The professor announced class was over, and the students got up to leave. It was like my entire life had been on a ninety-minute pause.

"Jimena," Nic said. He said nothing more, so I turned to face him. He looked so casual, resting his head on one arm as he studied me. "Join us for lunch? I'll count it as our public date."

"I have work directly after class," I said. "I was—"

"What time?" He draped an arm around my shoulders and pulled me close. "What time do you need to be at work?"

I didn't want to admit that it was two hours away, because if I did, then I was admitting I had time to eat with them.

"Is our relationship going to be founded on lies? Don't you want to prove to me that you're serious? That you're willing to spend time with me in public?"

The hoodie blocked me from any skin-on-skin contact he was trying to achieve, but it still felt like his attention was boring into me.

"I can't be late," I said.

"We eat quick," Alex offered. "Only twenty, maybe thirty minutes. You can spare that, right?"

He was looking at me like he was sincerely trying to help. I wasn't sure how to interpret their behavior. Were they all in on some massive trick? Or did they want to protect me from Nic? Or would they passively try to prevent me from joining their social circle?

I'd never planned on interacting with his friends, so this was new territory. He was supposed to be tied up and isolated in my basement. I wasn't supposed to be here trying to figure out how feasible it would be to share him with his friends.

Share.

This was so fucked up.

"Jimena." Nic pulled me closer, and it felt like he was nuzzling my neck, though, I couldn't be certain since the cloth of the hoodie was between us. "You are serious about this, right? Being my proper boyfriend?"

"Yes," I said. "I'll eat lunch with you."

Publicly dating.

I felt like I was in fucking middle school.

But if we were both murderous monsters who might kill each other, then the only way to have any degree of insurance that one of us wouldn't kill the other was to make it known in the public eye that we knew each other.

I could still kill him, but I would have to be smarter about it. I had a lot more at stake than he did, because if there was any degree of an investigation, they might discover all the other bodies on my property. Although, he might have skeletons in his closet as well.

"You're over thinking this," Nic said. He selected some food on the cafeteria line and placed it on my tray. "You haven't said a word since we left the classroom." He tried to tug my hoodie down but I swatted him away.

"Just think of it like you're back in high school having lunch with your friends. You ate lunch in a cafeteria in high school, right?" He put a carton of milk on my tray and one on his, then added a cup of fruit. He wasn't even asking me what I liked or didn't.

The line got held up as the person at the register fished for exact change in their pocket. Nic ran his fingers along the edge of my hoodie again.

"I really wish you would put this down. I like seeing your face."

I pulled away and stared at the food he'd selected for me. Some dumb sandwich that might've been a poor man's attempt at a sloppy joe and an unidentifiable casserole—or was it simply macaroni and cheese? The food here was horrible. How could he eat this every day?

The line moved again, and Nic paid for mine. If he expected a thank you, he was going to be waiting a while for it.

I followed him to the table where his friends sat. Suzie was smart and had brought her own sack lunch. The two men had gone to the snack line and got pre-heated slices of pizza. I sat across from Suzie as Nic sat next to me.

Suzie wore a turtleneck sweater even though the weather wasn't cold enough to warrant it. I wondered what the bruises looked like today. If I'd done my job properly the first time, I'd have put him in my basement, and she wouldn't have gotten hurt.

Would his friends miss him if he died? I'd initially thought they would, but what if they were instead relieved?

"Why are you staring at her?" Alex asked. "Are you using Nic to get closer to Suzie?"

I froze like a frightened rabbit and wished my heart would just give out. I couldn't admit that I knew about the marks on her neck. But what else could I say?

"Are you jealous he isn't staring at you?" Nic asked. "Are you hoping he secretly wants to suck your dick?"

Alex scoffed, and instead of being agitated, he looked... amused?

"Mine is better than yours. Yours is totally a starter dick," Alex said. He looked at me, and pointed to Nic. "After you learn how to give his tiny dick a good blowjob, you can upgrade to mine. It's too big for beginners."

Jake laughed so hard that he coughed up some of his soda. "What the hell is all that cocky talk? I've seen your dick. It's what they use in the encyclopedia to define a micro-dick. I think it might even be the photo they use."

"The hell it is! And why are you looking at my dick?"

They were insulting each other, yet it was all in jest. They weren't actually upset. I picked up my fork and stirred the casserole around, realizing I knew very little about how friendships worked.

"I try not to listen to them. They're idiots," Suzie said. "Completely rude."

I nodded.

"It's better," she said. "My neck. That's why you were staring, right? It's better."

I glanced up and saw the kind smile on her face.

"How did he know about your neck?" Nic asked.

"We saw each other in the library," I said. "When you sent her to give me the note, I noticed it. Her shirt was disheveled from how she'd rushed to find me."

If he was going to be mad at someone, I wanted it to be me, not her. The fact I'd found the courage to speak up like that, well, I wouldn't have thought I'd had it in me.

"Yeah, I guess I did get a bit too rough when I was fucking her," Nic said. He bumped his shoulder into mine. "I was thinking of you and remembered how hard you like it. Completely forgot that Suzie is more fragile than you are."

Even though I'd already known that was likely what happened, I wasn't prepared for him to blatantly admit it like that. Even Suzie paled as though she was embarrassed and surprised he'd said it.

"I have to go to work," I said. I rose, but Nic yanked me back down. "You haven't eaten."

"I sat here, didn't I? I never said I would eat."

He pulled the hoodie off, exposing my entire head to the world.

"I ate your shit cooking even though it gave me food poisoning," Nic said. "I paid for your lunch. Be polite and eat it."

"I'll pay you back for it." I reached into my pocket for some cash, and he grabbed my wrist to stop me.

"I don't want that. I want you to sit here and be with me. Just… *sit here*." His hand where he gripped me gave a tremble.

What exactly was this?

"You treat your friends like shit, and you're treating me like shit. Unlike them, I don't want to *sit here* and tolerate it. So. Let. Go."

His friends had stopped talking and gawked at us as we stared at each other.

It was then I realized.

Nic didn't know how to do this either.

Kidnapped

What was I doing?

I let go of his wrist.

He was trying. For whatever his reasons were, he actually was trying. And I was doing everything I could to make it as horrible for him as possible.

I knew it was unlikely he had friends in school, so I'd made it a point to bring it up. I knew mentioning having slept with Suzie would hurt him, so I said it. And I could tell he didn't want to eat the food, so I wanted to force him to eat it.

All because I was pissed that he wasn't slathering me in love and feel-good emotions like he normally did. He was all scared and agitated, and it was pissing me off.

I only wanted him because he loved me.

But I didn't know how to make him love me or trigger those emotions within him. I didn't even know why he'd fallen in love with me in the first place.

Maybe the only time he would feel love for me would be when he was trying to kill me.

"You're right. I'm sorry," I said. "You can, uh, you can go."

He stood and stared at me for a long time, his hair tousled from the hoodie, and I wondered what horrid things he was imagining doing to me.

"You can punish me tonight, alright? I'll come by, just say the time."

"Is that why you did it? Did you want to upset me? Do you want me to punish you?"

I felt it then. The first wave of attraction I'd felt from him all day. He liked the idea that I wanted to be punished.

"You don't have to act out." He put his hand on my head and tightened his fingers in the strands, pulling hard enough to hurt. "I already know you deserve to be punished."

There it was. His desire and want. Just feeling the small bit he was experiencing was enough to get me hard. After so many days of nothing, I could barely restrain myself from grabbing him and feeding on him right now.

"Yes, that's what I want," I said.

"I'm going to work," he said. He let go of me and took a step back. "Your first punishment is that you have to wait until *tomorrow* night before you can come over. I'll text you a time."

What? An entire day and half? Why were his recent punishments all about keeping me from going to his house?

He left the cafeteria, and I found myself stared at by Suzie, Jake, and Alex.

"What the hell was that?" Alex asked. "Are you into BDSM or something? Is he, like, your dom?"

"That's not your business, Alex."

Suzie had finished her salad and got up.

"Where are you going?"

"That's not *your* business," she quipped, tossing my words back at me. I gritted my teeth but didn't follow her.

I could barely pay attention in my afternoon classes, and the idea of having to wait until tomorrow to see Jimena was making my skin itch. Wasn't he supposed to be obsessed with me? Shouldn't he be the one tossing in his bed, unable to sleep because I wasn't safely tucked in his basement?

I pulled out my phone and messaged him.

How about I stay in your basement tonight? You can chain me to the post.

His response was immediate.

No.

I groaned as my cock swelled. I wanted him. How did people do this? I needed release. I went to Suzie. Even though it was two in the morning I knew she'd be awake studying.

She stayed in the dorms, but her roommate was often not there because she was involved in so many clubs. It was coed dorms, so I went directly to her room and knocked. She answered, dressed in cotton pajamas.

"It's late," she said, rubbing her eyes, but I could tell she hadn't been asleep.

"You need a break. You were studying, right?" I pushed my way past her into the room.

"Nic, not—"

I grabbed her neck, my fingers perfectly fitting into the marks that were fading from last time. I backed her up and used her body to push the door closed.

"I can't see Jimena until tomorrow. So, how about we have some fun, yeah?" I slipped my hand under her top and squeezed her breast. I leaned my head over her shoulder and sniffed. She smelled of fear. I hated the smell on Jimena, but on others, it was the strongest flavor I could get. "I'll be fast so you can get back to studying."

I let go of her and gave her a push toward the bed. I undid my fly, my cock eager to be inside someone. This would at least sate my hunger until tomorrow.

She was on the bed but not undressing as she should be.

"I-I want to call off our arrangement," she said.

I froze. "What?"

"Our deal, I want out. You have Jimena now, and you still have Alex and Jake. Three is all you need, so… I want out."

"We made a deal," I said. "I saved your mother when she was dying of cancer. She's alive and healthy, no sign of cancer. Do you want her to relapse? Cancer can come back. And I'm telling you, it will. If you—"

"If she knew the price I was paying, she wouldn't want me to keep doing it. I want out."

"Thyroid cancer is a horrible way to go… she won't last long. It'll spread fast. I'll make sure of that."

"But you don't have to. I've been doing everything you wanted for three years. Haven't I—"

"Our deal was ten."

She broke into tears.

"You serve me for ten years, and I keep the cancer away for the rest of her life. You're lucky you made the deal with me. Someone else could have easily tricked you and had your mother die from something else. Then they get you and have ..." I stopped talking because I realized she was no longer listening.

"Fine," I said. "She won't get cancer. She'll stay healthy."

I stuffed my unsatisfied cock back into my trousers. She ceased the sobbing and peered at me between her fingers.

"Really?"

If a deal was asked to be broken, we were obligated to break it. But the cost of ending it was completely up to us.

"Your mother will be fine. Our deal is over." I turned and pulled open her door. Under my breath I muttered. "But you won't be." My eyes flashed demonic as I spread the first contaminated cells into her uterus. I'd give her a chance. If she went to a doctor quickly, they could save her by removing her uterus. I mean, I could have been a real dick and put the cells in her brain.

Kidnapped

"I'm not waiting," I said as Jimena opened his front door.

I was completely drenched from the rain since he'd kept me out here, pounding on his door like a lunatic for a good twenty minutes.

"I said tomorrow," Jimena said. His eyes roved around my body, taking in my haggard appearance.

Alex and Jake had different arrangements with me, nonsexual ones, and I wasn't in the mood to go find a stranger to seduce.

"And I want *you. Now.* So, let me in."

He narrowed his eyes at me. "You can't come in unless I invite you, can you?"

I grabbed his shirt and yanked him onto the front porch with me. He was an idiot.

"You can either invite me in, or I can fuck you here on the porch. Your choice."

His eyes bulged. "I thought you were coming here for—"

I didn't let him finish. I kissed him and it triggered that rush of emotions from him that I was craving. He did like the idea that I'd come here because I couldn't stay away. In fact, I was pretty sure he loved the idea.

I moved to kiss his neck, and he rubbed his body against me, instinctively wanting the same thing I did.

"You can come in," Jimena said.

Kidnapped

I was a bit surprised when I woke up in his bed and was still intact. It was a rare thing and one I wasn't going to take for granted.

He was lying next to me, but I knew he'd been up for a while. He was fully dressed and a steaming cup of what smelled like coffee was behind him on the side table.

"Good morning," I said. He reached over and brushed some hair from my brow. I was still naked and wondered if I was allowed to get dressed. The morning after was always when he pulled out his harsher punishments.

"I let you do what you wanted last night," Jimena said. "You were quite aggressive."

I hadn't hurt him. I'd pleasured him in every way I could. A normal person would be thrilled. If I'd treated Suzie like that, she wouldn't have risked death to free herself. But Suzie didn't love me. Unless I inflicted pain on her, her soul tasted like nothing but obligation.

She knew I was a monster who had taken advantage of her situation. I wasn't certain what Jimena thought I was.

"So, today we do what you want? More games?"

He stroked the side of my face where he had once cut it. He gave a sad huff.

"No," he said. "Breakfast and then you need to go." He reached behind him and grabbed the coffee. "Here. To wake you and get you moving."

This was… not like him.

"You want me out?"

"There was a reason I wanted you to wait until tonight to come over. I have other… things in my life."

"Things I can't be part of?" I took the coffee as he stood. He hovered in the doorway.

"Don't be so sensitive. It's not another guy or anything."

Did that mean…? *Was* someone coming over? And why did that bother me so much?

"I don't have to leave. You can lock me in the basement until they're gone."

"What? Why would I do that?"

I crossed the room and tried to approach him but he seemed afraid of my nudity so I stopped.

"You can just tell them I'm your roommate. That's what you wanted, right? For me to live with you?"

"Stop talking weird and just leave. You wanted this to be normal or whatever, so, uh, you leaving is normal. That's what—"

I kissed him gently, the way I knew he liked but also hated. He pushed me away and moved into the hallway.

"Am I just a one-night stand to you?" I asked.

"I'm being polite and offering you breakfast! Go take a shower and at least stop being naked."

He turned from me and went to the kitchen. I let him go and decided his request wasn't completely unreasonable. He had washed my clothes and they were neatly folded on top of the dresser. I grabbed them and went to the adjoining bathroom.

I turned on the shower and stared for a moment at the soaps and shampoos.

They were mine.

Well, not literally stolen from my house, but they were the same brand and scent I used. How had I not noticed it before? I quickly searched and realized he had the same toothpaste, mouthwash, deodorant… hell, even the toilet paper looked like the brand I used. Had he taken inventory when he'd been in my apartment that one time? Had he memorized it all?

I quickly showered and used the toiletries that were all too familiar to me. Part of me wondered if I opened a few drawers on the dresser, would I find clothing inside that was identical to mine? *Were* these the clothes I had worn yesterday?

I uneasily made my way to the kitchen and hesitated. Was I supposed to eat on the floor like a dog or at the table like a person?

He placed a large omelet on the folding table near the counter. A glass of orange juice sat next to it.

"Go ahead," he said. "We don't have time for games. I already told you."

Still, it felt weird. I settled into the chair and picked up the fork. How could it feel so weird to have him treating me normal?

"Do you really want to move in?" Jimena asked. "Like, be my roommate?"

If we were able to actually figure out a way to make this work that didn't have me so on edge, yes. Living here would be nice compared to being at my brother's apartment.

"I think we could make it work, yes," I said.

"You would be implicated if anyone found out about the bodies."

"You're planning to take me down for your crimes?"

"I'm just making sure you're aware."

He wasn't eating. I didn't like that. And I hadn't seen him cook this. I took a third mouthful, already knowing I would regret it. I chewed slowly and noticed his defensive posture. He'd had his arms crossed all morning.

"I don't like you hurting Suzie. I want you to leave her alone."

"That's already been handled."

"Handled?"

"My arrangement with her is over. I knew it was bothering you." It seemed smart to let him assume I had broken things off for his benefit.

"What was she to you?"

"Nothing. Okay? I said it's over."

"What are you?"

"What are you? What kind of question is that?" I'd eaten half the omelet, and my stomach wasn't upset. Maybe he hadn't poisoned it.

"I've seen you do some weird shit. So—"

"You do weird shit too, Jimena."

We stared at each other, and I waited to see if he'd have the courage to be more specific. He stepped closer, and I couldn't get a solid read on him. Was he going to slap me?

"Do you want to tell me what is specifically bothering you?" I asked.

He unfolded his arms, and I saw the glint of metal that had been previously tucked up his sleeve. Before I knew what he was doing, pain lashed my hand, and my breath came in a staggered gasp.

I stared at what he'd done.

My hand had been lying flat on the table. He'd driven the knife into it. It was a serrated knife, the kind that went in easily but when pulled out, had hooks that would get caught. And he'd pushed it deep enough to wedge it into the folding table.

And the metal was burning. It had no handle covering, so when I went to touch it, my fingers burned.

"You stabbed me with a hunting knife."

It hurt as if the thing was coated in chemicals that were burning my skin.

"It seems I did," he agreed.

"What's on this?" I tried to touch it, but the pain on my fingers was too intense for me to grip it. "I need you to take it out."

My entire body started sweating. I wasn't sure how long I could last before I passed out.

"Why would you react so strongly to a lead knife in your hand? Why don't you just vanish like you did when I whacked you with a lead pipe? Vanish, Nicodemus."

"What?"

"Do like before. Turn into the black smoke and leave."

"I don't know what you're talking about, Jimena! Please, calm down and take the knife out. It's hurting me. Please."

We both heard the knock on the door and the subsequent clink of a lock as the front door was pushed open.

"You have to go," Jimena said. "Do your black mist thing and leave."

Is that why he stabbed me? Because he thought it would make me leave like when he'd hit me with the pipe?

"I can't." I gestured to the knife with my good hand. "Lead keeps me from doing that. It hurts me, okay? Is that what you wanted to learn? Now. Take. It. Out."

"Hemy?" a woman's voice called from the foyer. Two sets of footsteps came toward the kitchen.

"Mom, just a minute!" Jimena shouted. He grabbed the metal handle of the knife and yanked. I managed not to scream but just barely. My world went white for a brief moment, but I stayed on my feet. I sagged against the table as I waited for the room to stop spinning.

Jimena threw the knife into a drawer just as his guests reached the kitchen.

"Did you make us breakfast?" a man asked. "Your omelets are always—"

The man stopped speaking, and a woman peeked around him. Her entire expression changed as she saw me.

"What happened?" the woman asked.

"He's fine, Mom," Jimena quickly said as he moved to stand in front of the table where most of the blood was visible. I was too disoriented to bother doing anything to stop the bleeding that was now flowing quite freely.

"He's the guy from the mall," the man said, I recognized him now. "The one that was being all creepy and said—"

"He's my boyfriend," Jimena blurted. Perhaps he thought throwing that news at them would distract them from the fact I had a horrible wound that was gushing blood all over the kitchen.

"We were having a fight that day. But we are all good now. I mean, emotionally. Obviously, we had this little, uh, accident." Jimena looked over at me, and he flinched as if he hadn't expected my wound to be as graphic as it was.

"I was a nurse for thirty years. Let me see." His mom came around the table and reached for my hand but stopped. "Can you get up? We should wash this at the sink."

"You have a boyfriend?" his brother said. "Why were you keeping this a secret? This is great. It's great to meet you. I mean, not under these circumstances. Wow, that looks bad."

His mother guided me to the sink and turned on the water. She flushed the wound out and I was surprised at how little it hurt. That probably wasn't a good sign.

"Paul, get the first aid kit," she said.

"It's still in the bathroom, right, Hemy?" the brother asked, now identified as Paul.

"Yeah, under the sink." Jimena moved a chair under me, and I sat in it without thinking. I hadn't realized how dizzy I was. I hadn't lost that much blood, had I? No, it was the lead and possibly whatever he'd put in my food if he had poisoned it, which I now suspected he had.

"This is deep. Did you cut it clean through?" She couldn't get enough of the blood away to get a good look at it. "We should take you to the emergency room."

"Mom, that isn't necessary. He's fine."

"Why do your friends always get hurt? I feel like every time I meet one of your friends, they are bleeding."

"I'm not his friend," I said. I must have paused longer than I intended because they both seemed to stare at me with a mix of puzzlement and horror. "Did you not hear him? I'm his *boy*friend."

Jimena visibly relaxed. "Now isn't the time to worry about that kind of clarification, *Nic*."

Paul was back with the kit, and he handed her a roll of gauze, which she skillfully used to wrap my hand until it became three times its normal size.

"Hold it above your heart," she directed. "And let's get you to the hospital."

"Mom, no." Jimena seemed adamant about this, but I was actually thinking it might be a good move. I would eventually be able to absorb enough souls to regenerate, but not until I recovered from the lead. Until then, I was going to be in pain. Some modern medicine sounded pretty good, because even now, I wasn't certain if my inability to focus was due to the pain or poison.

"He needs a doctor."

Jimena was battling an internal fight. We could all see it. I wondered if I was the only one who knew the true extent of that fight.

"You came over for a reason," I said. "I wouldn't want to ruin whatever your plans are. I can call my brother, and he can take me."

"No!" Jimena shouted viciously as though it was the worst idea he'd ever heard. "I'll take you. They're just here to try to convince me to go to the family reunion."

"It's not a reunion," Paul said. "I've explained this. It's grandpa's ninetieth birthday." He held up an envelope. "I brought the plane ticket with me and," he spread his fingers and displayed two pamphlets, "brochures telling you all about the resort we'll be staying at."

"Everyone is going. You'll be the only one not there," his mother added.

"I'm not actually related to any of you. No one will miss me. I'm not going," Jimena said.

"You know I don't like it when you talk like that. You are as much a part of this family as anyone. And you are always missed when you don't attend our gatherings," his mother said.

"We can get another ticket," Paul said. He pointed at me. "You can bring your boyfriend. How about that? You two can even sneak off and do, uh, well, not this, I hope." He eyed my hand, as if unsure the incident was an accident. "You'll enjoy it more if a friend is with you, so you aren't stuck with the family the whole time, right?"

"That's right," his mother said. She looked at me, a stranger who had suddenly become their leverage. "You can show off your boyfriend to everyone. Weren't you always annoyed by how everyone said you'd never get a, uh, significant other? Well, now you can come prove them wrong."

Their pitch was getting rocky and awkward for all involved, even I could see that. Why did they want him to go so badly? Was this normal for a family? Did they really just want to see him happy and together with the rest of them? It seemed odd for someone to care about Jimena like they were. Did they not know he was a psychopath? Did he hide it that well? Or were these people just *that* kind? Did they love him despite his flaws?

They were nervous, and I could see they feared him, but I was confident they also cared for him. Their attempts seemed sincere. How did he turn out so angry at the world when he had people like this supporting him?

"I don't need their acceptance," Jimena said. "Can I take him to the hospital now? Weren't you insisting I do that just a few seconds ago?"

"I'll leave this here." Paul put the papers on a clean spot of the table. "Think about it, okay?"

CHAPTER seven

Kidnapped

My hand kept throbbing, and if I moved my head too quickly, the room spun a bit. My stomach swam, perhaps from the dizziness. I wondered if the hospital would run a tox screen and see what drugs were in me. They had to, right? Before they could give me any drugs?

Am I finally going to learn what you've been giving me?

I blinked my eyes and focused on Jimena who sat on the hard plastic chair next to me in the waiting room of the ER. He had a clipboard and scribbled furiously on the medical screening forms the receptionist had given him.

I was still in a bit of disbelief that he'd actually brought me here. Didn't this go against everything he believed? Didn't he want me to die?

"Your family seem nice," I said. "I'll go with you to that reunion-birthday thing if you want."

He didn't look up from the paper as he wrote.

"You should have left when I'd told you to."

"You didn't want me to meet them. Yeah. Sure. You sorta botched that up stabbing me. Why did you do this anyway?"

"It was just a stupid article I read. I didn't think it would…" He took a moment to glare at me before resuming his scribbling. Like the article was my fault.

"It's a lead allergy. The shit is toxic to everyone. Ever heard of lead paint?"

"Little kids eating lead paint chips is different. You didn't eat the fucking knife," he grumbled.

"Don't be so irritable. You shouldn't be mean to me when I don't feel good." I leaned closer and nuzzled his neck, perhaps because my head felt so heavy that I wanted a break from supporting it. "You're my lover."

"I'm your what?" Jimena got up from the seat as if I'd poked him with a lump of hot coal. "I am not your lover. I am your stalker. How do you not understand the difference?" He flipped the forms around and thrust them in my face. "I completed your entire medical history paperwork without needing to ask you a single question. How does that not bother you? A lover doesn't do things like that. A stalker does. An obsessive stalker. What we have, it isn't love."

Why would he say that?

It had felt like love. Why would he say it wasn't? And to say it so loudly and openly in front of everyone else in the waiting room. I blinked back the tears quickly. I was being emotional because of the pain and overall feeling of unwellness. He couldn't possibly have hurt me that much by simply saying that.

Unless.

Did *I* actually love him?

"Nicodemus Greene?" A woman in a smock held a door open leading to the rooms beyond the waiting room.

"Come on," Jimena said. He held my forms in one hand and looped the other around my good side to pull me up. He led me to the awaiting woman and handed her the forms.

"You'll need to wait out here," the woman said. "There's not enough room for the patients to bring family with them. I'll get you when he's in a room."

I expected him to put up a fuss, but, instead, he nodded. The woman took me to an area in the hall where she wheeled over a cart covered in various things. She pulled up a tablet and input the data off my forms as she took my vitals.

"Can I see the forms for a moment? I want to make sure I completed it all correctly."

She'd already finished putting the information in the computer, so she handed them to me.

"We need to take you back for an X-ray," she said. She grabbed at another employee. "Can you take him to radiology?"

I skimmed the medical history that Jimena had written while the nurses rounded up a wheelchair. He knew my brother's phone number and had put him down as the next of kin. Of course, he had put himself down as the emergency contact. He listed my mother's last known address, which was the only flaw on the form. I knew she'd moved out of state and changed her name. He'd even noted my tonsil removal from ten years ago and my broken arm during high school. Allergies, he'd listed lead and other various metals. He knew my birthday and social security number. He even knew who my medical insurance carrier was and my blood type.

He was right. He did know more than any normal lover would. He knew more about me than a wife who'd been married to me for fifty years would know. And he hadn't even referenced anything. He'd had it all memorized. Exact dates. He knew the exact fucking day my tonsils had been removed. I didn't even know that. I'd been twelve at the time.

"Ready to go?" the man had returned with a wheelchair.

"Uh, yeah. Here, you need this back." I handed him the forms. "It's all correct."

Kidnapper

Why had I said that? If he wanted to call me his lover, why should I stop him? It was just a word.

But still, even now, as I sat in the waiting room thinking about the word, it aggravated me. Whether there was emotion involved or not, I did not want to assign it a word.

I waited. After two hours, I decided they'd either forgotten about me or Nic had told them he didn't want to see me. I went to the reception desk, trying my best to look friendly.

"Can you check on a patient for me? I've been waiting a while now, and no one has told me his status."

"Name?"

"Nicodemus Greene." I waited patiently as she typed the name in.

"He's been admitted and should be in surgery prep now. We had a bit of a delay in getting an—"

"What? He's in surgery? Why did no one tell me beforehand?" I glared at the woman, wanting to reach across the counter and strangle her.

"Are you family?"

"No. I'm the one who brought him here, which apparently means nothing to you people."

"I'll be sure you're notified when he comes out of surgery."

I didn't believe her acidic words for a second. But her shift wouldn't last forever, so perhaps the next receptionist would be more understanding. I shuffled back to my plastic chair and sulked. My stomach rumbled, and I considered leaving for food, but what if I did that at the exact time Nic came out of surgery?

I groaned and clutched my head, fighting the dehydration and hunger that nipped at me as the hours passed. My phone vibrated, and before I even answered, I knew it would be my work. I put it to my ear and spouted a mix of truth and apology until my manager hung up. He ended up feeling guilty for having bothered me when he probably should have fired me.

"Is there someone here for Nicodemus Greene?"

I jumped out of my seat and raced to the reception desk where a different lady stood, but she had the same callous expression on her face as the other woman had.

"I am," I said. "Is he okay?"

"They'll be bringing him out shortly for you to take home. If you want to get your car and pull up to the front entrance, they'll bring him out in a wheelchair and meet you." She barely met my eyes as she gave me the directions. I wanted to ask her questions because shouldn't someone have come out and told me how it all went? They knew I was more than just Nic's driver, right?

She hadn't even waited for a response. She had already returned to her computer. I bit the fleshy skin of my lip and turned around. I stomped out of the waiting room and retrieved my car. I pulled up into the loading and unloading area, where an elderly couple had taken the closest spot next to the doors.

I slouched behind the steering wheel, silently wishing the tottering old man, slowly getting out of the car, would stumble and die. If he fell at the right angle, his head would hit the open car door and—my eyes darted away from him to the wheelchair coming outside, pushed by a young man in light blue smocks.

I swung my door open and waved.

"Over here." I hurried around the car and opened the passenger door. Nic was dressed back in his blood splattered clothes. I hadn't noticed how much blood was on them before. His right hand, the one I'd so elegantly stabbed, was wrapped in so much gauze that it looked like he'd put on five mittens. Three fingers had the tip of a needle poking out of each of them.

Nic held the hand close to his chest as he rose from the chair to slide into the car. The orderly handed me a slip of paper.

"His prescriptions. You'll want to get these filled on your way home," he said.

"Thanks." I took the paper and went to my side of the car. I glanced up. The old man had made it a whole two feet away from his car. "How are you feeling?"

"Just take me home," Nic said. I noticed he'd put on his seat belt, and he now slouched with his forehead resting against the window of the passenger door.

"We should get your prescriptions first." I held up the paper to show him. "It's probably something for pain and infection."

The car ahead of us finally decided to abandon the old man, and I was able to follow them and also depart.

"I'll have Marc fill the prescription," Nic said.

"Why would your brother do that?"

"I trust him more than you."

"Ha! Huh, that… uh, you're saying that because you don't feel well. They probably gave you some pretty strong stuff."

"To be clear, take me to my brother's apartment. Not your place."

I swallowed deeply. "What are you talking about? You agreed to move in." I tightened my grip on the wheel.

"I can't be around you when I'm like this. I don't trust you."

"Of course, you can trust me."

"Jimena, you're the one who did this to me. I can't be around you when I'm unable to defend myself." He sat up and looked at me with his blurry bloodshot eyes. "Take me to my brother's apartment."

"You—you can trust me. I'll take care of you. I'll nurse you back to health."

"You had a lead knife in your house. That isn't a common household item. You were planning this. I can't deal with you right now. Please, take me to my brother's."

I flexed my jaw. If I took him to my house instead, there wasn't much he could do about it. But if I wanted to earn some good faith, then I would need to listen to him.

"I'm sorry I said those harsh things to you before. You can call me your lover if you want. I'm okay with it."

"Jimena, please. I just can't with you right now. I just can't." He banged his forehead against the glass window a few times, not super hard but the action alone disturbed me.

"I'll take you to your brother," I said. I turned the car in the direction of his apartment. "So, what did they do to your hand?" Silence was my only answer. I glanced at him, and his eyes were closed. I could take him to my house so easily. Chain him in the basement with my new lead cuffs and choker.

"No." I flexed my hands on the wheel. He *could* trust me. I would not hurt him when he was in this vulnerable state.

We reached his brother's apartment complex, and I pulled up to the closest legal spot I could find. I wanted to park in a handicap space but avoiding any and all conflict with the law was a bit of a must at the moment.

I went around the car and opened the door. I gently shook his shoulder until his eyes fluttered open. He moved to rub his eyes with his hands and instantly winced and clutched his injured hand.

"We're in the parking lot of the apartment complex," I said. "I brought you here just like you wanted. But I really think I can keep you more comfortable at my place. You can sleep in my bed. It's better than the floor mattress you have."

"Help me get up." He leaned on me as he got out of the car. "My script for the meds?"

"Right here." I made a display of showing him and tucking it in his front pocket. "I can get it filled for you if you'd like.

"I'll do it later." Nic pushed away from me and walked on his own toward the gate that surrounded the apartment complex. I fell in step behind him. "You don't have to walk me up."

"You're dizzy, and your apartment is on the third floor. I'm making sure you get there safely."

He didn't object as I followed him, but he shook me away every time I tried to steady him when I noticed he was wobbling. He got the apartment keys out of his pocket but fumbled with them for several minutes. I had wounded his dominate hand, after all.

"Let me do it," I said. I gently took the keys from him and used them to unlock the door. I pushed it open and let him enter first. As he passed me, he yanked the keys back.

"You can go now."

"Let me tuck you in." I followed him inside, and the brother was there, loafing on the couch. Was that all he ever did? Did the man have no job?

"What the fuck happened to you?" He pointed at Nic's hand.

"Slight accident." Nic curled the hand against his chest as he walked past him and went directly to his bedroom. I trailed him without comment and helped Nic take his shoes off as he laid on the mattress. He didn't bother undressing beyond that, and I agilely slipped my hand into his pocket and retrieved the prescription.

Nic mumbled something, but I couldn't understand it. I pulled a blanket up over his shoulders.

"What was that? Do you want me to stay with you?"

The hood on my jacket was yanked, and I was pulled to my feet. The force swung me around and shoved me into the hall.

"Nice try, but no." The brother stood in the doorway, blocking me as he released my hood. "I am not leaving my brother alone with his perverted boyfriend that likes to fuck unconscious people. He's in no state to have you raping him."

"I wasn't going to."

"Yeah, sure. Get out."

"Nic said I could stay."

"If Nic wants you here, he can call you when he wakes up." He reached for my hoodie again, and I twisted out of his grasp. Whatever. It wasn't like I needed his permission to come back. I could sneak in the window again.

"Fine, I'm going." I didn't trust him enough to turn my back to him, so I walked backward toward the exit.

"If you come back without an invite, I'll call the cops. Understand?"

I reached the door and yanked it open.

"I'm his boyfriend. I'm allowed to check on him."

He laughed. "You're his stalker." He slammed the door in my face. My own words tossed back at me. I was a bit offended by the sting.

Kidnapped

The hard tip of my brother's shoe tapped my forehead until I roused enough to push it away.

"So, what did he actually do to you?" Marcanian asked.

"He stabbed me with a knife coated in lead." I managed to glance around the room. "Where is he?"

"I kicked him out. I told you he was no good. He did his homework, huh? Or did he just get lucky?"

"I don't want to talk about it." I wanted to roll over and away from him, but my hand hurt too much to lie on that side.

"You went to the emergency room? You need a shaman to treat the poison. That Wiccan shop downtown will probably have what you need." He grabbed my arm and held it straight up so he could stare at it. He took his free hand and tapped the needle poking out of my index finger.

A lightning bolt of pain rippled down it and through my bones. I suppressed a groan and tugged my arm away from him.

"Don't."

"Did you want me to get the stuff for you?" He kneeled and eyed my hand as though he wanted to touch it again. "Or are you going to send your boy toy to get it?"

"I'll go myself. Go away, will you?"

Marcanian grinned in a way that he didn't normally aim in my direction. "Whatever. Don't die in here. It would be annoying."

Kidnapped

I pushed open the door, and the small bell hung above it chimed musically. I rubbed my nose, already feeling a sneeze coming on. The place was always filled with the smell of herbs. Intentional or not, I doubted it could be avoided when most of their products were fragrant. I tried to hide my disgust at the scent and proceeded inside the small Wiccan shop.

Most of the customers were normal people who wanted to try earthly or natural remedies. I had no idea if the people running it were supernatural or not, nor did I intend to ask questions to find out. I went down a few rows of factory-sealed bottles, things likely filled with diluted quantities of what they advertised.

"Can I help you?" a woman asked. She had on a flowing dress, similar to one a belly dancer would wear. Dozens of bracelets were on each arm, and loops equally as large hung from each ear. Her frizzy hair could benefit from a wash using actual soap that her store likely did not sell.

"Something for a detox," I said.

"Liver or kidney?"

"No, more for poison," I corrected.

"Oh, I have just the thing." She rounded the corner, and by the time I reached her, she held a jar filled with something black. I took it from her with my good hand, surprised by its lightness.

"Activated charcoal," she said, "It will—"

"No." I put the jar on the counter. "Lead poisoning. I need something for lead poisoning."

"The charcoal will—"

"It's not good at absorbing metals. Do you actually practice this stuff, or did they put you at the counter just to look the part?"

"Damn, you're in a mood," a woman said behind me. I turned, not realizing I knew the speaker until I saw her face.

"Arimathea," I said.

"Nicodemus," she replied. "You look horrible. Who poisoned you?"

"No one," I said. "I had an accident and fell onto a jagged lead knife."

She laughed, and the clerk took a few steps away from the counter, as if the sound startled her. Arimathea walked closer, her heels clicking with each step. She'd dressed modestly, and a passerby would dismiss her as a suburban mother shopping for a few pills to help her lose weight, but even the clerk could sense there was more to her than that. Or maybe the clerk *was* a wiccan or shaman that could see certain auras. If so, why hadn't she reacted to mine?

"Seriously, who did this?" She stepped closer and pointed at my hand.

"I know you're in the business of avenging, but this wasn't something like that."

She looked at the clerk. "Give him calcium and iron supplements." She looked at me. "It slows the body's absorption of lead. I take some every day, as a precaution."

"I suppose it's not surprising that people want to shoot you full of lead," I said.

"It's not surprising that's your view. I'm trying to right wrongs."

"I think the proper term is a vigilante," I said.

"Deferasirox," Arimathea said. She looked at the clerk. "He'll be wanting some of that too. It's what people take for lead poisoning. You may need a prescription from your doctor for it."

My prescriptions. Shit. That damn pickpocket had taken it.

"I have it," the clerk said. She put a bottle on the counter.

"How much for all of it?" I asked.

"You'll want to eat well during your treatment," Arimathea said. "Have you and your brother been—"

"Let's skip the pleasantries," I said. "If you're in town, then it's because a bunch of girls have gone missing, and you're trying to figure out who is doing it. I know that's your thing, avenging girls who go missing. My brother and I don't kill our victims, so it wasn't us."

She placed a paper on the counter. "You know her?"

I glanced down and was more than relieved when I did not recognize the woman.

"No, and I doubt I would. My social circle these days is more on the gay pride side, so I don't know anything about missing girls."

"What about your brother?"

"He's running with Ana these days. You know she prefers the gothic scene, unless your missing woman is into that."

"Your brother is with Ananias? If they're hitting up local clubs, they might hear something. Take the flier and ask them, okay?" She tapped the paper. "She's only been missing for three days. There's a good chance she's still alive."

I picked up the missing person's poster and looked at the woman closer. The description listed her as thirty, and the photo showed her as neither pretty or ugly. I couldn't see the appeal someone would have in taking her.

"Sure you don't want to tell me who did this? If someone is targeting people like us, I'd sure like to know about it. I would enjoy the distraction of beating up the punk, since all my leads haven't panned out in trying to figure out who took this girl."

"She's not a girl. She's a grown woman. She probably left of her own accord, and I already told you no." I folded the paper and put it in my pocket. The clerk had rung up my things, so I swiped my card to pay. "Thanks for the treatment advice."

"No problem. Feel better. Be sure to take the deferasirox with a full glass of water."

I grabbed my bag and left, stopping only to get a drink from a vending machine outside. I took the first deferasirox pill and drank the bottle of water, which I had to open with my teeth because of my jacked-up hand.

The Wiccan store was close enough to the apartments that I was able to walk the distance. It was still strenuous enough that my hand was throbbing halfway there. I hugged the bag against my chest with my injured arm and attempted to text Jimena with the other.

I know you took my prescriptions. Are you going to fill them and bring them back? I walked up a small flight of outdoor steps and proofread my text before sending it. Did I really want him to come over? I could probably get the doctor to write me a new script. Jimena would probably bring me the medicine whether I ask him to or not.

I pushed send and heard a receipt chime from a different phone. I paused and looked at the parked car next to me. Unbelievable. The window was cracked and slumped inside, sleeping, was none other than Jimena. Had he spent the night here? Lurking in his car a block away from my apartment building?

I couldn't knock on the glass window, not while I was holding everything in my sole good hand. Instead, I leaned close to the window crack and shouted his name. He yelped and jumped. His frenzied eyes met mine.

"What are you doing?" I noted the empty fast-food containers scattered around the passenger seat. I couldn't believe I hadn't realized this was his car. I'd walked by it on my way to the store and hadn't noticed it or him inside it. Had he been sleeping then too?

His mouth trembled, and he didn't seem able to formulate a response.

"Do you have my prescriptions?"

"Y-yes," he said. He rummaged through some of the garbage behind the passenger seat until he found a small pharmacy bag. He jammed his thumb on the unlock button and held it out for me. We both remained there as I waited for him to realize I couldn't open the door. I was holding my vitamins and phone in my good hand, and I wasn't about to put them down just to open the door when he was capable of doing it for me. He rolled the window down instead and held the bag closer.

"Open the door for me, Jimena," I said.

"Oh. Oh, right." He glanced at my hand, which had been perfectly visible this entire time. He leaned across the car and pushed the door open. He swept the array of food wrappers onto the floor so I could sit.

"Did you sleep out here?" I put my items in my lap, so I could take the bag he offered. I used my teeth to rip the stapled top open, then dumped the two bottles out.

"I went and filled your prescriptions. I thought you would message me for them, and I didn't want you to wait long for me to respond. I would have come up and given them to you, but your brother threatened me, and you'd also told me to stay away. So, I was waiting."

"I did message you. You missed it because you were sleeping." There was no way for me to open the child proof cap on the prescription medicines. My teeth would not suffice.

"You did? You…" He grabbed his phone and hurried to check the messages. "You just sent this."

"But I did send it." I held the two bottles out to him. "Open these."

He grabbed them and quickly obeyed.

"Do you have any water?"

"Uh, yeah." He rummaged behind my seat and produced a sealed plastic bottle.

"Give me one pill of each."

He tapped them out onto his palm and held his hand out, the pills exposed for me to pluck them with my fingers. Instead, I lowered my face and scooped them up with my tongue, being sure to give him a nice sloppy lick in the process. I swallowed them dry since he wasn't offering up the water. He was too busy looking shocked by what I'd done.

"Water? Can you open it?"

"R-right." He took the cap off and held it for me to take. This time I did take it from him, drinking half of it before handing it back.

I leaned back in the seat, closing my eyes, and waiting for the pain killer to give me some relief from the throbbing.

"Are you feeling well enough to be around me? Can I come over? Or can you come to my place? I want to earn your trust. Please, Nic. I'm sorry about what I did. I won't do it again. I'll throw it away. The lead knife, that is."

"You can keep it," I said. He might need it if someone like Arimathea ever crossed paths with him. "Just don't use it on me."

"Do you forgive me? Can I bring you back to my place?"

"I'm going to need some sort of gesture, Jimena. Something beyond camping out in your car all night." I lifted my head and looked at him. "I want you to be my boyfriend not my stalker. Can you think of a way to differentiate between the two?"

"What?"

"When you figure it out, we can try to make this work again." I scooped my items up into the bag, then pushed the door open.

"Go to the resort with me," Jimena said. "Th-that's a boyfriend thing. I'll take you to my grandfather's birthday celebration. You said you would go."

"I thought you weren't going?"

He grimaced. I wasn't certain which part was more unappealing: having to take me with him or having to go at all.

"Taking you would be a boyfriend thing to do, right? A stalker doesn't take their prey to meet their family or on a weekend getaway. So, will you come? Can we do that?"

"When is it?"

Kidnapper

I followed behind Nic as he led me up to his shared apartment. My offer had earned me a respite, and he was allowing me to join him.

"I have to attend classes tomorrow," he said as he unlocked the door. He passed me a warning glare. "I already missed two days. That can't happen again, understand?"

I nodded.

He hugged his bag of drugs against his chest, his injured arm unable to grip anything. He tucked the apartment keys back in his pocket and used his good hand to coil his fingers behind my neck. He pulled me in close, pressing our foreheads together and sniffing.

"You smell like BO," he said. "How long has it been since you showered?"

"A few days," I admitted.

"It's hard to wash myself with my hand like this. Will you wash me?"

My heart raced at the idea. Him naked in a tub with me washing him? Or was he thinking more of a sponge bath? Either way, the idea of slowly washing every inch of him was extremely appealing.

"Y-yes," I agreed.

"Great." He pulled away, turned the knob and kicked the door open. "We'll take a bath together."

Together? Did he mean both of us? Naked? Memories of showering in locker rooms after gym in high school flashed in my mind. Forced baths as a child by my mother and later by my stepmother. As a child I was one of those weekly bathers, not daily. As an adult, it was a twice weekly event, unless circumstances required otherwise.

And that wasn't even addressing the fact that being completely nude with someone under the invasive light of a bathroom was a level of intimacy and exposure I was not prepared for.

"Ah, shit, he's back? Why?" Marc pointed at me.

"He's my boyfriend, that's why," Nic said. He pulled a folded paper out of his pocket and put it on the counter. "I saw Arimathea. She wanted me to show you this and ask that you let her know if you'd seen the woman or know what happened."

I shyly walked into the apartment and shut the door behind me. Marc glanced at the paper, his attention completely off me.

"She's on another rampage to avenge women who are abused, eh? She's so annoying." Marc squinted at the paper. "I don't know her."

Curious, I approached the counter and peered at the paper, staying as far away from Marc as possible. My heart raced as I saw the familiar face on the missing person's flyer. She was the woman I had snatched off the street when Nic and I had been fighting.

"Why are you looking like that?" Nic asked. "Do you know her?"

I stepped away from the paper and shook my head. Technically, I didn't know her. I didn't even know her name. She was just a nameless, faceless corpse buried in my flowerbed.

"Good thing you're into boys," Marc said, bumping into my shoulder as he passed me. "Arimathea doesn't avenge them."

"I've kidnapped women," I said, my need to defend my attraction to both genders outweighing the fact I was exposing myself to accusation.

"And you think Nicodemus is better than a woman? You're crazier than I thought." Marc shook his head and settled onto the couch, his attention going to the program on the screen.

"Come on," Nic said. "Let's clean up."

I glanced one last time at the missing poster, reading that the woman's name was Terri. I looked away from it before I could see anything else. The less I knew about her, the better. Although, if I knew her favorite kind of flower, perhaps I could plant that above her grave. It seemed fitting, and she might appreciate it.

Nic sat on the toilet as he attempted to remove his clothing with only one hand. He'd gotten his shoes off so far. I hovered in the doorway.

"Do you think Terri liked marigolds?"

"Who?"

"The woman in the poster."

"How would I know?"

"Would your friend Arimathea know? She knew her, right? Do you think you could ask her?"

Nic stared at me long and hard as if he thought if he studied me long enough, he would find answers hidden somewhere.

"What's the real reason you didn't want me to come over to your place earlier in the week? You said it was to punish me. Was there another reason?"

"My family was coming over. You saw that."

"And the days before that? Did you have someone else over?"

"No."

"Did you have Terri over?"

"I told you I don't know her."

"But did you have her in your house?"

"Why would you ask me that?"

"Because she went missing the day you were pissed at me and then you didn't want me to come over. Is Terri in your house right now?"

"No."

"Did you kill her?"

"Why are you asking me this? What difference does it make?"

He stood, and his eyes changed into that light bronze shade as he approached me.

"Did you kill Terri? Yes, or no?"

I pried my eyes away from him, but it actually hurt my brain. It hurt to break the eye contact. He leaned close and inhaled deeply at my neck, sniffing me, like my odor was a lie detector.

"Did you really get over me that fast? You already took someone else?"

"No!" My voice was a high shrill, and I made the mistake of looking back at him. Our eyes locked, and this time, I couldn't look away.

He grabbed my shoulder with his good hand and squeezed. "Stop being scared. That's not what I want from you."

"Then stop interrogating me."

"I need your help undressing."

I focused on the task at hand and began taking his clothes off. First his pants, then his shirt, which had to be carefully maneuvered around his hand, then his underwear and socks. I started filling the tub next, making sure the water was a good temp before he got in.

"You need to strip too," he said. "You're getting in here with me."

"There's not enough room."

"Get in." He slumped, laying down in the tub and closing his eyes. "I'm too tired to argue, but you smell too much to get in my bed in your current state."

I bit my lip and decided I could try. I took my clothes off, shaking like a frightened puppy by the time I had the last article of clothing off.

"W-where?" I asked.

He opened his eyes, and they popped a bit as he saw me standing there completely nude, one arm across my chest to hide my nipples, the other cupping my privates. His mouth opened, and I expected him to comment on how he'd never realized how unattractive I was until now. The sharp edges of my bones poking out at every angle matched with the pathetic marks of muscle that babies had more of than I did. Or maybe, he would save the narrative until he saw the small nub that passed for my cock.

"On top," he said. His right hand, the casted one, hung out of the tub, so he waved for me to come closer with his left. "Face me, on top."

I wasn't certain what he meant by that, but I came closer and put one foot in the tub, thinking I was going on the opposite side from him.

"No, your legs on the outside. Straddle me." He pulled on my calf to move it. Was he serious? I would barely be in the tub if I was sitting on his lap. I put my leg outside, and after a quick breath through my teeth, removed my hands from their locations that had provided me with some modesty, needing to use them to keep my balance as I lowered myself.

I dropped quickly, wanting to get my nub under the water before he could get a good look at it. The water sloshed a bit onto the floor and went up above his chest, rising a bit above my hips. I reached behind me to turn the water off. I managed it in two quick twists, then turned back to him.

"Well, start washing," he said. He was still laying back, looking relaxed, likely from the meds he'd taken. Mixed with the drowsy expression was a smirk of pride. Did my ugliness boost his own ego? Did it make him feel better about himself? Like how the ugly fat girl finds uglier fat girls to be her friends so she doesn't look as ugly? Not that Nic needed to do that. Few could compare, and if anything, I was lowering his appeal.

I was more on his thighs than his lap, and his dick bobbed above the surface of the water as it grew larger. My vision blurred for a moment as I tried to grasp what was happening. Was some aspect of what we were doing, arousing him? It couldn't be from my appearance, and I hadn't touched him. Dominance? Because he'd told me what to do, and I was doing it?

"Do with it what you want," Nic said. "You can pretend I'm asleep if that'll help. I actually think I could nod off. Those meds are really hitting me." He rubbed his eyes. "Would you enjoy this more if I was unconscious?"

"I…" I couldn't bring myself to touch him. I kept my hands gripping the rim of the tub on both sides. "Why are you aroused?"

He opened his eyes into small slits. "I suppose I'm hoping we have sex. Am I not turning you on? Shit. You really are over me, aren't you? I was joking before. Why are you looking at me like that? Are you going to drown me?"

"No, no, I am, I mean, I'm not. I, uh." I grabbed his hand with mine and intertwined our fingers. I guided him under the water to touch my own erection, however small it was. "I want you to stay awake." I forced the confusing thoughts in my head away, and tried to say what I thought he wanted to hear. "It would be a boyfriend thing to do, for us to both be awake."

"That's a good delineation, yes," Nic agreed. "You want me to touch you?"

I rubbed his hand against my erection and nodded.

"I'm not going to do a good job of it." His eyes fluttered closed. "I really am…"

His body went lax beneath me. Unmoving I stared at him. Had he really fallen asleep? I hadn't drugged him this time. If anything, he had drugged himself.

"Hey, hey, you have to wake up. You can't sleep in the tub." I slapped his cheek, not hard but enough to get his attention. He didn't respond.

I couldn't very well leave him like this, but I wasn't confident I could lift him either. I looked at the closed bathroom door and thought of the brother beyond it. I wasn't about to yell for him to come in here when I was in such a vulnerable state.

"It's fine, it's fine," I muttered to myself. I grabbed palmfuls of water and splashed myself, then used some soap to do a quick lather. I washed myself in a hasty manner, all posed above Nic and keeping him from potentially slipping under the water.

I drained the tub and turned on the showerhead. I turned the temperature to cold and stepped out of the tub. Nic cried and thrashed about. I turned the water off and handed him a towel. He ignored the offered towel and scowled at me from under his damp hair. He brushed it back with his good hand and held up his cast.

"You got it wet. We were supposed to keep it dry," he said. I was pretty sure he had done that when he'd woken up in a panic from the cold water. I helped him step from the tub and aided in drying his hair.

"Don't put your dirty clothes back on," he said. "You can wear some of mine."

He stumbled toward the bedroom, not bothering to dress. I followed him, wrapping myself in the towel I'd used on him. He went to a pile of clothing and pulled out some boxers.

"Here." He tossed them at me, and I managed to catch them. Then, still naked, he fell atop his stacked mattresses. He landed on his side and ceased moving. Had he passed out that quickly?

I put on the offered clothing, then returned to the bathroom to hang up the damp towel. I collected mine and his discarded clothing and brought it to the bedroom with me. I considered going to the kitchen where I thought he'd left his medicine, but I was worried the brother was there, and I didn't want to face him alone.

I laid on the bed next to Nic, covering myself with one of his blankets. I draped it carefully over him as well, not wanting him to catch a chill.

CHAPTER eight

Kidnapped

I woke to the pain in my hand throbbing a bit worse, likely due to the painkillers wearing off. I reached my hand out, fumbling for the bag full of drugs and vitamins but grasped at nothing. I sat up and reflexively moved my hands to rub my face. My hand erupted in pain. I grimaced and lowered the injured one.

The room was dark, but I could hear Jimena breathing next to me. I cradled my wounded hand to my chest and scooted closer to his sleeping body. He was curled away from me. I put my face to the nape of his neck and inhaled, breathing in his soul, flavorless, since he was asleep, but still useful to ease my pain. It only took the edge off and increased my craving. I wanted the heady rush he provided when coating me in his love.

"Jimena," I said. I slipped my good hand under the boxers he wore and rubbed his cock. He muttered as he started waking up. "Tell me how much you want me, Jimena."

"Nic?"

I kissed his neck and grazed my teeth along the bumps that raised in response. He reached his arm up and managed to touch the back of my head, ruffling my hair.

"I like when you touch me," Jimena said. I didn't sense the rush of obsessive love I normally did. There was adoration in it, but it was coated in fear.

"Why are you afraid?" I inhaled more of him, disliking the bitter fear spoiling the taste but too hungry not to proceed.

"I'm afraid this isn't real. Or worse, it is, and…" His breath hitched as I stroked him.

"And what?"

"It's only real to me." His body shuddered as he climaxed and his ejaculate coated my fingers. His woes were overshadowed by the hormone release, and I only tasted the goodness now. I drank it all, mending my hand to the point where the sticks in it were now annoying because they prevented me from healing completely.

I rolled away from him and touched the metal sticking out of my fingertips with my good hand. I wondered if I could pull them out with pliers.

"Jimena? Are you awake?" If there was anyone who would enjoy pulling these out, it would be him. I pushed his shoulder, but he didn't respond. I'd likely drained a bit too much out of him.

Kidnapped

"They make you look cool, like a cyborg," Jake said. I held my hand up as Jake and Alex gawked at my hand. I'd yet to remove the pins, but it was my goal to accomplish that before the day was out.

Attending class had taken priority when I'd woken, and I hadn't had time to deal with them. I didn't have any classes with Jimena today, but I found myself still searching for him. I'd left him sleeping on my mattress, still unconscious from how much I'd fed on him. I kept reminding myself that he was the reason I was injured, so it was fitting he be the one to heal me. But I couldn't help the nagging feeling that I had caused him harm.

I didn't like that idea.

I wanted him to wake up, so I felt assured he was okay. I barely paid attention in class, and by lunch I could tolerate it no longer. I sent him a text to check on his status. After ten minutes of no reply, I tried my brother.

"Who are you messaging? Suzie?" Jake asked. He took a large bite of his burger as he waited for my response.

I put my phone down next to my untouched tray of food. "Suzie?"

"She's been giving us the cold shoulder," Alex said. "She could at least tell us why."

"She and I had a falling out. I doubt she'll be around much longer." I meant that in more ways than one.

"What did she do?" Jake asked. "Was it something with that creepy kid?"

"She did seem a bit sweet on him," Alex agreed.

My phone flashed with a message. I picked it up. My brother had responded. *He woke up a few hours ago and left. He seemed a bit haggard, but doesn't he always?*

He was fine. The relief I felt was stronger than I'd expected.

"Stop talking about Suzie," I said. "She's not important."

Kidnapper

I was so tired. Like, coming down with the flu kind of tired. And the last place I wanted to be sick was in Nic's apartment with his creepy brother. I put on my best game face, dressed in my dirty clothes from the day before, and managed to stagger home.

If asked how I'd gotten there, I couldn't recall. But my car was parked outside, so I'd likely driven home. I stared at my phone in disbelief. I'd somehow lost two days. I rubbed my forehead, trying to work out the last of the fog but failing. There were dozens of missed calls, texts, and voicemails on my phone. I took some aspirin, guzzled some water, and began listening to them.

It was a mix of my boss calling from work and family members calling to find out if I was coming to the reunion. The last message from Nic had been from the day I'd left his apartment. I'd never responded to it.

How are you, today? That's what he'd written. How could I respond to that now? Two days later? Did I just ignore it?

I put on a pot of boiling water and called my boss to explain how I'd been sick. Then went thru a rotation of annoying concerned family members' messages. By the time I'd gotten through them all, my instant soup was done, and the last person I needed to contact was Nic.

Did I text, call, or go over? How could I have ignored him for two days?

"He must hate me. He must think I hate him."

I ate my soup as I mulled over what to do. I had to do something. Our flight for the stupid reunion was tomorrow morning. And during all those phone calls, I'd assured my family he was coming.

"I'm an idiot." And far too cowardly to call him. I typed out a text.

Sorry. I've been sick. I quickly deleted it, realizing it sounded like I was apologizing for being ill. *Sorry I didn't respond sooner. I have been sick. Really bad flu. How is your hand? Are you better?* That still sounded lame. Not to mention fake. I deleted it.

"It'll be easier to just lie to my family," I said, speaking to my soup bowl.

A text suddenly appeared under Nic's last message.

Is our flight tomorrow? What time should I meet you there?

I stared at my phone. Was he not upset? Was it not abnormal that I hadn't spoken to him in days?

I typed a single word. *Yes.*

... and? A time? Airliner?

I pulled up the email confirmation from the airliner and sent him a screencap of the information. He replied with a thumbs up.

How is your hand? I typed it, then deleted it.

See you tomorrow, then, Nic's message said.

I replied with a simple, *Yes,* hating myself for not being able to say more.

Kidnapper

I waited at the airport, holding the second plane ticket like an idiot. I flipped between the two, shuffling mine on top, then Nic's. I'd known all of his information, so buying the ticket hadn't been a problem. But was he going to show up?

I sat outside on one of the plastic benches and waited. My rolling suitcase sat next to me. My carry-on item was a backpack already on my shoulders. I pulled out my phone and confirmed the text I'd sent him with the airline information. He would know where to go, right?

"I should have picked him up," I said. Why had I agreed to meet him at the airport? There were so many things that could go wrong.

Are you delayed? How close are you? I texted and then stared at my phone, waiting for a response. It didn't even show as read, just sent. I unslung my backpack and unzipped the top. I started rummaging until I found the clear plastic container with my medications.

I didn't normally take them, but if I was getting on a plane today and later, augh! I shuddered at the mere thought of how I would be spending the next four days with my adoptive family. Cousins, aunts, and every extended family member a person could imagine. All giving me that sympathetic look and expressing fake gratitude that I was there. Sometimes I thought my parents had adopted me for the attention it got them. How many times had I heard the words, "You're such a good person to be doing this," as though adopting me made them saints. And then there were the envious glares the others cast at my parents because they knew the gesture couldn't be outdone. Well, they could have adopted someone themselves, but then it would simply be a copycat gesture, which would make them look even worse.

It was why they always demanded I attend reunions. They needed their show pony present and on display. And now, they could boast that they'd adopted a gay son. *Look here at his boyfriend. Aren't we amazing? We took in a gay.*

"If they're wearing damn Pride t-shirts…"

"Are we against that?" Nic asked, his shoes coming into view next to my bag. "And are we talking about a lion pride or LGBTQ Pride?"

"What?" I looked up at him, his white t-shirt and freshly trimmed hair making him look like a poster boy for college students. He should be in admission brochures; it was bound to increase attendance applications.

"You were muttering about Pride shirts. Should we be wearing those when we arrive?"

"No, I was, that—that wasn't what I was saying. I don't, uh, pay attention to those things."

"Oh, good. Neither do I, but if you wanted to, we can. Remind me again, are we aiming to make your family comfortable with this or uncomfortable? Or has that already happened? Is your family already comfortable with it? Are there other gays in your family? How new is this concept going to be for them?"

"Can you please stop talking about it?" I dropped my untaken medication back in the bag. "We're late, and we need to check our luggage."

"I only brought a carry-on." He gestured at his bag, the same one he brought to class every day.

"That's all you're bringing?"

"I'll buy more clothes there. Souvenirs and stuff." He glanced at my roller luggage. "I suppose you need to check a bag because you're bringing an arsenal of torture devices to use on me."

"No," I snarled the word as I got up. "Stop being so open about everything. People can hear you."

"I can't talk about BDSM in public? I thought it's a fairly known thing now."

"Stop it." How was I ever going to get through this? I walked ahead of him into the airport. I refused to look back to see if he was following. I went to the check-in line and impatiently tapped my foot as we waited.

"I know this is a big step for you," Nic said. "Are there any ground rules you want to set?"

"What do you mean?"

"Things that are off limits." He reached over and threaded his fingers with mine. "Holding hands, kissing…"

I jerked my hand away. "We do those things."

"I'm talking about in public. What are you okay doing in public and in front of your family?"

I stepped forward in line as it shortened. "I've never done this before, so I don't know. We'll figure it out as we go and do what feels appropriate." I shifted around a bit. "What have you done in the past? When you've dated someone?"

He shrugged. "I've never taken someone home to meet my family before. Or dated anyone seriously."

"But you've gone on dates."

"There's a difference between dating someone and taking someone on *a* date with the intent to seduce them. Besides, I'm trying to find out what sort of impression you want to give your family. Are we going to make them think we're so in love they'll be nauseated by it? Or so uncomfortable they won't ask any questions?"

"You're putting too much thought into this." I stepped forward as the airport attendant waved for me. I hefted my bag onto the scale. "One bag to check."

She printed a claim ticket for me, and I shoved it in my pocket. I led us to the tram that would take us to the airport security check-in.

"Anything I should know before we go through security?" Nic asked.

"What's that supposed to mean?"

"Outstanding warrants? Weapons in your bag?"

"No. Should I ask you that?"

He grinned. "Nope."

He thankfully remained silent as we rode the tram.

"I'm sorry about not reaching out more during the last few days," I said, breaking the silence.

"It's fine. You weren't feeling well, and neither was I," Nic said. "You look good now, though." He brushed a hand across my face, and I realized with a fright that it was the hand I'd stabbed. The stints and cast were gone.

"How did you?" I lifted his hand, turning it around and seeing no trace of the wound. "Two days? You can't… You can't show up like this."

The tram stopped, and the crowd pushed us with them to get off.

"My mother and brother saw you get stabbed. My mother is a nurse, she knows—she knows this is impossible. You can't—you can't show up like this."

"Will you stop saying that." He pushed me to the security line. "We'll wrap it up before we get off the flight. And if I suck at faking the injury, you can just stab me again." He winked, but I found no amusement in it.

I bit back my shock and anger and concentrated on the task at hand. I put my bag on the rollers that fed into the X-ray conveyor belt, then pulled out two clear plastic bags filled with my medications and my travel sized liquids. I took my shoes off and put them in the bin with everything else.

Nic dropped his backpack next to mine and snatched up my medication bag. "What are all of these? Is this what you've been drugging me with?"

"Hey, put that back." I reached for it, and he turned his back to me. Eyes went in our direction, and I resisted fighting harder to get them.

"Haloperidol? Isn't that an anti- psychotic?" He pushed the bottles around in the bag so he could read them. My items reached the X-ray machine, so he tossed the bag back in the bin. "Why didn't you tell me you take medications like that?"

"Sir, it's your turn," the security officer said. I turned away from Nic and walked forward. I stepped through the metal detector and collected my bag on the other side. I slipped my shoes on quickly and charged toward the gate we were assigned, not waiting for Nic. I didn't want to listen to his comments or questions. I reached our gate and sat down, dropping my bag between my feet. A few minutes later Nic sat next to me.

"Are you supposed to take those every day?"

"I don't want to talk about it."

"As someone in a relationship with you, I have a right to know if you are taking your medications as you are supposed to."

I closed my eyes. "I am supposed to take them every day, but I normally do not. I brought them because I know being around my family will be stressful. I was planning to take them."

"Those aren't the kind of medications you are supposed to take on a whim. They only work if you take them every day."

"I don't like taking them." I turned my head to look at him. "I have my reasons."

"Oh, really? Do they have side effects like lessening your desire to murder me?"

I wanted to smack him for saying such a thing so openly in public. How dare he? I didn't think anyone would actually take his words as truth, but still.

"No," I said, calmly. "Sometimes I have trouble knowing what is real and what isn't. Like this, you here right now. I don't fully believe you're here. I'm scared if I take the haloperidol, I'll be forced back to the real world, and I'll have to accept that you aren't here."

He stared at me. "You can't tell if I'm real or not?"

"Sometimes you do things that I know can't be real, but you still do them."

"I'm here, Jimena. Take your medication."

I huffed and unzipped my bag. I looked at the clear package inside that contained the meds.

"Why don't we ask her." He pointed to the woman sitting across from us. "You see me, right? I'm here. Tell him."

The woman ignored him.

"People are just rude. That doesn't mean anything. I'm going to get some water for you to take that with. I want you to take your medications." He got up and went to one of the food vendors. I pulled out the package of pills, knowing my anxiety would get the better of me if I didn't take it before I boarded the plane.

It would be okay if he wasn't here. It would be okay, and it would be best if I found out soon. I swallowed the pill dry and stifled the sob that went with it. It had been nice believing in the fantasy while I had been able.

Kidnapper

I waited until they were doing the final boarding call. He still hadn't come back, and I didn't see him at any of the stands. The pills worked fast, but I'd hoped the fantasy would have lasted a bit longer. He had never come to the airport. Had he even agreed to come? I passed my boarding pass to the attendant and walked down the tunnel to the plane. I nodded politely to the flight attendant as I entered and shuffled down the aisle to the row I was assigned. I pushed my bag into the storage compartment and scooted to my window seat. The aisle seat was empty; that was the one assigned to Nic.

I slumped in the seat and stared out the window. What would I tell my family when I arrived? He changed his mind? We broke up? I looked at my phone and all the unanswered texts. I turned it off and put it back in my pocket.

"Sorry, I had to buy some gauze. I completely forgot." Nic tossed his bag up in the overhead compartment and plopped down in the seat.

"You're here."

"Yeah, I'm here. I've been here." He had opened the bandage package and the roll unspooled in his lap. He glanced up and paused. "Wait. Were you serious about thinking I was a figment? Oh. Here." He handed me a bottle of water from his side pocket.

I reached across the space between us and pulled his lips to mine. There was no way I was imagining this.

"This is real. You're here." I rested my forehead against his.

"Jimena."

"Yes."

"Can you wrap my hand?"

The flight attendant recited the standard safety brief as I wrapped Nic's right hand with the gauze. His palm had a barely visible scar in the middle where I'd stabbed him, but otherwise it was completely healed. In two days. It was impossible and made me wonder if I should take a second pill.

"Is it only me?"

"What do you mean?" I wrapped the gauze a few more times, going between his fingers and around his thumb.

"You said sometimes you hallucinate that I'm with you when I'm not. Does that happen with other people or just me?"

"I've noticed it with you, but I've mostly stopped trying to sort it out." I tied off the wrap. And he clasped my hand with both of his.

"I want you to tell me if anything ever happens that makes you question your reality when it's not me. Okay? Can you do that?"

"Uh, sure."

"Sir, can you please buckle your seat belt?" The flight attendant gestured to Nic's lap.

"Oh, right." Nic lifted his hands so he could look under his arms for the belt.

"Oh, my, I didn't notice. Let me help you." Her tone completely changed and she gently reached around him to find the two buckles and clasp them for him. "If you need anything else, just let me know. Can you press the call button? Can you reach it?"

"Yes, I'll be fine," Nic said. The behavior wouldn't have bothered me so much if she hadn't been so young and thin. The more I looked at her, the more she looked like a model who had walked off the runway a few hours ago. She stayed bent over Nic, one hand still touching the buckle, for far longer than needed. "Can I have one of those blankets you guys offer?"

"Of course, I'll bring one by after we take off." She patted his lap and gave him the kind of smile normally reserved for private moments.

I'd put some of my medications in my pocket. I retrieved one of the bottles and shook out two pills. I popped them in my mouth and followed them with the water Nic had gotten me.

"What were those? I thought you'd already taken your meds?"

"Something to help me rest," I said. I closed my eyes and sagged in the seat, trying to get rid of the image of that woman's smile.

The pills did not work as promptly as I'd wanted. I kept my eyes shut as I felt the plane move across the runway and eventually gain speed until we were in the air. The first nips of sleep started to tug at me when her voice returned.

"Here's your blanket," she said. "Would you like anything to drink or a snack?"

"No, this is fine, thanks," Nic replied.

My eyes opened as I felt a warm hand wrapping the blanket around me.

"What are you doing?" I tried to shove the blanket off, but he pulled it back.

"Ever heard of the mile high club?" Nic asked, leaning closer so only I would hear him. "I was thinking you should join." His fingers rubbed my crotch under the blanket.

"No," I hissed. "How have you not learned I don't like public shit like that?" I pushed his hand away with the blanket.

"Come on, it'll help you relax." He flopped the blanket back over my lap.

"I said stop." I pushed again, and he finally relented.

He balled the blanket up in his own lap and stared forward. "We haven't seen each other in a few days. I thought you'd want to get some release before we arrive."

"I'll be fine. That's why I took the pills and started my injections again."

"What do you mean?"

"Just let me sleep." I turned away from him and embraced the lethargy from the sedatives.

CHAPTER nine

Kidnapped

What the hell had he meant? I stared at him as his body relaxed into a true slumber. I unfastened my belt and stood. I opened the compartment above us and pulled his bag out. I dropped it onto my seat and rummaged until I found the medications. I'd only been able to read a few of the labels before. Leuprolide Acetate was unfamiliar to me.

I snapped a photo of it along with the other medications, then tucked them all back where they belonged and placed the bag in the overhead bin. I paid the overpriced fee for Wi-Fi access on the flight and searched the medication and its uses.

Primarily used for the treatment of prostate cancer. Jimena didn't have that. I'd have sensed it if he did. I searched alternative uses for Leuprolide Acetate. The mention of using it to treat anemia appeared followed by something much more startling.

Decreasing the amount of sex hormones that a child makes. It was a castration drug. My vision blurred red for a moment as a rush of rage passed through me. How could he start taking something like this without telling me? I put my phone away and glared at the seat in front of me for the duration of the flight.

It was only a two-and-a-half-hour flight, but it felt much longer. When we touched the ground, the jolt was enough to rouse Jimena from sleep. He rubbed his eyes and peered out the window.

"That went quick," Jimena said.

"For some of us," I said.

"Do you want me to get your bag down for you?" a man asked, already pulling it from above without waiting for an answer. Right, my damn hand injury. I forced a fake smile.

"Thanks," I said, taking the bag from him and putting it on my lap.

"I hate this," Jimena mumbled.

"What?"

"How nice they all are to you."

"It's called sympathy," I said. "If you don't want people to feel sorry for me when I'm hurt, then you shouldn't hurt me."

"They wouldn't feel sorry for you if you were in my basement."

"What?"

"I mean they wouldn't see you, so they wouldn't. Augh! Never mind." He placed his head against the seat in front of him. People had begun deboarding, but it hadn't reached our row yet.

"You should have told me about the castration drug," I said. "As your partner I have a right to know."

"The what?" He lifted his head and looked at me, seeming confused.

"Leuprolide Acetate."

"You said you wanted normal. This is—"

"I said I wanted to be treated like your boyfriend. I never said anything about normal."

"This weekend is going to be hard for me. I'm doing what I need to do to get through it. It's only four days, then I'll stop."

Our turn came, and I stood, mistakenly using my wrapped hand to carry the backpack. I switched hands as I reached the corridor leading to the terminal and slung it over my shoulder.

"Nic, wait, are you really that mad? Nic." Jimena trailed behind me. We passed one of the restrooms, and I grabbed his arm, yanking him in with me. I pulled him toward one of the many stalls, but he jerked free.

"Why are we stopping?" Jimena asked. "You know I don't like public stuff, so nothing is going—"

"Can you even get hard while you're on that?" I turned and folded my arms. "Can you? Did you not think you should inform me that you were planning on a sexless weekend?"

"Why would you be expecting sex on a weekend we are spending with my family?"

"I'm hungry, Jimena, and I don't like being hungry."

"We'll get you some food then. Airports have lots of places to eat."

"That's not—" I raked my fingers through my hair. "That's not what I want."

"Why is it every time you get hurt, I get sick?" Jimena asked.

I froze, my gut prickling with needles.

"Does it have something to do with your hunger?" He pointed to my hand. "And your quick healing?"

The focus was back in his eyes as the sedatives he'd taken for the flight wore off.

"Even if the two are related, you're usually the reason why I'm injured, so it's a bit of balance, wouldn't you say?"

"You aren't injured now, are you? So, we shouldn't have a problem."

"No more drugs," I insisted.

"Give me a straight answer, and I'll consider it."

I clamped my jaw shut. He smirked.

"That's what I thought." He twisted his neck until it popped. "I'm going to the baggage claim. Our ride should meet us there."

Kidnapper

My confidence was a thin veil provided by the haze of drugs I'd taken, but it had worked. Did the cloud that dulled my thoughts and feverish obsessive desires also lessen Nic's ability to feel them? Is that why he seemed so annoyed?

I reached the baggage claim as the luggage from our flight rotated on the carousel.

"Hemy! You made it!" The girlish voice squealed behind me, and I inwardly flinched. Her arms were thrown around me from the side.

"Cousin Trixie," I said, my voice laden with annoyance. "They sent you to pick me up?"

"Yup, I got here yesterday, and I've been the honorary commuter." She let go and took a few steps back, hands on her hips. "I've got a three row SUV rental. This run is you and Cousin Vern. You remember him, right? His flight landed ten minutes before yours, so he went to find a smoking area."

She was short, in the under-five-foot range. Her freckles and bouncy hair made her seem like a child at first glance. She certainly had enough energy in her to still be one.

"I didn't actually think you'd show. You haven't come to one of these since your broody teen years."

"We're the same age, Trixie. They were *our* broody teen years."

"I was a happy teen."

"Uh-huh." I grabbed my bag as it passed us.

"Is it just you? Your mom mentioned you were bringing someone." She searched the crowd, as if she could spot my companion without knowledge of his appearance.

"Yeah, he's in the bathroom," I said.

"Shit, you came," Vern said. He had the first four buttons on his shirt undone, exposing his sparsely arranged chest hair. His cap boasted of the branch of military he'd chosen to serve in, as if his haircut wasn't already doing that for him. He was even wearing his military issued combat boots.

"Hey, Vern," I said. "How many people thanked you for your service today? Did anyone comment on the squadron patches you sewed on your backpack?"

"What? You jealous? Sad you couldn't sign up and shoot some terrorists? Too bad you're too bipolar, or whatever, for anyone to take you."

"And how many disorders do you have from serving? Have you caught the PMS yet?"

"It's PTSD, and you know it, shithead."

He took a step toward me, pointing at my chest with his long gangly arm when another arm snaked around my chest and pulled my body against theirs.

"Am I missing the family drama already? Don't start the show without me," Nic said. "Are these relatives?"

"Cousins," I said. "By adoption only."

Vern rolled his eyes. "We get enough of that thrown in our faces by your parents."

"They wouldn't do it if it didn't bother your parents so much," I countered.

"Besides, what is this?" He pointed to Nic. "We can bring friends to the reunions now? Or is he your emotional support animal? A new form of therapy?"

Trixie blushed, a sign that she had been briefed on the situation.

"If I'd known we could have brought friends, I would have brought a few," Vern added.

"I'm his boyfriend," Nic said. "And I'm guessing with your attitude, long-term relationships aren't a thing that works out for you."

"You expect me to believe you two are dating?" Vern laughed in that rowdy way of his. "I always figured Hemy ate his partners after he fucked 'em."

"Oh, wow! Okay, there are kids around, so let's get going, yeah?" Trixie said. "The car is this way."

Nic kept his arm around my shoulders, and we fell a few paces behind Vern and Trixie.

"I may need some of your meds to help me get through this," Nic said. "I thought your family was nice."

"They're competitive," I said. "My mother has four siblings, and each of them wants to be the shiniest toy in the collection, which means they've been pitting their children against each other from birth."

"And where do you fall in the lineup? Who is the current boy wonder?"

"I'm more the winner in the black sheep department, which gives my parents an advantage in sympathy because they adopted me."

"Hmm, bonus points for taking in the troubled kid with mental disorders, eh? You coming out as gay must be a nice layer of icing for their cake."

"Yeah, it won't compare to when they discover they are parents of a serial killer," I mumbled only loud enough for him to hear.

Trixie opened the back hatch on the SUV so I could put my luggage in. Vern shoved his camo patterned bag in with mine and glanced at Nic.

"No bag?"

"I travel light," Nic replied. They exchanged a look I couldn't identify, then went to opposite sides of the car to get in. Vern got in the front seat with Trixie.

"Did you all have good flights?" Trixie asked as she started the car. Vern answered first, going into a long ramble about how the pilot had announced he was a veteran, and all the passengers had applauded him. I leaned my head back and dozed while she drove, the sedatives still making me drowsy.

Nic poked my shoulder when we arrived, and I rubbed my face to wake up a bit. I got out of the vehicle as Vern and Nic pulled our bags out.

"I think you took too many pills," Nic said.

"I'll be fine," I muttered. I fell in step with Trixie as she led us across the parking lot to the six-story resort we were staying in. It was co-located with the amusement parks and a water park, with shuttles ferrying guests every hour to and from the park entrances.

We walked into the lobby, where I saw a handful of my relatives sitting at a table, acting as if they were handing out passes to a convention. One of them was talking to my mother, who immediately detached herself and rushed over.

"Jimena! You made it." She gave me a brief hug, our bodies barely touching. "And Nic, I'm glad you could join us as well. How is your hand?"

Nic raised the limb to hold it above his heart.

"Recovering well," Nic said. "Thank you for inviting me."

"I recognize that wrap job." She pointed at the gauze. "I'm glad Jimena is taking good care of you."

"The best," Nic said, glancing at me.

"I'll see you at the supper tonight," she said. "Trish will get you set up with your room and explain the signups. I'm just so glad you're here." She gave my shoulder another gentle brush before she walked away.

I turned back to the table to a big-nosed Trish staring me down, clipboard hugged to her chest. I'd always thought she would grow into that nose, but such was not the case.

"Hi, Jimena," she said. She was a cousin, but not an immediate one. I wasn't quite certain the family tree branch that connected her to me.

"Hi, Trish," I said. Her eyes went to Nic, urging me to do an introduction. "This is Nic."

"Hi, yes, I heard you were bringing someone. It's nice to meet you," she said. "I do have a bit of bad news. We had a bit of a hiccup. See, we weren't one hundred percent sure you were coming, and by the time we heard you were and went to make the reservation, all the rooms were booked at the resort."

"We don't have a room?"

"It's okay. I've been asking around, and I found someone who has two queen beds in their room and is willing to share with you. We can add a roller bed if you need. I wasn't sure, uh, how you prefer…"

"Who are we bunking with?" I asked.

"Uncle Wade," Trish said. "Are you okay with those arrangements? I asked around, but no one really has the spare bed except him. We can put a roller bed in with someone, or if you'd prefer, I can get you a room at a nearby hotel, and—"

"It's fine," Nic said. "Isn't it?" He looked at me but his glance made it clear my only option was agreeance. "Not like we'll be having any sex on this vacation." He didn't say it loudly, but he said it loud enough for Trish and the three people behind her at the table to hear. They all turned various colors of red.

"Okay, uh, great," Trish said. She scribbled our room number on an envelope, then handed both it and two plastic keycards to me. "Here are your keys. Sarah has the signup sheet for activities tomorrow, and tonight, we have a formal dinner planned in the ballroom. Cocktail hour starts at four."

I heard Nic thank her for us as I turned toward the elevator since our paper said we were on the fifth floor. I hit the call button and waited.

"So, what should I know about Uncle Wade?" Nic asked.

"He's a forever bachelor, not a blood relative, not that any of these people actually are. He's the brother of one of my aunt's husbands. He doesn't have any kids of his own, and I'm guessing there isn't much of a family tree, so he's sort of attached himself to the one his brother married into. He's at every gathering."

"Do we like him?"

The doors opened, and I entered, pulling my roller bag behind me. I shrugged.

"He's not part of the competitive whatever, so he's fine, I guess." I slumped against the wall as the elevator moved.

We rode in silence and maintained it as we went down the hall to the room. I took out the keys and handed him one. I knocked, in case Uncle Wade was in, then swiped the card and entered.

"Hello?" I asked walking past the entryway and into the room. The bathroom was to the right and beyond that were the two queen beds. The room wasn't much larger than the two beds, an additional dresser, and the mounted television.

"Little Hemy!" Uncle Wade said. He had his suitcase open on the bed closest to the bathroom. The nightstand was overwhelmed with a large device with tubes. "I hope you don't mind I took the bed closest to the bathroom. This old bladder isn't what it used to be." He patted his stomach. "Also, I have one of these sleep apnea machines. I hope that won't be a bother to you guys." He pointed at the contraption. "Keeps me from snoring and dying throughout the night."

"It's no problem at all," I said. "Thank you for letting us stay with you. This is Nic."

"Hi."

"Of course, no problem. I like to think of myself as plenty open-minded. Not that the gay bit is why most people were saying no when Trish was asking around for an open spot." He fumbled around in his bag, likely regretting bringing up the topic.

"Why were they skittish about it then?" Nic asked. "What could possibly have deterred them more than the idea of waking in the middle of the night to see two gay men fucking?"

"Don't give the man a heart attack," I snapped. "I apologize for him."

"No, no, he does make a, uh, valid point," Uncle Wade said. He closed his bag and zipped it. "I'm going to take a stroll around the resort. I'll leave you two to, uh, discuss and get settled."

He shuffled past Nic on his way out, leaving us alone.

"I'm going to take a nap before the dinner thing." I shoved my bag against the far wall and dropped to the bed, still fully clothed and not bothering to go under the sheets.

Kidnapped

He passed out moments after hitting the mattress. He hadn't even bothered to use one of the pillows. And I was left wondering what Uncle Wade meant. I mean, I sort of knew, but I wanted details. Had Jimena killed family pets? Did family members get mysterious injuries when playing with him? Or did he simply creep them out by acting oddly?

It wasn't like I had a lot of other things to do to pass the time, so asking around seemed as good of a pastime as any. I freshened in the bathroom and went downstairs to where the ballroom was being prepared for dinner.

I didn't know any of the people, but it was easy enough to identify the resort workers based off their uniforms. The others, I assumed, were relatives in some way.

"There he is, the great Nickolas."

The voiced sounded familiar. I turned to see Paul, the brother.

"It's actually Nicodemus," I said. "But you can call me Nic."

"Oh, wow, that's an exotic name," Paul said. He took a step back. "I know you and I got off to a rough start with the whole misunderstanding of—"

"How I thought you were Jimena's new boyfriend?"

"Yeah." He frowned. "It seemed a bit like I might have strained things between you two, so I wanted to apologize."

"It was a short-lived misunderstanding," I said. "Nothing to worry about."

"Jimena has never introduced me, or really any of us, to his boyfriend or girlfriend, barely any friends, really. So, I want to make this—"

"I get it Paul," I said, raising my hand. "You don't want to be the reason I leave Jimena or create some reason to discourage him from introducing *y*ou to future partners. I can assure you, if I stop being in Jimena's life, it will have nothing to do with you or this family."

"Oh, good, I mean, I'm glad to hear that." He raised his hands above his head. "It's just so much pressure, you know? It all has to be perfect."

"I don't think it does, actually, Paul." I spotted Uncle Wade entering the ballroom from a different set of doors. I took a step toward him but was blocked by three children who lined up in ascending height, all boys.

"Let me introduce my kids," Paul said. He spouted off their names as he pointed, all of which I immediately forgot. "This is your Uncle Jimena's boyfriend, Nic."

"Does that mean he's our new uncle?"

"Should we call him Uncle Nic?"

"Ah, are you okay with that? It's too much too soon, isn't it?" Paul asked. "You've only been together a few months, right?"

Considering I'd been told to call Wade an uncle and hadn't hesitated, I figured it was commonplace for this family.

"It's fine, they can call me that," I said.

"Great to meet you Uncle Nic!" All three shouted in unison and hugged my legs since they weren't tall enough to reach any higher. I stood there awkwardly and patted their heads.

"Do you have any nieces or nephews?" Paul asked.

"Uh, none that I'm aware of," I said. "I have a lot of siblings I don't speak to, so, who knows. My father, he was rather unfettered when it came to spreading his seed. I do live with one of my brothers. He's the only one I'm close to."

"I hope we can meet him sometime," Paul said, his smile actually looking sincere. "Maybe he can come to the reunion next year."

My returning smile was not like his. "I'll mention it. Um, if you'll excuse me." I pried myself away from the children and resumed my approach to Uncle Wade, who had seated himself at one of the tables.

"Finished your walk?" I asked. I sat across from him.

"Oh, yeah, sure," he replied. "Nice decorating, yeah?" He gestured around at the various balloons and streamers that had been taped to the walls.

"It actually looks a bit half-heartedly done," I said.

"Well, they do have a few more hours."

The three Paul minions were busying pumping air into balloons with the assistance of who I assumed was their mother, judging by the similarities in appearance.

"What happened to Jimena?" Uncle Wade asked.

"Napping," I replied. "Can I ask you what you meant earlier? Your theory on why no one wanted to room with—"

"Oh, my gawd, you're him, aren't you?" A young woman, either late in her teen years or beginning her twenties, leered closely at me. Her eyeshadow was bright pink along with her blush, an unnatural look that matched with a pink ribbon curled and dangling in her blond hair, equal to her hair length that went past her shoulders. She batted her glitter-enhanced eyelashes at me, and I resisted the urge to lean away from her. "You're Hemy's boyfriend, right?"

"That I am," I said.

She sat and nestled close to me. "I was wondering why it was such a big deal, dang!" She gave a whistle and made a show of looking me up and down. "You are something to brag about."

"Mind giving me an introduction?" I asked, leaning into her by letting our shoulders touch. I refused to shy from her intrusive nature, both physically and verbally. "Are you an acquired trophy like myself or here by blood?"

She laughed, a chittering sound that was actually quite pleasant.

"Wow, you are good." She pressed more into me, the entire length of our bodies now touching.

"Courtney, seriously, try to control yourself," Uncle Wade said. "She's married to Evelin and Mark's son, Dale. Evelin is a sibling to Marissa, who is Jimena's mother."

"So, a fellow trophy," I said. "Are you trying to create angst by doing all this touching then? Get the cousins to fight?"

"She hits on every newcomer. Sometimes does more," Uncle Wade said.

She lifted her leg and put it over mine. "You're just jealous I never hit on you." She turned to me. "So, what's the story? There's no way someone like Hemy actually caught you. Did his parents hire you to come here and make this production? I would think Jimena paid for you himself, but he's never cared about impressions. Does he even know you're a paid escort?"

"Exactly what is the gain to be had from my being here?"

"The attention boy-o. You're the star of the show, or did you not know?"

"And I suppose if you seduce me, and we have a little affair, you'll claim some of that stardom? Or merely muck it up for Jimena's family?"

"What's it to you? You're paid for already, right? And wouldn't I make for a better partner than—"

I put my hand across her mouth, clenching it tightly.

"I think I've listened to you insult my lover more than enough. Judging by your age, I assume you haven't been in the family long enough to have the proper trepidation regarding Jimena that everyone else does. So, why don't we listen to Uncle Wade as he tells us why no one wanted to share a room with good old Hemy." I moved my eyes to Uncle Wade. "That's your cue."

"This really isn't a proper forum," Uncle Wade said. "And I think you're hurting her."

"Not nearly as much as Jimena will if he finds out she touched me. So, tell her."

"He's just a bit clingy… creepy clingy."

"The truth Uncle Wade."

His mouth twitched a bit. "There are a few stories about childhood pets." He shifted in his seat. "They thought they were running away at first, but then they started finding them." He twitched and rolled one of his shoulders. "It's not a topic any of us like to discuss."

"Has he hurt any of you?" I asked. Courtney gave a groan of protest under my still-in-place hand gag.

"There have been accidents, but it's really nothing. He just makes people uncomfortable."

I turned my attention back to Courtney. "Touch me again, and I'll tell Jimena. Understand?" I removed my hand so she could respond. She nodded and touched her face where my fingers had been. "You should go fix your makeup."

She covered her face with her hands as if she feared her lipstick was smeared to a nightmarish level. I watched as she fled and noticed Cousin Vern glaring in my direction.

"What just happened stays between us," I told Uncle Wade. I got up and went to Vern who promptly turned and went into the hall before I reached him. He waited for me a few paces from the entrance.

"What?" Vern asked.

"I could ask you the same thing. What's with the glares?"

"You mean besides what I saw you just do to Courtney?"

"I did that in front of over a dozen people," I said. "Why did it bother you and no one else?" I stepped closer. "What's this really about? You've been rude to Jimena since you met me. You expect me to believe you've always hated him?"

"No." He crossed his arms and slouched. I expected him to have some childhood horror story about Jimena that likely ended with Vern in the hospital and running away to join the Army in an attempt to escape his psychopathic cousin. He muttered something I couldn't hear.

"What?"

"I'm gay," he repeated the words forcefully.

"And I'm bi, what does that have to do with anything?"

"No, that's not…" He huffed. "I'm not out." He pulled a pack of cigarettes from his pocket and used the pack to keep his hands busy. "And now when I do announce it to the family, I'll be coined forever as the copycat. The guy who came out after Jimena or with Jimena. It won't be the same. You stole the moment." He put a stick in his mouth. "And let's be honest, Jimena isn't actually gay. He's just obsessed with you or whatever."

There was still something missing. He was pronouncing his sexuality, but there was no hint of attraction. Sure, my ego wasn't so large that I expected every gay man desired me, but this…

"You're either lying or not telling me the whole truth. Did you have some production planned at this very reunion, and now you're thinking you can't do it?" He didn't look like he was prepared to come out of the closet any time soon.

"You're a perceptive asshole, aren't you?"

"Not everyone would agree on that." I shrugged. "Jimena was stalking me for six months, and I didn't figure it out until he'd… spiked my drink so he could get my attention. I don't notice everything, but I am noticing your extreme angst, and I'd like to know how big of a problem it's going to be for me."

"Now, that sounds like the Hemy I grew up with. Did he club you over the head and drag you back to his cave?"

"Back to his basement; chained me to a support beam."

"Fuck! I can't tell if you're joking or serious."

"If I can claw my way out of Jimena's basement of death, then I can help you piece together whatever plans we derailed. So, tell me, what did we mess up?"

"I have a boyfriend," he admitted. "I met him while I was doing a tour in Afghan."

"Afghanistan? He's in the Army with you?"

"No." He shook his head. "He's a local."

"Hmm. I can imagine that creates a few difficulties."

"Local interpreter assigned to my unit. I've been trying to get him over here on a travel or immigrant visa for over a year now, and there's a lot of red tape. I'd marry him so he can become a resident, but since he's not here, and it's not legal there, it's difficult. I was going to ask Grandpa if he had some connections and could help me, but now that Jimena has come out of the closet, the timing will look bad, and everyone will think I'm just trying to push him out of the spotlight."

"What if I use my connections instead?"

He gaffed. "Grandpa used to be a State Senator. I doubt you—"

I stepped closer, intimately close. "I can get him here within the hour if you want. You'll just need to make a deal with me."

CHAPTER ten

Kidnapper

An alarm went off on my phone. I didn't remember setting it but reached over to turn it off. I sat up and rubbed my eyes. I was in a strange room and fully dressed, even my shoes were on. I took a deep breath and took a moment to recall the events of the day.

"Family reunion, *fuck*." I was already struggling to recall why I had decided to come. Why, of all things, had this been what I'd spouted out of my mouth when Nic had demanded a gesture to show I could treat him like a boyfriend?

I freshened up in the bathroom and proceeded to trudge downstairs. I'd get through the customary family dinner, then feign illness and spend the night in the room delightfully floating in a drug induced haze.

I wandered into the ballroom and stopped, thinking I'd entered the wrong one. Did this resort have more than one? Probably.

Helium balloons lined the ceiling so densely the lights were dimmed by their ominous cloud. Cheap sound poppers—the ones that spit out mini confetti—were being used by every child present, a good half of the attendees. Music played softly enough to be spoken over, and multicolored laser lights moved around on the walls, adding to the craziness. It was a bit more party-ish than I remembered these gatherings being in the past.

I recognized a few relatives here and there and was comforted to know I was in the right location. A loud cheer went up at Aunt Janessa's table, my mother's eldest sister. A few people tapped glasses with utensils, and the movement spread quickly across the room until everyone had silenced. The music was even turned down.

My skin prickled seconds before a hand rested on my shoulder and words were whispered near my ear.

"I sorta did a thing," Nic said. He'd been down here with them? Hanging out with my family? He smoothly moved to stand next to me, and I saw a lively sparkle in his eyes. I couldn't quite place what that look meant, but I'd seen it before. When we were fucking. When he was urging me to tell him how much I loved him.

I didn't understand what he did to people. Mostly, out of denial. Deep down I knew he'd fed on someone. Struck a new deal, seduced new prey.

Fed on someone who wasn't me. And it felt worse than any adultery could.

He was usually tapped into my emotions. He should have felt my agony, but the pills I'd been taking stifled my reaction and subsequently his ability to sense it. So, while I internally suffered, he maintained his grin of pride.

"I want to thank my sister Marissa for adopting our darling Jimena," Janessa said, pointing her fork in my direction. "Because if he hadn't been brought into our lives, we never would have met Nicodemus Greene, and without him, my dear son Vern would still be separated from the love of his life. Everyone, please, welcome Fazlullah! My future son-in-law!"

The cheering went up again, and this time I saw Vern and a deeply tanned man standing in the center of the gathered crowd.

Vern waved bashfully, then locked his eyes on me. Eyes that seemed extremely grateful and joyous.

"What did you do?" I growled. I looked at Nic who only had a second to flash an expression of puzzlement before Vern and Fazlullah approached us.

"I don't know how you did it," Vern said. "But you and your brothers, your father, whoever your connections are, I am in your debt."

"We made our deal, Vern. We're good," Nic said. The couple were clutching hands. I'd never seen a happier, more in love couple. It dazed me a bit.

"All the same, we want you two to be the godparents for our first child. In your honor, Jimena, we are going to adopt," Fuzlullah said.

Like they had other options; they were both men. I bit back the comment and forced a smile I would never have been capable of if I wasn't drugged.

"Let's not get ahead of ourselves," Nic said, likely thinking of how a serial killer shouldn't be a godparent.

"Yes, let's not," I agreed. "Can I talk to you for a minute?" I pulled on his arm and backed us out of the ballroom. Vern and Fuzlullah were sucked back into the spotlight, and we faded into the background of the hall.

"What did you do?" I grabbed him and forcefully slammed him against the nearest wall. "What is that? Any of that?"

"Well, if you weren't high on whatever your therapist prescribes you, maybe you'd be able to catch up," Nic said.

I slapped him, the smacking sound loud enough to be heard in the ballroom as it echoed in the hall. A server passing us uttered a gasp, and the tray of salads she carried clattered a bit as she struggled not to drop them.

Nic's eyes flashed the golden color, and he clenched his fists.

"That." I pointed to his eyes. "That's what I want to know. What the hell is that, and what did you do? What is it you do?"

He grabbed my wrist and pulled, walking briskly to the single stall handicap bathroom. He pushed me inside and locked the door. I flexed my palm as it still stung, yet I itched to hit him again.

"I did your cousin a favor, and you hit me for it?" Nic turned from the closed door, his eyes that light color again. "Why don't you explain why you're so pissed?"

"What exactly did you do?" I asked.

"Vern explained to me that he is gay and in love with a foreigner. So, I pulled some strings and brought them here. In a few days the paperwork should catch up, and—"

"No, not that. How? I've always thought it was me hallucinating, but it's not, is it? Your eyes, your healing, I was right before. You fed on me and healed yourself. You fed on Vern and, somehow, supernaturally brought his lover here, didn't you?"

The golden shade faded, and his demeanor relaxed.

"That's what this is really about, isn't it? That I, as you put it, fed on someone else. You're jealous."

"That is not what this is. I want to know what you are."

He grabbed my chin, holding me in place. "I don't like this drugged, dulled version of you. It doesn't taste right. Get off the meds, and I'll leave your family alone. Fair enough?"

"Who said I wanted you to feed on me?"

"It's intimate, and you want me so completely to yourself that you wanted to hide me in your basement. That implies a lot, like you don't want me to—"

"Stop, just stop it." I put my hands over my face as a headache began throbbing at the base of my skull. "I can't talk in all these circles right now."

"Because you're drugged," Nic said, the irritation clear in his voice.

"Let's just get through dinner, then…" I didn't know what, but I'd figure out something. The dinner. "Shit, my mother is going to be pissed. You put all the attention on Janessa's family."

"I thought you didn't care about that."

"I don't, but she's going to be upset about it, and now we have to endure it the entire trip." I rubbed my forehead again.

"Well, the spotlight isn't entirely on them. *Your* boyfriend is the one who made it happen." He put his hands on my shoulders. "Doesn't that count for something?"

"Yeah, I guess." I could tell by his expression that my response wasn't what he wanted. He stepped away, the look on his face similar to the one he'd had the last time we were in a bathroom together. The one when he'd been upset at my reaction to our public bathroom fuck.

Whatever it was about me that kept him coming back, despite my ill treatment of him, I currently wasn't providing it. Enduring my family while sober was torture for me, but watching him seek others to satisfy him because I no longer could, was far worse.

"I'll stop taking the drugs," I said. He'd unlocked the door and paused to glance back at me.

"You will?"

"Yes, but that means you have to help me endure my family."

"Deal."

We walked back into the ballroom to find everyone seated. I went to my mother's table and plunked down, with Nic next to me.

"Are you okay?" Paul asked, looking at Nic, not me. The table was solemn and unease spread within me. I glanced at Nic and saw his reddened cheek from my slap. And even if that trace of evidence hadn't been there, they would have known I'd been the one to do the assaulting because Nic's dominate hand was still wrapped in gauze. At least, that was the logic my brain came up with because I knew the sound of the slap had been loud enough for them all to hear.

"I'm fine," Nic said. "He's done worse, remember." He waved his wrapped hand and flashed a smile as he picked up his fork in his left hand.

"That temper," my mother said, shaking her head. "It's rare for us all to be here together. Would it be so much to ask for everyone to get along?"

"This happens every year. How is it rare?" I asked.

"It's rare for you to show up," Alexia said, my younger sister by two years. She was well on her way to being one of those lifelong students who keep changing their degrees.

"Did you slap him because of Courtney?" Piper asked, Paul's youngest son. He batted his eyes innocently, but he was fully aware of the pot he was attempting to stir.

"I slapped him for meddling in Vern's affairs," I said. "What did you do to Courtney?"

"She sat on my lap," Nic said, following the statement with a mouthful of lettuce.

"What? Are you Santa Claus now? Having people line up, sit on your lap, and tell you their wishes?"

"That would be a very productive way to do it."

"Unbelievable."

"I didn't do anything for her."

"Only Courtney would think she could sleep with a gay man," Paul's wife said. "She flirts so unashamedly."

"By the way, I don't think we've been properly introduced," Piper said. She waved at Nic. "I'm Jimena's younger sister."

"I'm Ashley," Paul's wife said.

"And Rick," my father said, raising his hand.

"He speaks," Nic quirked.

"But is not spoken of," my father said. "I'm more a behind the scenes man."

"More like behind the mother," Piper said, more to her salad than to anyone at the table.

"I apologize if what I did for Vern upset anyone," Nic said. "I understand there is a social order at these events, and what I did put Vern's family at the top."

My mother shook her head. "It's fine. It's obvious that man is just using Vern for a free ticket to America. I give it two months, and then Vern will be a raging alcoholic living in some veteran homeless shelter. Janessa will get pity, but it's not really a bragging thing to have a child that's such a failure."

"Such positivity. Do I dare ask how much time you give us?" Nic put his fork down, his salad plate empty.

"Well, I'm not a fortune teller," my mother said. "But I imagine you'll be with us for as long as you can endure our little Hemy here."

Her tone shifted from irritated to soothing as she spoke of us versus her sister's children.

"Let's shift topics, shall we? How is school going for you, Piper?" I asked. "Nic also thinks education is important. He's a full-time student."

"Really? I don't suppose you caught the learning bug?" Piper asked.

"I'm in a class with him," I said.

"And he's going to be in more with me next semester, aren't you?" Nic asked, but I knew it wasn't a question.

"Of course," I said, trying to keep my tone even.

"Well, that would be just great," my mother said. "If you two have degrees, we'll have more at our table than either of my sisters do."

"Nearly done single-handedly by Piper," I said. That earned a laugh from my father, who had paid for most of her education.

The servers came and cleared our plates, replacing them with the main entrée of steak or pasta, depending on if they'd requested vegetarian as Piper had.

The conversation drifted to other topics as we filled each other in on what we'd done over the past year, all edited versions to highlight successes, except when one of us who knew the truth took an extra stab. After dinner was finished, the three-tiered birthday cake, which looked more like a wedding cake, was wheeled out. We all sang Happy Birthday to our grandfather who soaked it all in like he was a king being given tribute. It was his ninetieth birthday, but he didn't look it. He was the annoyingly youthful-looking elder who would probably live well into his hundreds. He was also wealthy and well-connected in politics. Part of the sucking up everyone did was because of wanting to solidify their spot in his inheritance.

He did his birthday speech, which I mostly ignored because my head was throbbing. They served slices of cake that I took two bites from and shoved away, then the party moved outside, transforming into a pool party.

"Looks like I need to buy a swimsuit," Nic said. Of course, he would want to go swimming. The children were already throwing off their clothes and running for the pool, some of them grabbing floaters. They'd been smart enough to wear their swimsuits under their clothes. "Did you bring yours? Are you going to change?"

"I'm not getting in the water," I said. I stopped at the nearest outdoor table and sat, rubbing my temples.

"Do you want me to do something about your headache?"

"No, just get your suit or whatever." The sun was barely visible on the horizon, and the outdoor lights were on. Every bulb pierced my eyes like miniature daggers of wrath. Nic sat next to me and scooted his chair closer.

"You're going through withdrawals for me, at least let me help, please?" Nic put his hand on my chin and turned my face to him.

"So, now you can magically heal people?" I asked.

"No questions." His eyes turned that bronze color, but under the pool lighting it was harder to notice. He ran his hand over my head, and it felt like the strands of pain were being pulled out, attracted to his palm as if it were a magnet. He removed his hand, our eye contact never breaking. My headache was gone and so was the comforting haze the drugs had given me.

"You could have done that this entire time and you didn't? If you wanted me off the medications that much, why didn't you just do this?"

"Unlike you, I don't feel the need to control everything. I'll order you a water before I go. I'm going to go buy a suit." He kissed the top of my head as if I were a child, then walked back inside after speaking to one of the servers.

I huffed and closed my eyes, trying to get the world to calm down now that the haze was gone. A clink came from near me, and I assumed someone placed a bottle of water on the table. I muttered a thanks and reached for it, opening my eyes as I did.

My hand wrapped around the handle of a woman's beach bag, not a bottle of water. A woman I didn't know stood in front of me, dressed in a bikini that barely covered anything.

"Oh, sorry," she said. "All the tables are full, and I saw you were alone, so I'd hoped you wouldn't mind if I sat my things here."

I uncoiled my fingers from her belongings.

"Come on, Sandy," another woman said, waving at her. "I told you to leave all that stuff in your room."

"Yeah, one minute," she said. "Do you mind?" She pointed to her bag. I managed to shake my head, which was apparently enough of a confirmation for her. She flashed a smile, showing teeth that could only be that straight after years of dental work. The attention only lasted a moment before she turned back to her friend who stood at the pool's edge. "I'm coming, Dani."

I watched her join a group of four girls, all looking similar in age, probably early twenties. It was fall break, so it made sense if they were college kids on vacation.

Sandy had pale skin, bright blue eyes, and long blond hair. She was much like a Barbie doll but with realistic body features. She pulled her hair up in a bun as she approached the pool.

"I like to have my stuff handy," she said. "I don't want to use the hotel towels. You never know how clean those are."

She wasn't wrong. Hotels never cleaned or took care of things to the degree a person does in their own home. I looked at her bag, containing a beach towel, various bottles… I slipped my hand inside and pulled out her wallet. How trusting was this girl? I flipped it open.

Sandy Brown from Newtucket, Kentucky, age twenty-two, very young indeed. I slipped my finger in the area where the money was and found her keycard, still in the folded paper they gave you at the desk. Room 241. My fingers moved of their own accord. I swapped her keycard for mine, which looked identical. She would merely think it was programmed wrong.

I dropped the wallet back in her bag and glanced up to verify she hadn't been watching. She and her group were in the pool, facing away from me, ordering drinks from the bar located in the middle of the shallow end. She'd need her wallet for that wouldn't she? No, wait, they'd probably charge it to her room. And with her flirty ways, she wouldn't need to flash any proof of age. I could already tell that by the way she exchanged glances with the male bartender.

"Did they not bring you the water?" Nic asked. I jumped, guilt wafting off me in waves that I hoped he wouldn't detect.

"They probably didn't figure I was with you," I said. I turned and was relieved to see he was wearing a shirt. His swim trunks went to his knees.

"You need to stop that," Nic said.

"What?"

"Thinking you aren't good enough to be with me." He moved as if planning to kiss me. I turned my head, so he was forced to kiss my cheek instead. "Why do you have a beach bag?"

"Some girl left it," I said.

"Did she even ask?"

"It's fine."

"You really are just invisible, aren't you?"

"Are you trying to make that a compliment?"

He grinned as a response. "Are you going to come in the pool with me or not?"

"Not. I'll watch."

"Shirt on or off?"

"I get to decide?"

"I wasn't sure if you'd want the view or if you'd be jealous of all the others looking."

"Your ego is suffocating."

He laughed as he backed away from the table. He pulled the shirt off and tossed it at me. When I saw his rippled abs and perfect chest, part of me regretted not voicing an opinion.

Kidnapped

I neared the pool's edge and heard the sharp tone of a mother chastising her child. I figured it was meant for one of the many children running around, but then a firm hand grabbed my wrist.

"What are you doing?" I looked up and found myself face-to-face with Marissa.

"Did you not hear me? What are you thinking?"

"I don't follow."

"Your hand." She raised the limb she was clutching. It was still wrapped in the gauze. "You can't go into a pool full of chlorine when you have an open wound."

"It's not an open wound. It's completely sealed. I—"

"I saw you stabbed less than a week ago. Not only is it not good for you, but no one wants to find your bloody gauze floating in the water. No pool for you." She scowled in the way only a mother can. But unlike my mother, there wasn't an underlying fear in the mannerisms.

"I will be fine."

"No." She reaffirmed her grip on my wrist and led me away from the pool. I thought she would take me back to the table Jimena was at, but instead she took me to her table. Her husband was there, sipping a beer and looking wholeheartedly bored. Next to him was a child I hadn't been introduced to yet.

"Welcome to the first-aid station," Rick quipped.

"I can't go in the pool either," the kid said. She, or possibly he—it was hard to tell—had to be no more than eight. "I have a skinned knee that's still bleeding. What's your story?"

"Sit down, let me give you a fresh dressing," Marissa said. I plopped down and tried to think of a means to stop her since there was no actual wound for her to find under the wrap.

"The doctors said the dressing shouldn't be changed," I said.

"And you were going to get it wet? Didn't they speak to you about that?"

"Well, yes, they did." I glanced over my shoulder, hoping Jimena would be coming to my rescue. Instead, I saw him looking at the swimmers in the pool. I focused on the area he was staring—a group of four girls.

"Are you listening to me?" She waved a hand in front of my face until I looked at her instead of Jimena.

"I won't go in the pool," I said. "Let me go back to Jimena."

She sat next to me. "I want to have a real talk first."

"Me and the other prisoner are going to take a lap around the pool," Rick said. He got up and the child went with him.

"What kind of talk?"

"We all know what happened earlier." She waited, as if expecting me to say it for her. I shrugged. "He hit you. Jimena hit you, and I doubt it was the first time. Your hand, it was no accident, was it?"

"I'm an adult, Marissa. I can take care myself."

She put her hand over mine. "You aren't the first he's hurt. I want to help you, Nic. You can get out. It may not seem that way, but—"

"I appreciate what you're saying, I do. But you've no idea the relationship I have with your son. He and I, we're fine."

"I worked at an ER for ten of my thirty years as a nurse. I know what abuse looks like, and you have it. You can't let him treat you like this. It's no way to live."

"Your insistence on this makes me believe you are projecting," I said. "I suggest you drop it, lest you want me to begin prying."

I watched the muscles in her jaw flex as she struggled against her impulse to keep arguing with me.

"As I said, I appreciate your concern." I stood and went to the table Jimena was at. His eyes were still on the woman in the pool. "Hey." He didn't respond. I repeated myself louder.

"Oh, hey," he said. "I thought you were going in the pool?"

"Your mother had other ideas." I held up my hand. "She's pool-blocking me because of my wound."

"Tough luck."

I sat down, grabbing my shirt back and putting it on. "She also wanted to have a heart-to-heart about the abusive relationship I'm in… with you." His eyes had gone back to the pool. "The passion your mother had about it leads me to believe she speaks from experience. Is Rick abusive?" If anything, I'd suspect Rick was the one being abused by Marissa.

"No, not at all. He's very passive," Jimena said, his eyes searching the bodies of the pool occupants. I'd watched him enough that I was confident it was the young blond-haired woman he was eyeing.

"Who abuses her then?"

"I don't know."

"Well, if not her spouse and not you…" She'd be in far worse shape if Jimena was her abuser. "Then maybe it goes back farther. What about Grandpa?"

"Grandpa?" That pulled his attention away from the pool. He looked at me, like the suggestion was forbidden. "That." He looked across the pool patio at the umbrella covered one that his gracefully-aged grandfather sat under. "I could actually imagine that, yes. It would explain a lot. He is quite controlling. He and I have never spoken much. I always figured it was because I wasn't blood, but maybe it's more, like he and I are cut from the same cloth, and instead of looking in the mirror, we've both looked away."

"How poetic," I said. "Well, I definitely think it's time to break the silence between the two of you. It seems more a task for tomorrow, though. The pool is a bit boring when you aren't allowed in the pool. Let's head up to our room. If we go now, we should have some alone time before Uncle Wade shows up."

"But what about Sandy's things?"

"Sandy?"

"The girl who left her bag." He pointed to it.

"Did she tell you to watch her things?"

"Well, no, she asked if she could put it there, but it was implied that she wants me to watch it."

"If she didn't ask you to, then it's not your job. Just leave it."

"I should tell her I'm leaving, so she knows her bag is unguarded."

"It was never your place to guard it."

"It was implied." He got up and approached the pool. I could see his hands trembling. Why would he be so nervous to tell her? She was a complete stranger. I got up and fell in step behind him. He reached the pool's edge and hesitated.

"What now, slick?" I asked. "I can't go in, and you can't either. So, you'll have to yell her name, which will be such an awkward thing for her."

"Do you think you're helping?"

"I think I'm preventing a social suicide."

He gave me a sideways glare of annoyance.

"Would you prefer I help?"

"What do you suggest?"

"This." I put my hand on his back and pushed. By the time he realized what I was doing, it was too late for him to adjust his balance. He fell forward, face and belly down with hands doing twirls at his sides, straight into the pool. I knew I would pay for it later, but the fleeting moment of humor was well worth it.

He popped back up, swiping his hair from his face and coughing.

"We have her attention now," I said, nodding behind him. He turned quickly, the water up to his chest as he churned in place. The group of four girls all looked at him, not laughing, more surprised and uncertain about what had occurred.

"I—uh, I wanted to let you know your bag, I mean, the table, is free now. Your bag is, uh, still there," Jimena said.

"Oh." She was silent for a moment, then she seemed to remember him. "You were the one at the table where I left my bag. Right. Uh, thank you."

Jimena nodded then returned to me. I reached a hand down to help him out, already suspecting he might pull me in. It would upset his mother, not me. He jerked, using all his strength. I could have resisted, but it was more fun to allow him to do it. I fell forward, pulling him under with me. We both came up, my wrapped hand a soggy mess. I looked through the crowd, most of which wasn't paying us any attention, and found Jimena's mother glaring at us, hands on her hips.

We swam back to the edge and climbed out. I avoided glancing in Marissa's direction. We went to the rack of beach towels and each took one.

"First impressions are important," he said. "Now, this is how she'll remember me."

"You'll likely never see her again. And if anything, I helped you become memorable, so she *will* remember you."

He dried his hair first, then tried to soak some moisture off his clothes so he wasn't a dripping mess.

"First impressions may not mean much to you, but they mean a lot to me."

"Is that a jab at the fact I can't remember the first time we met?"

He didn't look up. He focused all his concentration on the drying.

"Tell me about it then," I said. "Every detail you remember. When did you first see me?"

I expected him to tell me he'd seen me across some vast distance. He likely hadn't even spoken to me.

"We met at a gas station," Jimena said.

"Really? Should we host our wedding at one? Serve hot dogs at the reception?"

"Do you want to hear the story or not?"

I wrapped the towel around my shoulders and nodded politely. "Go ahead."

"I was walking in, and you were walking out. You were with Alex. You had a case of beer in your hands, and you weren't paying attention to where you were walking. You bumped into my shoulder, and I dropped my wallet. I wasn't paying attention, either, and I'd been walking while looking in it for cash. I wasn't sure I had enough to pay for a full tank. When we collided, you stopped to help me collect my fallen cards and cash. In way of an apology, you took out one of the beers and gave it to me."

"You remember all of that?"

"I could tell you what you were wearing that day." He copied me and wrapped the towel around his shoulders. "You don't remember any of it, do you?"

"No." I saw no point in lying. "But that doesn't make it any less meaningful to you." I put a hand on his shoulder. "Let's go to our room, yeah?"

On the walk, I noticed his eyes went to the woman in the pool. It made me wonder if his encounter with her was going to be as memorable as the one he'd just recited about me. Was she his new victim to stalk?

CHAPTER eleven

Kidnapper

"I'm going to need new shoes," I said. I took them off as we entered the room. They had squished the entire walk, and I didn't want to get the floor wet. "I didn't bring a second pair."

"The hotel has dry cleaning," Nic said. "And the gift shop probably has shoes."

"Cheap stuff, like flip flops," I said. "I should have brought a spare set."

I grabbed one of the dry-cleaning bags from the closet and sat my shoes on it. Nic grabbed a second bag and started putting his damp clothes in it as he undressed. He tossed his shoes next to mine.

"You only brought one pair of shoes too," I said.

"It's not a problem. I'll get us new shoes," he said. "It'll be like Christmas morning when you wake up. You'll have a brand-new pair of sneakers."

We were down to just our underwear. I fumbled with the waistband but didn't remove them.

"I'll call downstairs and tell them to pick up the laundry, that way it doesn't sit for too long outside our door," Nic said. With no modesty, he stripped completely naked, shoving his last item of clothing in the bag.

"We should have done this in the bathroom," I said. "My uncle could come up any minute."

"We're all men," Nic said. "I'm sure he's seen naked men before."

He picked up the phone and punched the number for the front desk. While he was distracted, I removed my boxers, placed them in the bag, and scurried off to the bathroom. I shut the door and instinctively locked it. I paused there at the door, my hand still on the lock. Should I lock him out? Like me, his skin reeked with a coating of chlorine and chemicals from the pool. He couldn't get dressed until he rinsed off in the shower, just like me. And he was my boyfriend. I shouldn't lock the door. Or did couples still lock doors when they were using the bathroom?

A gentle rapping of knuckles came on the door.

"Yes?" I asked.

"You gonna let me in?" Nic asked.

I unlocked the door and opened it. "Sorry, instinct."

"You live alone, is it really that instinctive to lock a bathroom every time you enter it?" He slipped inside and shut the door behind him. His fingers flipping the lock.

"I haven't lived alone my entire life," I said. "And maybe I do lock the door when I enter the bathroom, even in my own house. You don't know."

He put a hand on my chest and pushed me backward so he could reach to turn the shower on.

"Locks won't keep me out, Jimena, you should know that by now." He kissed my forehead, lingering despite the chlorine taste my skin had. He moved closer and bumped parts of his body against me. "I really have missed you."

"Nic…" I wanted to say more to deter him from pushing things further, but his lips mashed into mine, silencing any objections. His tongue invaded me, distracting my thoughts until the embrace was broken. My hands were now on the counter, my face close to the mirror as I leaned forward. His fingers prodded inside me, opening me up enough for him to put what he really wanted inside. His fingertips grazed the special nerves inside me that flickered with delight, and I moaned.

"That's better," Nic said. He pushed on that spot again. I cried out, nearly having an orgasm from just being fingered in the ass. He was on top of me now, his chest pressed to my back, his face against my neck, inhaling deeply. "I like knowing I'm the only one who has ever seen you like this, ever made you squirm like this."

It was still just his fingers pushing me higher. I wanted to ask him if he was going to put it in. Didn't he want to fuck? Hadn't that been his goal this entire time?

One of his hands grabbed my cock and squeezed. That pushed me over the edge, and I came, releasing hot spurts of cum onto the cabinets below us. I heard him take in a deep breath, like the smell of my orgasm gave him some sort of pleasure.

He kissed and licked my neck before he detached us. "We probably should have waited and done this in the shower, but I really enjoyed watching your face in the mirror."

I looked at my reflection, realizing how exposed I'd been for all of this. How had he changed me this much in such a short time? I'd gone from only being intimate with people who were unconscious to letting someone finger me while on full display in front of a mirror.

"Don't think about it too much," he said, as if sensing my embarrassment. "I could only see your face."

"I want to shower now," I said, pushing away from the counter and not looking at him.

"If you didn't like it, you can punish me," Nic said. "Cut me, hit me, whatever—"

"It's fine." I stepped into the shower, letting the hot water wash away the stink on me, both from myself and the pool. I closed my eyes and envisioned the woman from downstairs, remembering the girl's keycard was nestled in my wallet.

Sandy.

"I saw you were alone," she'd said. In my mind, she said it as a forward to then sitting down at the table. She gave me a smile. "You don't mind if I—"

"—join you, do you?" Nic asked, her words transforming into his as some of the water spray was blocked from me when he presumptuously entered the shower.

"You aren't the only guy who has touched me," I said dryly, wanting to take that fantasy from him. He stood in front of me, between me and the water from the shower nozzle. I refused to look down, but from my peripheral vision, I could see he had an erection.

I forced myself to glance up at his face, wanting to see the pain in his eyes as I tore that reward from him.

"What do you mean?" was the only prompt he offered as his face gave no hints to his potential pain.

"My second time at this reunion-birthday thing after I'd been adopted into the family, there was an incident." I'd blocked a good portion from my mind, not wanting to think about it, but brief flashes could be recalled. "A male relative, in-law to someone, he took me to the bathroom to clean me up after I'd gotten into something. I don't remember what—food, cake, sand, mud, whatever. He wiped my face clean and said stuff about me being dirty, and how I was probably dirty from the orphanage. He said,

'You probably had to do some dirty shit to survive on the streets, right?' I didn't know what he was talking about." I put my hand on Nic's dick and squeezed hard. "I remember he pulled this out and shoved it in my face, saying something about how I was probably real good at it and knew what to do."

Nic didn't move, his eyes were locked with mine as I unraveled a tale that was from so long ago, I wasn't confident how much had been warped from time. I was cold now since he was hogging the water, but I didn't make an effort for us to swap places in the shower.

"He told me to put it in my mouth, so I did, and I bit it so hard he bled. He shoved me back, and I hit my head on something, the counter or wall. He had a limp the rest of the reunion, but he couldn't tell anyone about it. I mean, how do you explain teeth marks on your dick when you're a married man? Everyone knew he'd started limping after our time in the bathroom, so they all assumed I'd kicked him in the groin or something. That's when everyone started noticing people got hurt around me. All because of that dick's dick."

I lowered myself and licked the tip of his penis, expecting him to flinch or pull away. He had to know my story was a lead up to what I was going to do.

"Now, every time I see one of these, it makes me want to…" I paused, glaring at the one-eyed snake as it hovered a hair's width from my nose. "Rip it off with my teeth, like I should have done to him."

I opened my mouth and put his entire tip inside, closing my teeth around the flesh and applying pressure. I clamped my jaw tighter, knowing I would leave an impression. I waited for him to pull or push me away, to at least squeal in pain. I bit until I tasted the first coppery droplets of blood, then I sat back to admire my work.

His face had turned red, his fists pressed against the glass door and shower wall, every vein in his body bulged. But somehow, he'd resisted the screams his body must have urged him to utter.

The indentations of my teeth went all the way around his cock, the bruising already evident and a few droplets of blood showed in the holes from my incisors. I wiped the drool from my face and grinned up at him.

"Guess I'll need a knife to actually cut the thing off," I said. "I wonder if you can grow it back like how a lizard can grow back a leg?"

He ripped his eyes away from me then and yanked the shower door open, slamming it behind him so roughly I feared the glass might break. I laughed as he went, my mind filled with the images of his lifeless cock flopping around on the shower floor like a dying fish.

Kidnapper

I laid in the bed next to him, both of us facing the ceiling. Uncle Wade was slumbering in his bed, the sound of his breathing assistance device filling the room. I couldn't imagine how he slept so well connected to it. I rolled onto my side so I faced Nic, whose eyes were open, no attempt made to sleep.

"Aren't you going to ask me if I was serious?"

"Regarding what?"

"Cutting off your dick," I said. I swept my hand under the sheet and grazed his groin.

"Would there be a point to my asking? You'll either do it or you won't." He didn't turn to look at me, he stayed focused on the ceiling. It irritated me. I wanted him to look at me. I wanted, no, *needed* to see the fear in his eyes. The trepidation at what might soon come.

"Why aren't you sleeping?"

"Why aren't you?"

"Are you trying to stay awake until I fall asleep? Is it because you're afraid of what I'll do when you're unconscious?"

"It wouldn't be out of character for you."

"My uncle is right there. I can't do anything. You're safe. Go to sleep."

"And why aren't you sleeping?"

"My sleep cycle is messed up from the meds. I slept most of the afternoon and the flight over here. I'll probably be up all night and need to drown in coffee to make it through tomorrow."

"I guess that's true," Nic said. He rolled away from me, facing the closed curtains.

"Are you mad at me?"

Kidnapped

Was he seriously asking me that? Was I mad at him? He'd chewed on my dick. What did he think my response would be?

I closed my eyes, not bothering to give him a response. The best I could hope for was that he didn't spend his sleepless night torturing me. I feared the loopholes he would find between what he'd said about my being safe because his uncle was here.

Either he'd grown tired or was presumably good at laying still and pretending. He didn't speak or move for quite some time. My body relaxed, thinking perhaps I would get to sleep in peace, then I felt the slight roll of the bed as he got up.

Was he going to pace in the room? Get something to stab me with? I remained motionless, not wanting my awareness to trigger a reaction in case he was doing something as innocent as going to the bathroom.

Light from the outside hall flashed in the room briefly, then the click of the door as it shut. I waited only a second before I threw back the covers and looked about the darkened room. He'd left? I stole a quick glance at the uncle to confirm he was slumbering before I dissipated into a black mist, nearly invisible with the low lighting. In my vaporous state, I slipped between the cracks of the door and into the hallway.

The rules of entrance did not apply to public places of rent like this. I could enter wherever I wished. I followed Jimena, staying above him, and dispersed enough to be dismissed as a shadow. I assured myself it was paranoia. Jimena was likely being considerate and taking his restless nature out of the room so his uncle and I could sleep.

I doubted *anyone* would believe such a farce. He hadn't put on his shoes, which made sense considering they were still wet. He wore only his boxers and an undershirt, not the kind of attire he would want to be seen in by others. Was this a run to a vending machine? He went to the stairwell and pushed the door, slipping through and descending. I followed, more confused than before.

We stopped on the second floor, then he strolled down the hall, glancing at the numbers until he found 241. He put his ear to the door and listened.

If I had been in my human form, my blood would have churned with fear, my heart clogged in dread. This was that girl's room. The one he'd kept staring at. There was no doubt in my mind that it was anything else.

She's safe. She won't open the door. He is a stranger to her. And she likely had one of her friends inside with her. I couldn't repeat the mantra any further because he slipped out a keycard and pushed it in the slot. The light turned green.

I nearly shifted human and grabbed him. I stopped only because of the security cameras and the likely scene that would ensue. And his questions. He turned the handle and pushed. The door moved forward but only a bit. The safety chain was in place.

He won't get past that, not quietly, at least. He won't risk it. He is careful to not get caught. He pulled a bent wire from some hidden place on his wardrobe and slipped it through the crack. Like a professional locksmith, he slid the chain off and pushed the door open.

It was then I realized how much I'd underestimated him all this time. How many people had he killed? How honed were his skills?

How lucky was I to still be alive?

I slipped in with him and briefly considered sweeping past the slumbering women. If I could rouse them, it might prevent whatever was transpiring. Or I might worsen it. Jimena could pretend he'd entered the wrong room. Instead, I resolved to wait and see what his ill intentions were. Not yet decided if I would stop him if he... Would I stop him if he...?

He walked silently through the room, doing a quick lap to get his bearings. Then he went slower, taking an inventory of everything laid out and in view. He studied it all without touching, like an investigator at a crime scene. He took nothing. He touched nothing. His fingertips passed over objects, leaving the slightest fraction of space between him and the surface. He went to the slumbering women, ignoring one completely and ghosting his hands across the form of the other.

Then he stopped at one side of the bed, the one which she faced, and he stood. He did nothing but stand there, staring at her while she slept. He stayed motionless. I watched him watch her until it went beyond creepy and into something else entirely.

No one stared at something for this long when the something was doing nothing. Except a person who is crazed and obsessed. A person hungering to memorize every detail of a person's being and relish every moment stolen by their side.

Had Jimena done this with me? I recalled how he'd moved in my apartment as if he'd known where every item had been, regardless of how dimly lit I kept it. I'd assumed he was observant and not clumsy. He'd broken in with the ease of someone who had performed the feat before. Had he ever stood in my room like this and watched me sleep?

And what did this mean for us? Now that he was doing it with someone else, was our relationship effectively over? Buried in one of the many graves he'd prepared for me?

Two hours he stood there staring at her before he retreated to the hall, slipping away as silently as he'd come. I went to our room before him, materialized, and pulled the sheets back up around me, then closed my eyes and pretended to sleep.

I should be grateful he hadn't harmed her.

But I wasn't.

It would have been better if he'd dealt with her swiftly. Prolonging it meant she held meaning to him. And the more important she was, the less value I had. I reflexively recoiled and moved to the edge of the bed when he climbed in.

It hurt.

The thought of him wanting her hurt far more than anything else I'd seen him do.

His hand touched my arm, and he used it as leverage to pull himself to me. He pressed his chest against my back and spooned me, though he was smaller and not able to fully encompass me.

His lips touched my neck in soft kisses as he grinded his groin against me. His stubble of a dick brushed against me. I knew that erection wasn't caused by me. It was from *her*.

I reached a hand up, gripping his skull tightly between my fingers. A surge rushed through me of anger and hate, of pure unbridled jealousy. I hit him hard with a rush of energy to knock him out and sate him into a slumber, because I could not deal with his shit right now.

I wanted to fucking sleep.

Kidnapper

My head hurt. The last time it had hurt to this degree had been when I'd woken in the basement, confused about whether I'd kidnapped Nic or not. Something wet flicked on my face for what I thought might be the second time. I forced my eyes open, knowing it would only embolden the throb behind my eyes. Nic stood there, fully dressed, holding a glass of water, his fingertips dripping with evidence.

"Time to get up," Nic said. "Your family is gathering downstairs for brunch."

"My head hurts," I said. I rubbed my temple and closed my eyes, but it did nothing to negate the pain.

"More side effects from the massive amount of drugs you consumed yesterday? Drink this. Perhaps it will help." He held the glass closer, the same one he'd dipped his fingers in.

"You fixed the side effects," I said. "Why do I suspect you caused this?"

"I give pain, and I take it away, do I? Oh, the powers you imagine me to have." He tapped a finger on my forehead, sending sparks of pain dancing across my scalp. "Stop making excuses to avoid your family. I'll buy you some overpriced pain reliever in the resort lobby, and you'll be fine."

He sat the water down and retrieved something from the floor. He held it up for me to view.

"I did get you some new shoes. Our dry cleaning won't be done before we leave for the amusement parks."

"The least you could do, since you are the one who got my shoes drenched," I replied. I braced myself for the expected pain as I attempted to sit up and was rewarded with a splatter of bright spots in my vision. But I was now successfully sitting upright.

"Someone is grumpy," Nic said. "Did you not sleep well?"

I decided not to respond and instead concentrated on pulling the sheets back and trying to get out of the bed.

"Exaggerating a bit, aren't you?" Nic asked. "Are you seriously going to fake a migraine so you can stay in bed all day?"

I swung my legs over the edge and dug my fingers into the comforter. "I'm not faking it."

He put a hand on the side of my face and pushed my head back, so I was forced to look up at him. There was something in his eyes I couldn't place. He looked… mad. An instinctive rush of fear ran through me before I remembered how good he was at sensing my emotions. I tried to stomp it back down, but the twitch on his lips gave away that he'd noticed it.

"You really think I did this." He pulled his hand away, and I quickly grabbed it with both of mine.

"Of course, not," I said, hoping his ability to sense my emotional state didn't also work as a lie detector. "That wasn't fear directed at you. It was worry that I might be too sick to partake in all the family fun. That would ruin my chance to show you I can be a good boyfriend."

"I suppose it would." He brought his face level to mine, as if daring me to betray my words. "Kiss me."

"What?"

"Does your head hurt too much for you to do such a simple thing?"

My eyes darted to Uncle Wade's empty bed, neatly made with the sleeping device tidied and tucked away on one corner of the side table.

"Never," I said. I reached up and put my hand behind his head, pulling him down so our lips would touch. A test, nothing had ever felt more like a test than this simple gesture. Something in me was still terrified because he truly did seem to be pulsing with anger, but I buried that knowledge deep and pushed my longing for him to the surface. I remembered the first time I'd met him, when our eyes had locked in that kind gesture as he'd handed me the spare beer.

He kissed me harder for a moment, then broke the embrace, and I realized dumbly that my headache was gone. "Hurry up, we're late for the brunch."

Kidnapper

We were back in the same dining hall as before. I wondered if Grandfather had reserved it for our entire stay. I sat down at my parent's table with a buffet plate full of traditional breakfast items.

"That's all your eating?" I asked. Nic had a bowl of cereal; flakes of some kind with milk. He took a spoonful but didn't answer. "They have omelets, pancakes, waffles, fresh fruit." I gestured to each item on my plate or to the plate of a relative as I listed them. "Cinnamon rolls, bagels…"

"I'm sure he isn't blind," my sister said from across the table. She narrowed her eyes. "Or maybe he is. That would explain why he's with you."

"I'm just making sure he knows he can eat anything he wants. Don't feel like you have to limit yourself."

"I'm surprised you didn't just get his plate for him," Piper said under her breath, but the malice was clear.

I clamped my jaw shut, realizing the situation I'd put myself in. They'd heard me slap him, seen me yell at him, knew about the abuse, and now my behavior only made them think I was obsessively trying to control every aspect of his life, including his diet.

A group of women, not family that I knew of, entered the ballroom. My eyes flickered to them, wondering if Sandy was among them. An employee intercepted the group, likely to tell them the hall was reserved for a private party.

"I like cereal," Nic said. "I'm just happy to be eating at the table instead of on the floor like a dog."

Piper laughed, taking his comment as a joke. One of Paul's kids started barking, and another asked if he could eat on the floor. I stared at the blond in the group of women, waiting for them to turn around so I could tell if it was Sandy. A hand blocked my view and fingers snapped in front of my face. I jerked and glared at Nic.

"Looking for someone?" Nic asked.

"I was wondering what those women were doing. They aren't family."

"You weren't hoping Sandy would be among them?"

"Who is Sandy?" Piper asked.

"Ten-minute warning!" Trish announced using a microphone. "Buses are outside to take you to the amusement park you signed up for."

"Better eat that food quick," Piper said. "I'll expect an answer about Sandy later." She winked before she got up and left. Paul's wife ushered the children with her, leaving Nic and me alone since the rest of the family had eaten and left before we'd arrived.

"Why would you bring up Sandy?" I asked. I hadn't touched any of my food, and now I didn't want to. Was Sandy why Nic was in such a foul mood?

He ate two more spoonfuls before he answered. "You were in her room last night."

"What?" I said a bit higher pitched than intended. "Why would you say something like that?"

"I know you were." He dropped the spoon, his bowl empty except for the milk.

"How would I do such a thing?"

"You're pretty good at breaking into my place, why not hers?"

"This is a hotel. I can't believe you are accusing me of—"

"Good morning, guys," Trish said, appearing between us and holding out two neon yellow shirts. "You forgot to pick up your family shirts. Please wear them today. And you haven't signed up for a park. Which one did you want to go to?"

Nic took the shirts. "Which park, Jimena?"

Why did this feel like another test?

"The Fairy World," I said, because I'd seen that it was the park Sandy would be visiting today. She'd had a map of it out on her table in her room. Nic had no way of knowing that was my reason.

"Really?" Trish asked. "That park is mostly kiddy rides and knick-knack stores with little ceramic collectable fairies."

"A grown man can't like fairies?" I asked.

"I've never seen a single fairy in your house," Nic said.

"Maybe I hide them to keep people from mocking me," I said. "We're going to the fairy world thing." I grabbed one of the shirts from him. "Is that okay with you, Nic?"

"I'd enjoy nothing more than to watch you gush over small sprites all day," Nic said, his tone flat.

"Uh, okay, great. That's bus four then. I'm sure Grandma Harris will be happy to have a few more adults along to help watch the kids." Trish spewed the words quickly before darting away, scribbling notes in her book.

"Grandma Harris?" Nic asked.

"They call her that but..." I stood up and flopped my arms in defeat. "She's not married to the grandpa we are here celebrating. I don't know how she's related. Probably married to a sibling of Grandpa, so she's Trish's Grandma. I've spoken to her maybe four times in my life." I turned from the table, my desire to avoid the topic of Sandy and fairies distracting me from the rumbling reminder my stomach gave me that I hadn't eaten anything.

Nic was silent, but I could sense him behind me. I kept focused ahead, intentionally not looking for Sandy in any crowds we passed. I walked through the two sets of automated double doors, and once outside, Nic grabbed my arm.

"Can you wait a sec?" Nic asked.

"Ten-minute warning means we need to get on the bus," Jimena said. "Or do you need a bathroom break? The bus ride is only twenty minutes."

He smiled, the innocent gesture not fitting our situation at all. He held out the neon shirt.

"Can you hold this for a second?"

I grabbed it from him, too irritated to ask why. His arms free, he grabbed the bottom of the shirt he was wearing and pulled it over the top of his head. He took a moment to roll the shirt up, then stuffed the end into his pants pocket, so it hung there like a dirty rag.

He held his hand out. "I'll take it back now."

"Why would you take your shirt off in public?" We were standing in front of the hotel, where people actively entered and exited. And there he stood, mister perfect abs and chiseled body, practically glowing in radiance. He had stopped us right where streaks of sunlight came down from the awning above, illuminating him like a beam from the heavens.

"I'm changing into the shirt your cousin gave us. You should be doing the same."

"You could put it over. That's what a normal person does. You put it over your other shirt. Like this." I hurriedly yanked the shirt on over my other clothes, treating it like a jersey rather than the regular tee it was. My clothes bunched a bit, but I was slender enough to make it work. I looked back at Nic to find that he was still shirtless, he'd paused his endeavors to watch me.

My eyes looked past him to the gawking stares I knew he was collecting. One set of eyes peered back, and for a moment, the world blurred. My breath stopped as my lungs seized and my heartbeat drowned out any words Nic might be saying. Sandy was there. She was watching us, or rather, she was staring openly at Nic along with her friends from the night before.

"P-p-put your sh-shirt on," I stammered, trying to find the air to get the words out and wishing I had the motor capacity to force the shirt on him myself. Nic's brow furrowed, and his eyes followed mine, quickly connecting with Sandy's.

"Sandy," Nic said. He waved at her. "We met last night."

She approached us, entranced by his bare chest, and if my feet had been capable of moving, I would have stood between them to block her view.

"Last night?" she asked his chest, not his eyes.

"By the pool," Nic clarified. He pointed at me. "My boyfriend watched your bag for you."

Her eyes skittered to me for a moment, as if just realizing my existence.

"Oh, that's right," she said, but it was clear on her face that she did not.

"I think we'll be seeing you at the Fairy World today," Nic said. He then reached over and looped his arm around my shoulders, his bare skin seeming to scald my neck.

"Great. Yeah, we'll see you there." A sly grin was on her face now, the kind you got when you were let in on a secret. She was excited to know a gay couple or some weird bullshit like that. Either way, this event would stick in her head. She would not forget Nic and by association me.

I could not kidnap or murder her. I couldn't do a damn thing to her. Because her gaggle of friends would remember us. I would be implicated if she went missing, and that was not a risk I could take.

She gave a parting wave and retreated back to her friends. When her back turned from us, I shrugged Nic's arm off me.

"You did that on purpose."

"What? You want to get to know her, don't you? I'm helping."

"You know exactly what you did." I lowered my voice, spewing the words with more force than needed. "You made us memorable. I can't touch her now."

The twitch on his face confirmed it. The smug flash of a satisfied smile.

My hand moved without thought. I slapped him. Hard. The sound echoed under the awning. My hand stung, and I heard a few gasps. The rage kept me from fully grasping what I was doing as I swung for a second time, intending to strike him until he begged me to stop.

My hand didn't reach his face. Nic's fingers coiled around my wrist as he held me inches from completing my task. He dared to stop me? My other hand twitched, ready to throw a punch this time, either the eye or nose. I hadn't decided which would be more satisfying.

"More than one hit," Nic said, "and someone will call the police. We don't want that, do we?"

The bystanders watching us came into focus. We were in front of the hotel. Not only did the people outside with us have a view, but also those in the lobby. And these days, nearly everyone held a cellphone. In moments, someone would start recording while others called the police. There was probably security inside the hotel already preparing to intervene.

"No, we don't." I wrenched my hand free and took a step back.

"We're fine," Nic said, not to me but to the closest people who looked about to separate us. He pulled his shirt on. "Shall we get on the bus?"

He grabbed my hand like nothing had happened, like his cheek wasn't still red from my abuse. He pulled me with him to the bus filled with a handful of adults and a dozen children wearing the same neon shirts as us.

"We're the last ones, right?" Nic asked.

"Sit by me, Jimena," Grandma Harris said, pushing the kid who had been next to her away.

"I'd rather—" Before I could finish Nic shoved me into the seat and smoothly sat next to one of the children several rows ahead of us.

"I think some time apart to cool your head would be wise," Grandma Harris said. "Plus, you and I haven't spoken since you were, what? Barely out of diapers?"

My jaw dropped slightly in mock disgust. "I was ten when I was adopted into this family."

"Oh, so it's been even longer than I thought."

"Who are you thinking I am?" The bus started moving, and I accepted my fate of speaking to a relative who was likely confusing me with one of the other cousins.

CHAPTER twelve

Kidnapped

For a moment there, I'd worried the police would be called. And with how upset he'd gotten, I'd feared he would storm off. But it had worked. The girl was safe. He wouldn't go near her now. I wondered if I'd have to do this every time someone caught his eye.

"We need to have a talk," the little girl next to me said.

I turned my head to look at her. She was no more than eight, curly brown locks in pigtails with blue ribbons. The pin, adorned to required neon shirt, displayed one of the fairies the amusement park was known for, the blue one with dark skin.

The kids in the row ahead of us both turned in their seats to face us, the freckled boy spoke first. "Did it hurt when he hit you?"

"I hurt when Chase slapped me on the playground, so I bet it did," the redheaded boy next to him said.

"It did hurt," I replied. "You should never tolerate someone striking you."

"Then why did you? I pushed Chase down when he hit me."

"Sit properly in your seats." The girl kicked the seat, and they both turned around, their heads vanishing behind the backs of the headrests. She turned back to me. "You don't belong in this family. It belongs to me."

"I'm a plus one and not here to—" I stopped as her eyes turned golden with a black slit focused on me. She kept the beast like eyes present long enough for me to see, then changed them back to her normal brown eyes. Fuck! "Jimena is adopted. I'm only here with him. I am only interested in him."

"Then why did you make a deal with Vern? You're feeding on my family, and I have a problem with that."

"I didn't know," I said. "I'll stop."

She looked at me, making it quite clear that wasn't enough. "You owe me a soul."

"What does that mean? I already consumed it to grant Vern's wish. I won't feed on him again, but I can't give you what I already took."

She leaned forward and glanced back at Jimena who chattered with the grandma. "You give me some of him."

"No."

"He's flavored like love, isn't he? You can make him taste like that when I feed on him."

"I made a mistake. I'll take your clan's punishment, but you can't have him."

"You either give him to me, or I tell my clan what you did, and they take him."

"Tell your clan then." I didn't know who her clan was, but I could hope, desperately, that mine was of higher rank.

"It'll be a bigger cost if I have to involve them."

"Keep up your threats, and I'll feed on you."

"You don't have it in you." She sneered, and I fought the trickle of fear because I had something to lose. She likely did not.

The bus stopped, and the children cheered, quickly clamoring off despite Grandma Harris shouting at them to remain civil.

"Nic, hey, we're supposed to get off." Jimena tugged on my sleeve until I got up and followed him. I watched the girl skip off to join the other children, blending seamlessly with them.

"Listen, I want to apologize for earlier. You're right, I was obsessing with someone else, and it was wrong. I understand why you lashed out like you did. Nic? Nic?" He snapped his fingers in my face and forced my attention back to him. "What's wrong?"

"The girl I was sitting next to, do you know her?"

He turned to look at the kids as they lined up to go through the ticket line to enter the park.

"Ah, I think so. She's a cousin's step-kid or something like that. I think her name is Stephie."

I moved closer to him, pulling the length of his back against my chest, and lowering my head to sniff his neck where I could smell the hint of his soul, a food only I would feed upon, no matter what.

"She's a demon," I said, "and she rightly has claim on your family. I've violated a demon rule by feeding upon Vern and making a deal with him. Her claim might extend to you. There will be punishments."

"What?" He broke free and looked at me, wide-eyed in what was his first negative reaction to what I was. "That little thing is feeding on my family? Oh, fuck, no." His fists trembled as he squeezed them. "If we kill her, you get claim right? We kill her." He nodded like the decision was simple in his mind.

"We're not murdering your cousin's kid."

"Step-kid, not actual kin." As if forgetting he was adopted and not true kin either. "Does it mean more demons are here? Would her mom be one?"

"No. The mothers rarely are. She was likely…" The words died in my throat as I recalled what my mother had endured, not once but multiple times, until…

"Nic, hey, come back. Just say it." He shook my shoulder.

"Some demons prefer the flavor of a soul that's… raw from rape, and it results in a demon child."

The answer was clear on my face, but he still said it. "That's what you are too, isn't it? A demon child of rape?"

Grandpa Harris whistled and pointed at us. "Come on, boys, let's get these kiddos in the park."

"We're killing her. Her whole damn clan if we have to," Jimena snarled. "Rapists are scum."

"You're a rapist."

"Yeah, but my victims are unconscious. That's different." He turned and walked to rejoin the group, his demeanor flipping back to normal with no indication of his murderous intent.

I followed them through the ticket booth, swiping my room key as a pass and shoving my hands in my pockets, while Jimena snatched a map and looked it over.

"Alright, let's split into groups," Grandma Harris said. "We'll go by age, so the ones who want the bigger rides can—"

"I missed breakfast," Jimena said. "So, whoever wants snacks can come with us. We'll watch whoever wants to hit up the fairly playground park thing since that's near the food trucks."

Five of the kids broke off with us as Jimena charged ahead to the food area. I glanced back and saw Stephie had stayed with the grandma. Jimena bought them all whatever ice cream they wanted, and one requested a pretzel instead. We sat at a bench so he could eat his own assortment of treats—a candy apple and ice cream sandwich. The kids quickly ate theirs and bounded off to the wooden canopies above us, and I hoped we managed not to lose any of them as they merged with other children playing in the area. They did have the neon shirts, so I supposed it wouldn't be that hard.

"So, how is this sort of thing normally handled?"

"A deal is made between the demons to compensate the loss. She's already told me what she wants."

"And you told her to fuck off, right?"

A woman who had parked her stroller nearby glanced sharply at us as she kneeled to check her sleeping baby.

"Yes. Not in those words, but yes."

"Good. We don't make deals with rapists."

"Her father is the rapist, not her."

"And you don't think she'll grow up to be one?"

The woman moved her stroller away from us.

"You need to calm down."

"How can I? That kid has probably been feeding on my brother, sister… She could even have fed on me. I wouldn't have known, would I? You have to broker a deal and get full rights to our family so no one else bothers them."

"You're okay with me feeding on them?"

"Of course, I am. I know you. You aren't going to hurt any of them. You didn't hurt Vern."

"I didn't think you cared about your family. You avoid them."

"They still adopted me when no one else would. Even stuck by me when I know I freak them out. Hell, they're letting us watch five of their offspring even though I... they all know or suspect I've done some shit that shouldn't warrant me being a babysitter. But we're family, so they trust me. If I can't protect them from other soul-sucking monsters, then what's the point? I can at least do this."

"Ah, yes, every family needs a member who is willing to murder to keep everyone safe. How lucky they are."

"It's not funny." He tossed half his sandwich in the trash and slumped. I watched his eyes do a quick count of the five kids and realized he really did care. He might not be capable of feeling the emotions of a healthy socialized person, but he still understood the responsibility of caring for someone, even if he didn't know how to value life properly.

"Do you think we could have a normal life together?" Jimena asked. "Like, do this for real? Come back here to the next reunion with adopted kids of our own? Would you trust me like that?"

"I want to." But I doubted I could. There was far too great a risk I would come home one day to find he'd slaughtered the children, or worse, taught them to kill. "We could start small. Perhaps a pet."

"Yeah, maybe. Not a dog, I don't want it digging up anyone in the yard."

A dog? I'd start him with a houseplant, and in a year, maybe a goldfish.

"I think I know how to deal with Stephie." He leaned back on the bench, resting his elbows on the table. "This park is dangerous. You use some of your magic to create a little accident, and bam! All better."

"I need you to promise me you won't hurt Stephie. Let me find out who her clan is first."

"Augh, fine."

I wished I could trust his words.

Kidnapped

We'd somehow survived the park outing with all the children intact and no further violence. I was even more relieved to see Stephie skipping across the sidewalk to rejoin her mother in the lobby of the hotel.

"We had so many opportunities," Jimena said, giving a little sigh.

"I told you, leave the kid alone." We approached the lobby entrance, and standing near the glass doors, casually smoking a stick that resembled a cigarette but smelled of products otherworldly, stood the last person I wanted to see.

His skin was aged but only to the point of handsome maturity, with little flecks of white in his hair. He'd found women were attracted to the so-called silver fox look, far more than an amateurish youth. The suit and tie ensemble looked out of place at the resort, and if he'd worn something more casual, I might not have noticed him.

He locked eyes with mine, and his lip twitched. I grabbed Jimena's arm to stop him. "You go inside without me. I need to speak to someone."

"Who? About what?" He saw the person staring at me and immediately straightened. I could practically see the defensive thorns sprouting from him. "I'm staying with you."

"No, you're not. Go inside. I'll be in after I get rid of him."

"Tell me who he is first."

"No." I pushed him toward the doors.

"Then I'm not leaving. For all I know he's an ex-boyfriend here to take you away."

"Nicodemus," he said, approaching as Jimena positioned himself between us. "You and I need to talk." He flickered a quick look at Jimena. "Alone."

"I'm trying," I said. I whirled Jimena around and pushed him toward the automated lobby doors. "Please. I'll get you in a moment."

"Who are you?" Jimena demanded, no longer asking me.

"I'm his sire. Who are you?" He didn't give Jimena a chance to respond. He put a hand on Jimena's chest and pushed, putting him on the other side of the automated doors that quickly shut and refused to work properly, trapping Jimena inside and us out.

"Getting quite friendly with the food, aren't you? You always were a charmer." He looped his arm with mine and guided me around the building, out of Jimena's view.

"The food tastes better when they like us," I said, yanking my arm free.

"Platonic desires barely flavor a soul. I taught you better than that." He flicked his hand dismissively. "I'm not here to discuss that. The Domenichini Clan contacted me. You made a deal with a human in their territory without permission. You know better than to feed on someone outside the territories I control."

"I'm here with a family. None of them are from here. It's a vacation."

"This resort and those in it are Domenichini property. He even marked this family by embedding one of his offspring in it."

"I was approached by that child today. She warned me about what I'd done. I was going to contact you."

"I brokered a deal to peacefully resolve things. You can't come here again, to this resort."

"Fine."

"And you leave that family alone. All of them, even after this vacation is done."

"I'll repay what I took, but they can't have Jimena."

"That kid you were with?"

"They can't have him."

My father's eyes turned demonic, and I could see his agitation even though his body didn't show it. "You aren't worth a fight with the Domenichini clan. You don't agree to this, I won't stop them if they want to kill you."

"Then don't get involved. I'll fix it myself." I turned to go back, and he grabbed my shoulder. The world dissolved around us, and when it came back into view, I was standing in a rock cavern with no visible entrances. A completely sealed-off, underground cavern. The home of demons.

"I promised them that if you didn't agree, I'd bring you here."

"You won't let me arrange my own agreement? Let me talk to the Domenichini leader."

"They already made an alternate proposal if you didn't agree."

"What?"

"That little pet of yours? They're going to kill it. Once he's good and dead, you're free to leave."

"Kill him." My reaction wasn't what it should be. I laughed. My father stared as I erupted with sound. When I'd regained the ability to speak, I wiped the tears from my face and looked at my bewildered father. "I'm sure you think that's a valid threat, one that will convince me to do what you want, but... I'm more afraid for the Domenichini's kin. Ask Domenichini if he's willing to place a bet. I'll obey his demand. If he kills Jimena, I will give up my claim to his family, and I'll avoid the resort, but *only* if he agrees to revoke his claim on the family if Jimena kills the assassin instead."

My father vanished in a mist of vapor. He was only gone for a few minutes before he returned.

"He laughed. A lot." My father was not laughing, though. "But your proposal amused him. He said if your human is still alive at sunset, you can have him and his family."

I sank to the floor, nearly laughing again. "Oh, if he's alive by morning, Domenichini will be begging me to take him back."

"Why's he so important to you? You're a charmer. You can easily get another human."

"Yes, but not one that loves me as much as he does."

"You understand you're to stay here until dawn? You can't help him."

"I wouldn't want to be anywhere near him. Not when he realizes you've taken me."

Kidnapper

They had to call someone to open the doors. A janitor had to override the system. By the time I was freed from the cage, stuck between the two sets of automated doors in the entry way, Nic was unsurprisingly gone. I still roved the parking lot just in case before I sent him a barrage of texts, asking where he'd gone and when he'd return.

I sat through the required, customary dinner gathering with my family, no food on the plate in front of me because I'd been too distracted to bother with the buffet. I checked my phone for the fourth time since I'd sat, and still no response.

So, I tried something different. I texted his brother. Keeping my phone on my lap, out of view from my family members who bickered about whatever had happened today that either increased or decreased their favor in grandfather's eyes, I typed a simple message.

Where is Nic?

Who is this? was the quick reply.

It's Jimena. Your dad showed up and took Nic. Where?

A bunch of laughing emojis came through followed by, *Dang, you are persistent. How did you even get my number?*

Nic isn't answering. Your dad took him. Where?

Probably to hell. Fuck off. I'm blocking you.

Tell me where they went.

I waited, wondering if he'd truly blocked me and ruined my easiest lead to getting an answer. It wasn't like I could go pound on his door since I was currently at a resort in a different state.

One sec. Don't spam the fuck out of my phone. I stared at that single message, my strand of hope. Would his brother truly get me an answer?

A hand gently squeezed my shoulder. "Honey, are you alright?"

I looked at my adopted mother and still marveled at the sincerity in her eyes. After all these years, I still didn't understand how she could love something like me. Maybe love was the wrong word, but she still cared and nurtured me.

"That had to be terrifying to be locked between those glass doors," she added.

"It was twenty minutes. I'm fine."

"He's freaking out because Nic left," Paul said, tapping his fork against his jaw. Everyone at the table fell silent and stared at him. "I didn't mean it like that. Nic just left, as in he's currently not here. I didn't mean to imply anything else." The flinch on his face indicated someone, perhaps multiple someone's had kicked him under the table.

"You should eat," my mother said, putting a plate of food in front of me.

My phone chimed, and I quickly unlocked it.

Family emergency. If all goes well, Nic will be back in the morning. Don't message me again.

My fingers itched to type something back, to beg him to tell me more. Did it have to do with Stephie? Should I interrogate her for answers? But I'd never spoken to her before, it would seem odd if I did now. It would... I'd never spoken to her before. Which meant if something were to happen to her, I wouldn't be suspected, not in the least.

Thank you, Marc. I typed the message and locked my phone.

"I heard back from Nic's brother. There was a family emergency. Nic will be back in the morning. I don't know any more than that, so don't ask." I jabbed my fork into the chicken breast. I needed to eat a good meal for whatever tonight might bring.

CHAPTER thirteen

Kidnapper

I went to the front desk when dinner was over. I'd promised Nic I wouldn't bring any lead to torture him with. Besides, a lead knife brought on a plane, even in checked luggage, was suspicious. I wasn't an amateur. I knew they x-rayed those things, and I wanted no trails.

"I should have a package." I recited my name and waited for the employee to find it. If I hadn't needed these items, I would have simply shipped them back to me. Nic would never have known.

The woman placed a twelve-by-twelve-inch box on the counter, and I signed for it. I stopped at the gift shop located in the hotel and bought a bottle of whiskey and two souvenir shot glasses. On my way back to the room, I glanced at the pool area where some of our relatives were, again, enjoying the resort's perks. Little Stephie was among them.

I went to our room and found Uncle Wade rubbing his feet on the bed. "Too much standing in lines for me. How was your day?"

"Uh, too much watching other people's kids have fun," I remarked. I went in the bathroom and opened the box. I opened the bottle of pills and dropped one in a shot glass. Then filled both with whiskey. I put the box on the floor and piled two used towels on top to keep curious Uncle Wade from it. Then went back into the room and offered him one of the glasses. "To ease our woes."

"Oh, no thanks. If I drink this late in the evening, I'll have horrible heartburn all night."

"You're on vacation. Live a little." I shrugged. "I also have antacids."

"Your day was that bad? You're up here drinking alone instead of down there at the pool bar? Where's the boyfriend?"

"Called away for a family emergency." I still held the glasses, refusing to put his down because I knew it would encourage him to take it if I kept holding it. "And I am apparently not close enough to his family to be worthy of knowing what the emergency is."

He shook his head slowly. "That is a tune I know all too well." He took the glass. "My ex would never tell me what was going on with her family. Deaths, births, not a peep." He swirled the drink. "She has full custody of our kids now. I see them twice a year if I'm lucky. The rest of the time, I have no idea what's going on. Hence, I am here with my sister's in-laws because I have no real family beyond her."

"To being the black sheep of the family," I said, holding my glass out to him so he could tap his against it. We both drank the contents in two gulps. "I'm sorry about your kids."

"Eh, it barely matters anymore." He handed the glass back to me. I put the whiskey bottle and glasses on top of the dresser. "She's turned them against me. I'm just the guy who gives them a Christmas present, forgets their birthday, and will fund their college."

He rubbed his forehead. "You know, today, I was with the group that went to Thunder Fun Mountain, and even though I was with people all day, this conversation is the most personal one I've had."

"I could say the same."

"Fuck these fuckers, right?"

"How about tomorrow we go to the same park?"

"Yeah, we black sheep should stick together." He rubbed his forehead again. "I must be more tired than I thought. I'm going to turn in early."

He barely got the sleep apnea machine on his face before he passed out. I finished tucking him into the bed and ensured he was comfortable. I needed to make sure he didn't wake up tonight in case anything happened that might be difficult for me to explain.

I'd considered going after Stephie, but if Nic was coming back, he would be unhappy if I had disobeyed him. I would wait for him to return before taking any action. But all the same, I didn't feel safe with him gone, and I'd gotten a feeling Stephie was avoiding me for the same reasons I had for avoiding her. Why would she not threaten me like she had Nic? Unless she was also wanting to ensure no one would connect her to me if I were to disappear.

I kept repeating to myself that I was being paranoid, but it wouldn't hurt to be a little cautious. I went to the bathroom and opened my box. A hotel wasn't a home, and I didn't know if the same rules applied about not being able to enter without permission.

Nic could enter rooms via the air and likely vents. I looked at the ones in the room and considered blocking them. I just needed to keep demons out of the room until morning. I moved a chair over to do so, then stopped. Did I *want* to keep Stephie out?

I was willing to accept a truce. I wouldn't pursue Stephie in honor of Nic's request. But if Stephie came for me? I wasn't going to stop her. I went back to my box and pulled out the supplies. I looked over the .22 pellet pistol for any damage it may have incurred during shipping, then loaded the CO2 canister in it along with one lead pellet. I tucked spare pellets in my pocket, then placed the weapon to the side. I checked my lead coated knife, the same I'd used on Nic, and put it on a holster around my ankle. I took out the wool lead blanket last, the kind made for protection against radiation.

I carried the blanket and pistol to the bed. I covered my entire body, including my head, with the blanket, so anyone who came would have to pull it off and hopefully endure some pain from the action. I put the pistol under my pillow with one hand wrapped around it.

In theory, if someone came, they would wake me when they tried to remove the blanket, and I'd be able to pull the gun on them. If I was able to put one lead pellet in them, they wouldn't be able to shift into air and retreat. I would, then, be able to finish them off however I saw fit. If things needed to go that far.

There were flaws in the plan. If the demon opted to kill me without removing the blanket, I would never have a chance to defend myself. But something told me demons were too greedy for that. They'd want to feed on me first. They wouldn't kill me outright. They would torture me to flavor my soul, then feed, and kill me last. Giving me plenty of chances to murder them.

And the lead blanket was useful in two aspects: after I used it for protection, I could also throw it over the demon. I wasn't sure what that would do, but I doubted they'd like it.

My only regret was that I'd bought a stupid bolt action pellet gun instead of one that could handle a rotary magazine. I would only get one shot before I'd need to reload, and maybe thirty before the CO_2 would run out. But the weapon was otherwise perfect. The lead wouldn't go through them, it would lodge in them and be quiet enough that no one would call police. Plus, acquiring pellet guns didn't have the red tape involved that regular guns did. The purchase was paid for in cash and untraceable to me.

I closed my eyes and waited, hoping nothing would happen but prepared for the worst.

Kidnapper

I wasn't aware I'd fallen asleep, but I must have. The muffled curse from someone near me woke me. I oriented myself and gauged which direction the person was. I didn't hear a second person, just one. I threw the blanket back and raised my gun, aiming it at the person's outline in the dark room.

"What is that blanket made of?" Stephie asked. I hesitated. Was I really about to kill a child? "Is that a gun? Really? Everyone in this hotel will hear you shoot it. Dumbass. Just listen to what I have to say."

I could shoot her in the foot. All I needed was to get some lead in her in order to equalize the situation. But if I shot to wound, she would scream, a sound worse than a bullet.

"Make a deal with me," she continued. "You made one with Nic, right? I'll make you a better one. Whatever you want. I have—"

Fuck this. I sat up, put the barrel of the gun to her forehead, and pulled the trigger. She didn't even try to move away, like she truly thought I wouldn't shoot her. Which was likely since she had never spoken to me.

The sound made a loud snap, but no more than if I'd hit her with a large rubber band. The pellet was projected by nothing more than air, and the impact was muffled since I'd had the muzzle against her skin. It wasn't enough to crack her skull or reach her brain, or so I thought. But maybe demons were different because her ass crumpled to the ground like I'd shot her with one of those stunbolt guns used on cattle before slaughter.

Blood trickled from the single wound, and I quickly reloaded in case there were other demons. I didn't move as I waited, expecting something more to happen. When nothing did, I realized I had a new situation on my hands. What did I do with Stephie?

I used one hand to check for a pulse and felt none, not that it told me whether she was truly dead. Nic had survived quite a few things. Granted, I'd never done anything this extreme. The longer I hovered here with the evidence, the more likely it was that Stephie's clan would send reinforcements. If that was a thing, I had no idea. Maybe she had gone rogue?

I grabbed a bandage from my toiletry kit and affixed it to her forehead, but the moment I touched her, the wound seemed to come alive and gushed with blood. I fastened the bandage on better, but it didn't stop the blood from getting on the carpet. She was a child, small compared to my other victims, so it was rather easy to pick her up and move her to a much more cleanup-friendly location, like the bathtub.

I decided my first priority was to get rid of the body so I wouldn't get arrested when Uncle Wade woke up. If other demons got pissed about this, I'd have to hope Nic could sort that out. I *had* killed her in self-defense if one understood what demons were. No human would believe me, though, so I needed to take actions to prevent them from accusing me of anything.

I grabbed my suitcase and shoved the contents into drawers. Then, I lined it with a plastic bag because, yes, I had packed some mostly to put my dirty clothes in. I put the bag over Stephie's head and taped it securely, adding suffocation to the list of problems she would encounter if she wasn't dead.

Her body hadn't stiffened yet, so I was able to tuck and fold her into the bag. I washed myself and the area of all blood. But that still left the blood on the carpet and my clothes, and I needed a reason to leave the room to get rid of the body. No body, no crime. It was ninety percent of the reason I'd never been discovered. Of course, I couldn't bury Stephie on my property that was several states away, and I didn't have the kind of time to rent a car, hope no one stopped me, get there, and drive back. So, I would need to improvise.

I would solve where to put her later. First, I needed a valid reason to leave the hotel, one that would not make people suspect or question why I had left on the same night a little girl had gone missing.

I went to the bedroom and looked at the blood. I wouldn't be able to get that clean enough to not be noticed. And if anyone tested the blood and connected it to Stephie, I was fucked.

I looked at my arm and realized what I needed to do. My boyfriend had left me. No one would question it. I was known for being mentally unstable.

I scribbled the note first, in case I fucked up and damaged some nerves, and writing was difficult afterward.

Went to ER, cut myself, but then regretted it.

Sorry, Uncle Wade. I'll be back after I get stitches.

Tell my mom not to worry.

I folded the paper neatly and put it on my bed. I pulled the knife out of the holster and paused. Maybe I would wait until I was at the ER before I cut myself. I still needed to deal with the fucking body.

I grabbed a towel, put some of Stephie's blood on it from the floor, and wrapped it around my arm. I tucked the pistol in my pants just in case and also put the knife back in its holster. I took a deep breath and opened the door, half expecting someone to be there, poised to kill me.

The hall was empty.

"Thank fuck." I closed the door behind me and moved to the elevator, being sure to favor one arm so my injury was believable on any security cameras. I reached the lobby and went to the front desk. Here, I put on my first big performance because I knew more cameras were watching.

I was in an Uber moments later, my bag next to me as we drove to the nearest hospital. I pulled out my phone and looked at the route we would take. I needed a secluded area to ditch this fucking bag and claim I'd been mugged.

"Hey, can you stop at this gas station?"

"Why? I thought you were hurt. Aren't I taking you to the ER?"

"I have to piss, which is taking priority over my arm. Just pull over. I'll tip you well or whatever. Just stop here." I'd selected one of those gas stations that had the bathrooms outside.

"Wait for me," I said. "Don't leave." It would look suspect if I had to call a second Uber. He pulled into a parking spot, and I dragged my bag with me toward the bathrooms. I didn't go in, and thankfully, the driver wasn't paying attention to me. I went around the building to the rear. According to the map, there was a river down here. It wasn't ideal, but it was the best I could hope for. Shove her into the river, and hope I never saw it again. Was the river deep enough to carry her somewhere? Or was a better option to try burying her in some damp soil?

"Whatcha got in the bag?"

I dropped the bag, and my hand went behind my back to clutch the pistol. The man standing there looked at me, and I tried to decide if this was idle curiosity or another demon.

"Depends who is asking," I replied.

"I was watching you, wondering if I'd get a moment alone, and I couldn't believe when you went back here. It's almost too perfect." He looked at my bag again. "Show me what's in the bag."

It seemed unlikely, but I had to ask because it would also make sense. "Are you… do you know Stephie?"

His eyes turned cat-like, and I pulled the pistol. He, like Stephie, was overconfident. I shot the gun aiming at his forehead, but since he was an adult and had been a few feet farther from me, he didn't go directly down. He cursed, grabbed for his head, and I dodged out of his path. While he flailed, I reloaded, put the gun closer to his head, and fired again. He swung for me, his screams a mix of anger and pain.

"Fuck, die already," I said. I reloaded and fired into his eye this time, and that did the trick. I dropped to the ground and looked at his body. Now, I had two of them to deal with. I didn't have time to handle this as well as I wanted. "I hope the police here really suck." I grabbed his ankles and dragged him down to the river. I pushed him in, getting my feet a bit wet, until the current caught him and swept him away to who knew where, but hopefully far enough away that my having been at this location wouldn't connect us.

I dumped the girl next, lifting her from the suitcase and removing the plastic bag from her head. I took those items to the dumpster behind the rest area and tossed them in. Was I leaving behind an annoying amount of clues? Yes. But how likely was it that someone would find that bag and get the great idea to test it for DNA? It was a common suitcase dumped in a roadside dumpster. The bloody bag? Better here, mixed with rotting trash, than with the body. Too high of a risk that my fingerprints would be on it somewhere. Again, unlikely anyone would pay attention to this dumpster.

I started toward the car and realized I still needed to cut my arm. I went to the bathroom only to find the door locked. I couldn't very well go inside and ask for the key since I was attempting to avoid leaving a trace of my having been here.

"This won't get infected," I muttered sarcastically to myself. I'd at some point lost my towel so I pulled my shirt off. I gritted my teeth and cut my arm, doing the swipe quickly before the pain could stop me. I did a good gash going from wrist to elbow. It was actually larger than I intended. I wrapped my shirt around it and put the knife away, wondering if they'd search me and take it away at the hospital. I clutched my arm to my bare chest and went back to the car. I slumped in the seat, and the driver glanced at me in the rear mirror.

"What happened to you? Your shirt? Luggage?" He turned in his seat and his eyes widened at the sight of me.

"I was mugged. Some asshole took my bag. My arm hurts like hell. Can you hurry up and get me to the ER?"

It wasn't until the car began moving that I considered the possibility that the person driving the Uber could have been a demon. It was probably bad for business to kill your passengers, though. These creatures seemed to have a main goal of not being discovered, which meant murdering people outright was frowned upon, or so I hoped.

My paranoia got the better of me, and for a short while, I feared he was taking the wrong route and not taking me where I'd requested. Then the lights of the hospital came into view, and he pulled the car into the loading and receiving area.

I quickly paid, leaving a nice digital trail by using a credit card, and gave him an abundant tip as promised.

"If anyone asks, we came directly here. The mugging is embarrassing. You understand, right?" I handed him an additional cash tip, and he nodded. I staggered out of the car and into the busy waiting room of the ER, where I was surrounded by witnesses and video cameras.

I'd never been so happy to be in a hospital. The dull orderly business of waiting, checking in, being examined, and finally treated took the entire early morning hours of the day. The nurse was taking out my IV as I signed the check out papers when my mother yanked the curtain back and gave an exaggerated gasp.

I hadn't been given a room, and my entire treatment had been in the ER bay, where the room beds were separated by curtains.

"Jimena, oh, my." She nearly pushed the nurse out of the way in her approach, grabbing my arm and looking at the fresh bandage. I could tell she wanted to inspect their work but didn't want to rip the bandage off.

"Twenty-seven stitches," I told her, knowing that's what she wanted to ask. "I took a photo after they finished if you want to see."

"I'll see it later when I help you change the bandage." She patted my arm gently. "They're discharging you into my care."

"Yeah, well, I almost got put on suicide watch," I said. The nurse left the area. "But I knew all the right things to say to avoid it, thanks to the years of therapy you've put me through."

"You never resorted to self-harm before. I can't believe you did this. No man is worth this." She ran her fingers down my arm, tracing where the wound was. "There's more to this than you're telling, isn't there?"

"Of course, there isn't." I got up from the bed. "Nic left, and I thought a stunt like this would catch his attention and bring him back."

She closed her eyes, her eyelids fluttering as she rolled her eyes under them. "You did this for attention. You weren't actually trying to kill yourself."

"So smart, Mom." I tapped her forehead as I passed her. "And suicide victims who are in it for attention are rarely put on suicide watch. Can we get back to the hotel?"

"I read your note. I can't believe you left that for Uncle Wade." She followed me out of the ER and into the waiting room, where I signed a few more discharge papers at the desk.

"There was blood all over. I had to leave him some sort of explanation." I rolled my sleeves down. "I should probably change shirts so I don't attract a lot of attention when we get back." I went into the hospital gift shop to buy whatever random shirt they might have. "Does everyone know what happened?"

"I left when it was still dark. Most of the family hadn't gotten up. Uncle Wade called and told me. I had to get a ride from Trixie. She's probably started a text chain to tell everyone."

I bought a long-sleeved button shirt and put it on while my mother paid for it. My mom neatly cut the tag off with nail clippers that emerged from her purse.

"I suppose it doesn't matter," I said. "Vern has already won the show for this year, right?"

She scowled and turned me around so she could do the buttons for me. "It isn't about that, and you know it. I worry about you—we all do—and this isn't helping."

"I'm fine." Although I was annoyed Nic hadn't shown up to get me. Not that I'd texted him where I was, but I had a feeling he would know.

Kidnapper

The ride back to the resort hotel was mostly uneventful until we pulled up, and I saw the police cars parked in front.

"What's that about?" I asked. "Were they here when you left?"

"No, but almost no one was up when I left."

Trixie parked the van and checked her phone for the first time since we'd left the hospital. She was one of those rare types who didn't use her phone while driving.

"Oh, no."

"What's wrong?" My mom moved to peer over her shoulder, but Trixie quickly summarized.

"When Marsh and Bill got up this morning, Stephie wasn't in their room. They haven't been able to find her, so they called the police. All the rooms are being checked."

That had unraveled fast. I wasn't sure how concerned I should act since, in truth, I did not know Stephie. My mother quickly set the tone. "They announced this after word of Jimena going to the hospital, didn't they?"

"Well, yeah."

"She probably isn't even missing. I bet they staged it to steal your spotlight. Her father probably came to get her."

"Steal my spotlight? You mean the attention my suicide attempt would have received? Mom, I did that to get Nic's attention, not the entire family. And they even called the police. Why would they do that if they are faking?"

"You got twenty-seven stitches, is that going too far?" She huffed and pointed at Trixie's phone. "Tell them we are back, and Jimena had to get stitches. Be sure to mention how many."

"Don't do that," I countered. "This isn't the kind of thing to compete about, Mom."

"You nearly died."

"And their kid did— I mean, could be... we don't know. You don't want to say something you'll regret, so just let them have this."

The two women were silent for a moment, and I wanted to kick myself for the misspeak.

"He is right. If it turns out to be something horrible like that..." Trixie looked at my mom. "It would be terrible if you came across as someone trying to one-up them."

"Augh, fine. We'll downplay the importance of your life since you insist." Her tone was drizzled with sarcasm, and she started off across the parking lot.

"We are worried about you," Trixie offered. "Everyone's been expressing their concern in the group chat. Do you want me to add you? I just need your cell number."

And give me a front row seat to the situation of the missing Stephie I'd murdered? *Yes, please.* I rattled my number off to her, and she promptly sent me an invite. I shoved my phone in my pocket. I'd review the chat room later. For now, I needed to plot how I would get past the police and distressed family members in the lobby. I'd managed to snooze a little at the hospital, but I planned to excuse myself from the day's events by claiming exhaustion and staying in the room.

I realized Trixie was still standing next to me. "I'm really not a suicide risk. You don't have to stay with me."

"Oh, yeah, sure. I just didn't figure you'd want to walk through all that by yourself. It's going to be a frenzy."

"Yeah, probably. Thanks." I stepped forward, short little Trixie at my side, and approached the hotel. Three police cars were out front, which seemed a bit excessive. It wasn't like Stephie was famous. She'd only been missing for six hours at most, and her parents probably hadn't noticed it that early. We got through the doors, and I scanned the crowds for signs of Nic. It was morning, after all, and his brother had said he would be here.

A pair of officers were seated at a table near the lobby, where people lined up to give statements, probably offering up the last time they'd seen Stephie. I saw another officer walking with a hotel employee, probably one of the many asking to check people's rooms. Our family and other random guests stood scattered throughout the lobby. No Nic in sight.

I was so busy scanning for Nic and ensuring I avoided the police—there was no reason to attract their attention—that I almost collided with someone. He loomed over me, the heavy-built type, not only tall but wide. His hand came down on my shoulder and locked me in place. Trixie gave a gasp of surprise, and I heard my mother's shoes as she rushed to my side.

Fuck.

I forced my eyes to look up at the damned asshole who forced us all to come to this resort every year for his birthday. I was pretty sure he'd only spoken to me a handful of times in my life, and now those brazen blue eyes that looked snagged right from a Nazi white power propaganda poster were aimed at me.

"Jimena," he said my name for what felt like the first time ever. "I'm glad you're alright. No pain in this world is worth taking your life for. I'm sorry if I've ever made you feel like you aren't part of this family. No one here wants to lose you." He tightened his grip. "Suicide is the coward's way out. It only hurts the people you leave behind."

"Fuck. Shit, I get it." My knees barely kept me upright under his gorilla grip.

"I don't think you do." He let go but ended his touch with several heavy slaps. "You're sticking with me today. I'm going on the river cruise. Tell Trish you are too." He gave me one last back slap before walking off as though he was the damn dictator of my life.

"I guess we're going on the boat tour," Uncle Wade said. I'd no idea how long he'd been standing there.

"We?"

"You agreed we'd spend today together. I already told your mom I'd stick close to you and make sure you are okay. I felt so horrible when I saw your note. I should have seen the signs."

"Wade, no, what I did wasn't your fault, and I'm not going on the boat tour. I'm exhausted. I'm resting."

"Not in our room, you aren't. They're cleaning our floor. They promised to have all the blood cleaned up before we get back tonight."

"Jimena." My mother turned me to look at her. "If my father wants you to go on the boat tour, then you are going on the boat tour."

Wait. Boat. River. Fuck-fuck-fuck, did the resort do boat tours on the same damn river I had dumped two bodies in? Please, oh, please tell me I dumped them downstream from where the tours are. As I tried to recall the geography of the area, my brain insisted I had not. Fuck!

CHAPTER fourteen

Kidnapped

My cellphone didn't work in the depths of the caverns. So, I had to rely on my father's reappearance to be the indicator that dawn had come. I stood and looked at his hardened face, unable to tell how the night had gone.

"Is he alive?"

"Domenichini wants to see you."

I couldn't help the grin that spread across my face. "He is alive, isn't he?"

"Don't be so cocky." He turned to mist, and I followed. We solidified in a larger room where a short, under four-foot man, round enough to probably still weigh the same as me, sat in a chair. A man of normal stature on either side of him.

"This is my son, Nicodemus."

"Nicodemus." The man wiggled out of his chair, his demeanor spreading the confidence of a man double his height. "I think you tricked me."

"I tried to warn you."

He raised a finger as if to contradict my point, then nodded instead. "Indeed, one could argue that."

"Are you going to honor our deal?"

"Two demons are missing."

"You mean dead."

"Unconfirmed."

"You made a deal. Whether he hurt or killed them, your people won't seek vengeance. Jimena and his family are mine now. No other demon can touch them."

"We'd like you to extend the window of our deal. We'd like more time to hunt him. We will offer you a greater reward in exchange, should he survive."

"No."

He looked back at the other two men. They nodded. "Very well. We demons are nothing if we do not honor our deals. No demon will touch your pet or his family. I suggest you mark them so others know. We want to know only one thing. How did you know he would survive?"

"He's a serial killer who's been trying to murder me for weeks." I shrugged. "Sounds like your goons gave him a chance to get it right. Thanks for that."

I turned, not wanting to answer more of their questions. I walked from the room into an adjoining cavern and sagged against the wall.

"Why are you with someone like that?" My father glared at me, and I could almost mistake the look for concern.

"You're going to pretend to care?"

"You've trained him to kill demons."

"He was already a killer before I met him."

"That's how you justify it? Does he hurt you?"

"Who doesn't?" I saw his lip twitch, the remark perhaps upsetting him at how accurate it was.

"Jimena is a serial killer?" Her voice was not one I'd wanted to hear. I turned and faced Arimathea. "He killed the girl I'm looking for, didn't he? And you knew."

"You're assuming that based on what? The fact they are from the same town? He murders a lot of people. I don't have a list."

"Don't dance around it. Did he kill her?"

"I don't know."

She stared for a moment, as if hoping I would utter a confession.

"He has killed people, though. You said that."

"Sure."

"So, he's likely killed people I'm looking for."

"What are you getting at Arimathea?"

"I'm a vengeance demon. If I've been contracted to avenge someone he killed, he won't be immune from my wrath. No matter his deal with you."

"Is that supposed to inspire me to give you a list of his victims?"

"It won't be that hard to find out on my own." She faded away before I could try to argue. I stood there in disbelief at how quickly things had reversed.

"What do I do?"

My father was behind me, but he knew the question was directed at him.

"You let her fulfill her contract. If a human traded their soul to her in exchange for her to seek and kill someone Jimena harmed, you can't stop her from doing that."

"Is that a rule or a suggestion?" I looked back at him.

"It's an impossibility. Vengeance demons are trained assassins. You can't beat her."

Kidnapped

I considered going directly to Jimena. I worried what state he would be in since I hadn't returned, but I needed to control the situation with Arimathea. I left the demon underworld and went to Jimena's house. I appeared in his backyard, my arrival concealed by his wooden privacy fence. Arimathea couldn't go in his house, but she could search everything else. Her black mist swirled in the yard, passing through objects and searching for any breadcrumb that could convict Jimena.

"Will you stop and talk to me? I'm sure we can reach an agreement."

Her mist went underground, and I wondered if the crawlspace under Jimena's house was off limits to her or if she'd be able to enter it. It was technically part of the basement and house, so… no? But if she tried to go under the house, shit, I didn't know exactly where he'd buried his victims.

She surfaced from the new flowerbed, the one he'd buried me under, and held out a necklace.

"Terri Jones was wearing this when she went missing. I was told to use it as a means to identify her." She pointed at the flowerbed that was on an elevated cement platform, not weird at all. "And the flowers planted here are her favorite. She posted about it publicly on her social media."

"That could be coincidence. It's not enough to convict and kill someone."

"I've seen enough bodies to know the rate of decay matches with how long she's been missing. Want me to pull her teeth out and compare dental records?" She tucked the necklace in her pocket. "Her best friend sold her soul to me in exchange for finding out what happened and avenging her."

"And you can't collect until you fulfill your end, which means if Jimena has more bodies in his basement that you've also been contracted to avenge, you won't get to collect those souls because he'll be dead, and I'll never let you in this house."

"You expect me to believe he put you in his will? The house will go to his next of kin, and when they sell it or it needs repairs, one way or another I will get in there."

"I moved in. We're roommates. The house is as much mine as it is his, and you will never enter it." I could tell she was considering but not completely sold on the story. "I'm on a vacation with him, meeting his family. I'm his boyfriend. Trust me, you won't get in if I don't consent. You already know I can grant you access right now if I wanted. I wouldn't be able to do that if I didn't reside here."

"How many bodies are buried in his basement?"

"I'm not confident on the number, but at least eight."

She set her jaw. "What are you proposing?"

"Revenge doesn't have to be death. I let you in. Let you identify all the bodies. I could even get Jimena to give you a list, like you wanted, and you can give all those families closure. You can have all their souls from any family member who wants to know what happened to their missing loved one, but instead of offering to murder the person who took their loved one, you offer them something better. A chance to forgive, to trust that the person who did this won't hurt anyone else. That will help them heal their loss more than a standard vengeance deal, and it might flavor their soul better than the temporary satisfaction they get from you murdering the person who wronged them."

"I could almost believe you if I actually thought Jimena could change. Can you actually promise me he won't kill again?"

"I can't. I'm actually quite concerned about how many people he may have killed while I've been gone, but that's not a bad thing for you. Every time he kills, that's another family you can make a revenge deal with."

"That's a sick system."

"But a profitable one for you, isn't it?"

"And how it is benefitting you? You're making a lot of sacrifices for one human, Nicodemus."

"I love him." I couldn't believe my confession was to her, and not Jimena. My first confession where I truly meant it, at least. "And he's the first human, demon, first anything to make me feel loved. So, make this deal with me, Arimathea, and let him live. Please."

Kidnapper

The boat had a clear bottom. Because, of course, it did. I swallowed in my all too dry mouth and looked at the various fish swimming beneath us, the seats arranged around the glass floor in the center of the boat. Some tour guide rambled about the various plants and aquatic life we were observing. I glanced at my mother sitting across from me and next to her father, poised like a proud crow shining in her glory. At least my suicide attempt had worked out well for her. I slouched back and looked at the cloth canopy above us because I figured it was best if I wasn't the one who spotted the corpses, nor did I want to get caught seeing a corpse but not mentioning it.

Uncle Wade slouched with me, bumping his shoulder into mine. "You should have been allowed to stay back and get some rest. You had a rough night."

"I'm glad someone realizes that." I looked at the bright-eyed tourists surrounding us, only a handful from our family. "If anything, we should be part of the search for Stephie." Most of the family had canceled their plans to either join in search parties or comfort the immediate family. It wasn't like we were the only family members to proceed with events, but still… if they knew what I did, they sure wouldn't be doing anything fun.

We'd spoken quiet enough that I knew my mother and grandfather hadn't heard us, but her prying eyes told me she was annoyed at how little I seemed to be enjoying myself. I pointed at my arm and winced, using it as my reason for my foul mood. The numbing agents they'd used had worn off, increasing my crankiness about being forced on this boat.

"Did you want to take something," Uncle Wade offered.

"They don't give drugs to suicide patients," I said. "They're worried I'll overdose on them."

"But you can take over the counter stuff." He pulled out a bottle of some generic anti-inflammatory pills from his pocket.

"Did you pay the outrageous prices in the resort gift shop to buy that?"

"I figured you would need it." He didn't seem deterred by my comment. If only he knew I had an arsenal of drugs that would very much take away my pain, far more than those little pills he offered.

"There's no need to suffer."

I couldn't take my drugs. I needed to stay alert for another demon attack or a corpse-sighting, but what he was holding wouldn't dull my senses. I doubted it would help the pain much either, but it would make Uncle Wade feel a sense of purpose, which it seemed he desperately needed.

I held my hand out, and he shook two pills into my palm. I popped them in my mouth before remembering how thirsty I was. My mother tapped my knee with her water bottle, a true nurturer coming to the rescue yet again. I forced a smile and took it, downing the pills in two swallows and then giving the bottle back.

We were an hour into the stupid boat ride, and I was beginning to think we'd end up in the ocean before the tour ended when the shrill scream came. I wished it was a shark. I wished it was a toddler who had fallen overboard. But I knew what it would be before anyone recovered enough to speak coherent words.

Kidnapper

We sat on the beach, not one intended for tourists. The sand was a dirty color and scattered about was debris washed up from the river. Today, a good dozen of us tourists were disrupting this otherwise secluded area because the police would not let us leave until each of us was interviewed.

I glimpsed Stephie's parents coming down the impromptu made path from the nearest street, proceeding to where their daughter's body lay. I didn't understand why they would want to identify it here or even want to see the body. But I supposed that was part of what was wrong with me. I sat on a washed-up log and pressed my fisted hands into my temples. How had the therapists phrased it? "Emotionally underdeveloped. May never express himself properly or empathize with others. Seems to mirror the habits of others so he can pretend to be like them."

How the hell was I supposed to be reacting in this situation?

"You must be overloaded, huh?" Uncle Wade asked. I covered my eyes so he wouldn't see the annoyed eyeroll as I resisted telling him that I was the only person here who wasn't an emotional mess because I didn't give a shit about the dead bodies or the people who were affected by it.

"Your boyfriend ran off, you tried to kill yourself, and now your cousin is…" He choked up, and I bit my lip to keep from laughing. This was hell. The demons had actually killed me, and this was hell.

A shadow covered the patch of sand I was viewing. I couldn't see who was casting it since I kept my hands up to shield most of those around us from seeing my face.

"Jimena, why don't you come with me." My mother pulled on my arm and got me up. I dropped my hands, forcing a blank expression on my face. She guided me to an area no one else was. "I know you don't handle situations like this well." She had read the reports from the therapists.

"That's a nice way of putting it," I said drolly, already knowing my tone was wrong.

"Stay over here, away from the others. I'll keep Uncle Wade away." She pushed me to lean against a tree. "I'll get you when the police are ready for your statement."

"Thanks." Isolation was probably best. I rubbed my back against the tree to get some kinks out and felt the pellet gun. *Fuck!* I had the damn weapon that had been used to murder Stephie and her dad still on my body, and there were dozens of cops around. I needed to ditch it. Right? No? What if they saw it on me? Would they be searching all of us? Why would they? We'd found the body, but the murder hadn't happened here. It also wouldn't make sense to toss the gun here unless I was aiming for them to believe the gun had washed up in the same place as the bodies.

But if I ditched the gun, I would have no protection against more demons, other than the knife, because the hospital, thankfully, hadn't checked me for weapons. Damn it all. I really needed Nic to come back. Why wasn't he back? I grabbed my phone.

No messages.

A man staggered through the brush and promptly vomited a few feet from me. I stared at him as he wiped his mouth and took a few deep breaths. He looked remarkably like the man I'd murdered last night.

"I just had to identify my brother's body," the man said, staring out at the river, but I assumed he was speaking to me since I was the only person nearby. "I never thought I'd have to do that."

What was an appropriate thing to say? Sorry for your loss? I knew if I said it, my inflection would be wrong, and I'd sound like a sarcastic ass, so I opted for silence. He was a complete stranger. I didn't have to comfort him just because he'd randomly chosen me as his confidant.

"You were on the boat, right? That found them?" He looked at me, and I wished there was some telltale means to verify if a person was a demon. Could demons have normal human brothers?

"Yes," I replied, cause how could I say that wrong. "I'm also related to the girl." Why had I added that last bit? Why? I clamped my mouth shut as he continued to stare at me.

"The girl. *That girl* is my niece. Someone murdered my brother and his little girl."

Shit, was it inappropriate to say girl instead of her name? I'd said it like she was no more than a flower I'd once seen in a garden. But really, I'd never spoken to her until the night she tried to kill me, so how sad was I supposed to be about all this?

"What's your name?"

"We should probably be with the others," I said. I turned to go back but noticed no one was in view, not from this little shrub area of privacy my mother had tucked me away in. He grabbed my arm, and I reached without thinking. I grabbed the pellet gun, already loaded—because, you know, everyone was trying to murder me lately—put it to his eye and pulled the trigger. The eye had worked well last time.

He didn't even get a scream out. There was a brief shimmer of black smoke, then it went back in him and his body collapsed. The river had swallowed the sound of the gun, so no one came running, but it wasn't like I could just gently push his body into the river and be like, "Oh, look guys, there's another one." Even the worst of detectives would piece together what I'd done.

There was no hiding the body or concealing that I'd murdered him.

"It is not my fucking day," I muttered. I took the remaining pellets from my pocket and stuffed them in his pockets, all but one, which I loaded in the gun, because claims of self-defense worked better if there are signs of a struggle, and the victim is injured.

I aimed the pistol at the top of my foot because it would make sense for me to have pushed his arms down when he first tried to shoot me. And odds were, the damage on the top of my foot would heal. I should still be able to walk and everything. It would bruise me through the shoe, at worst.

I stifled the scream as the pain hit me, far sharper than I'd expected. I limped to his body and wrapped his hand around it, hoping to God that statistics were on my side, and he was right-handed. He *had* grabbed my shoulder with his right hand, so *hopefully*.

After I felt there was an ample amount of his fingerprints on the weapon, I kicked the leaves and sticks around us, so it would seem like a scuffle had happened. I imagined the fight, playing out.

> *He'd grabbed my shoulder. I turned, saw the gun, pushed it down, and he fired. We grappled, likely on the ground.* Yes, it would make sense to fall. *We separated, he reloaded, I kicked and tripped him, then he dropped the gun...* I dropped it and kicked

some dirt on it so it would be dirty. *Then, I picked it up and shot him, while he...* Hmm... *While he was distracted because I'd thrown sand at his face.* I threw some at him to make it plausible.

It was a weak story, but hopefully he had some kind of record, and the cops wouldn't look too deeply into it.

Now, for the performance of my life. I needed to convince everyone, including all the police, that this man had murdered his brother and niece, then tried to kill me. I didn't have motive. Fuck motive. I couldn't do all the work for the cops. They'd have to figure that out on their own. It wasn't my job to know why he'd assaulted me, just that he had.

I kneeled, took a deep breath, and slammed my fist against the fresh bruise on my foot, allowing myself to scream in conjunction with the pain this time. I dropped the gun because, fuck no, I did not want to be holding that when the police came, and I continued wailing. Even managed a few crocodile tears as police rushed to the area.

"He attacked me, he attacked me," I repeated, aiming for shock since that was a state people often reacted emotionally incorrect in.

Kidnapped

The amount of police was unsettling. It felt wrong to be entering the area, but all the same, I knew if I waited for Jimena to return to the hotel, he would be even more furious at how long we'd been apart.

Yellow police tape was up in some areas, while others merely had a flag to indicate something of interest. I avoided those areas as best I could and stuck to the path I saw other people using. Arimathea stayed a few feet behind me, seeming more at ease than me.

"I suppose that's to be expected," I muttered.

"What?"

"You likely frequent scenes like this all the time, to scout for mourning humans who wish to make a deal of vengeance."

She sneered. "I was just thinking I might be able to pick up a new job while we're here. I wonder who died."

"I doubt anyone died. Someone probably fell overboard or—" I choked on my words as we reached the clearing near the beach and saw two body bags, the coroners sealing them shut as two officers prepared to lift them.

"Or you could be double wrong," Arimathea said.

"Excuse me," a youthful officer approached. "You can't be here."

"I'm part of the tourist group that was on the boat," I said. "I heard they got stopped here." The impact didn't sound strong enough if I said boyfriend, so I opted to exaggerate. "My fiancé is part of the group. Please, I need to see him."

The man, likely only a cadet, seemed convinced of the importance. He nodded but added, "Nothing is public, so no posting about what you see on social media."

I walked through the brush until I started recognizing people from Jimena's family. We neared the beach where the water rippled and made what would have been peaceful noises on any other day when I spotted Jimena. He sat on a collapsible chair as a medic prodded his exposed foot, which had a visible lump on it, already swollen and purple. My eyes also caught a glimpse of the white gauze wrapped around his entire forearm as a second medic took his blood pressure. His long-sleeved shirt rolled up past his elbows as he prattled, giving pointed answers to an officer who had his notepad open.

I'd assumed he would come through the night unscathed, and it horrified me to see he'd been harmed. I'd allowed this. I'd used him as bait to win the bet, and he'd gotten hurt.

Jimena's eyes caught mine, and for a moment, I thought he looked excited, perhaps even happy to see me. Then some twigs crunched behind me as Arimathea stepped closer. Jimena's eyes went to her, and his entire face contorted with restrained rage.

I shouldn't have let her come with me. I'd forgotten how jealous he could be of both men and women, and Arimathea was an attractive woman, even if she dressed like an average, middle-aged soccer mom.

"Can you give us a minute?" Jimena asked, hugging the blanket around his shoulders a bit tighter. The officer and paramedic glanced at me, unsure if they should obey.

"I'm his fiancé," I said. "I just arrived. I was away last night."

The officer flipped his notepad closed. "We'll need a statement from you before you leave the area." He looked down at Jimena. "Thank you for your cooperation."

"Anytime," Jimena said, his tone laced with annoyance, but I doubted a stranger would notice it.

I dropped to my knees in front of him. "They hurt you." My eyes went to the concealed wound, and I wondered how bad it was.

Jimena kept his eyes on the people around us, waiting until he was confident no one was close enough to hear him. "I did this to myself."

"Don't say that. If this is anyone's fault, it's mine. I made a stupid deal and put you in danger."

"No. I literally did this. I cut my arm and shot my foot. No one hurt me."

I put my hands on his thighs, worried that after I spoke, he might never let me touch him again. "The Domenichini clan wanted to kill you as my punishment for making the deal with your cousin, so I made a deal with them." I looked at his face, but it indicated nothing of how he felt. "I used their pride against them. I told them they wouldn't be able to kill you by dawn and that if they failed, I would gain rights to your entire family."

"I've been getting attacked by demons all night because you bet them that they wouldn't be able to kill me? You couldn't even be bothered to warn me?"

"It wasn't allowed. They had me confined all night."

"Whatever. They didn't try very hard." Jimena rubbed his bandaged arm. "I killed three of them. The girl came last night. I was waiting and picked her off quick, but there was a lot of blood, so I had to do this to explain it. No one would question blood in our room if it was mine." He used his finger to trace where he'd cut. "I told them it was a suicide attempt. The girl's dad found me when I was ditching the body, so I dumped them both in this river. Then I solidified my alibi in the hospital ER, which was fine and dandy until my grandfather insisted I go on this tour boat, which happened to be on the same river I ditched the bodies. The father's brother came to identify the body, realized who I was, so I killed him and shot my foot so it would look like self-defense."

"Shit," Arimathea said, her voice a bit in awe.

"Who exactly are you?" Jimena said, squinting at her.

"She's a revenge demon hired to kill you by the family of the woman you murdered and buried in your flower garden. You might recall me showing you her missing poster."

"Huh." There was no emotion in his voice, just exhaustion. "I'm not sure I can kill two people on this beach and keep the police convinced it's self-defense."

"You don't have to kill her. I made a deal with her."

His eyes went from her to mine, moving sluggishly. "Did you fuck her?"

Arimathea barked a laugh.

"No," I said. "She's agreed to give the family closure by a means other than your death. In exchange, we're going to give her a list of everyone you've murdered, the ones you can remember or have access to. She'll be able to go make deals with those families and offer them closure by telling them how their loved ones died."

"And she feeds on their souls in exchange for giving them answers and vengeance?"

"She feeds on the grieving families, yes."

"Nothing tastes better than the sharp pain of loss," Arimathea said. "Except the glimmer of hope a someone gets when they find out their loved one was avenged."

"I'm not sure I want to do this."

"She kills you and gets to collect one soul, or she lets you live and collects dozens."

"Or we kill her."

I considered trying to convince him that she wasn't as easy to murder as the three laying on the beach, but I worried his pride might have taken it as a dare. "I'd prefer you didn't."

"About time you showed up!" Uncle Wade stomped toward us, his footsteps exaggerated as he waded through the brush. "Do you have any idea the misery you've caused Jimena?"

I straightened to standing to remind Wade I was taller. "I had a family emergency."

"Her?" Wade looked at the woman.

"Why does everyone think we've been fucking?" Arimathea asked.

"Perhaps it would be best if you left," I said. "I'll contact you when we return to Jimena's house."

"Dolly Walters," Jimena said. "If you want to be proactive." He shrugged. "Might be useful to look into her."

"A good faith gesture. I like it." She bumped into Wade as she passed him in an accidental yet intentional manner.

"Thin ice." Wade waggled a finger at me.

"Uncle Wade and I have been bonding," Jimena explained.

"I should give the police my statement." I touched his shoulder. "Then, I'll see if I can take you back to the resort."

CHAPTER fifteen

Kidnapper

The foot hurt more than I expected. Every movement triggered a fresh rush of agony that lanced from the swollen knot down through my foot. A wiggle of a toe, the effort of lifting it, no matter how gentle I was in my efforts to walk, every step was hell. The indignity of using crutches or being wheeled off in the ambulance wasn't something I'd tolerate. I leaned on Nic as I finished convincing everyone to let Nic take me back to the resort. A few agonizing steps later, I concluded that it hurt whether I kept the foot elevated and hopped or simply walked on it normally. It was the jostle that caused the pain, and any method of walking would bother it.

I pushed Nic away and walked with the goal of speed, wanting to get it over with.

"Did you bring a car here?"

"No."

I turned and glared at him. Was his goal to infuriate me as much as possible? "Then why did you say you could give me a ride back?"

"I can get you to the resort. Close your eyes."

"Why would I do that?" I wanted nothing more than to be off this beach, and now the inside of the ambulance looked appealing. We'd only made it halfway to the road, a good thirty yards from the river's edge, and

I wasn't sure I could make it the rest of the way. Of course, turning back was the same distance as going forward, except there wasn't a damn car waiting for me like I'd thought.

"It's less jarring if your eyes are closed." He lifted a hand to brush over my face, like he thought he could close my eyes for me. I swatted at him and instinctively closed my eyes as his other hand swooped in toward my face.

When I opened them, the world had changed. We stood inside the hotel room, near the entrance door. My stomach lurched, and I probably would have hurled if the following stagger hadn't sent a jolt of pain so intense the queasiness was forgotten.

Nic moved to steady me, and I pushed him away, using the wall to support me instead. I hobbled the few steps to the bathroom so I could see my reflection and verify he'd reassembled me properly.

"You can teleport other people." I touched my face and pulled at my cheeks as I inspected my reflection.

"We don't do it commonly, but we can. Will you let me look at your wounds?"

"My mother wants to change the dressing on my arm." I hugged it close to my chest. "I don't want you to heal me. I can't let anyone think I faked the injuries."

"Because your wounds are your alibis." He stepped closer, and I could sense his hesitation as he neared. I'd pushed him away enough times he wasn't certain if he should try to touch me.

"I'm tired. I didn't get any sleep."

"I can help with that."

"I want a shower and sleep." I rubbed at my face, knowing all my aches would be worse tomorrow.

"I can help with that too." He slipped a hand under my shirt and kissed my neck as he pressed his body against my back.

"I said I'm tired." I elbowed him to get him to step back and heard him utter a sigh as he detached.

"Let me help you get undressed and showered," he clarified. "It will be hard to keep your bandaged arm dry if you do it alone."

I barely had time to nod before he'd lifted me to sit on the counter, somehow slipping my underwear and pants off in the same movement. I uttered a growl of protest as he slipped the shoe off my bruised foot, then nearly kicked him as he bumped the wound again while getting my pants off. I lifted my arms, and he slipped my shirt off, leaving me to sit completely naked.

"Don't pick me up again," I said. "I can walk to the shower myself."

"I think a bath would be easier." He went to the tub and started filling it as I carefully got down and limped to it. He hovered near me as I stepped in, acting as if I was elderly and might topple at any moment.

The warmth of the tub encompassed me as I slid down into the water. Nic got a washcloth and began using it to bathe me, which was fine until his hand went to my groin.

"Stop it." I splashed the water as I moved from him. "I'm far too angry at you to want to do something like that."

"I'm not asking you to pleasure me back."

"Do you not understand how not in the mood I am? You gambled with my life. I am allowed to be upset at you for however long I want."

"That bet kept you alive. They would have hunted you until you died if I hadn't—"

"They wouldn't have hunted me at all if it weren't for you."

He pulled his hand out of the water, starting to look a bit annoyed himself.

"How do you want to fix this then? Do you want me to leave?"

"I want to punish you. I want to hurt you. But I'm not allowed, am I?"

"You don't think what you're doing now is hurting me? How is this not punishment?"

I crinkled my face at him, hoping it portrayed my disgust. "Emotional pain? Don't be so dramatic. It's not the same as when I actually hurt you physically."

"I daresay it cuts deeper, but the concept seems lost on you." He tightened his grip on the side of the tub. "Where is the lead you brought that you promised you wouldn't?"

"I didn't bring it. I mailed it to myself in case I needed it. Which I did. I'd be dead otherwise. My lead-coated knife is in the holster you took off my ankle."

He got up and rummaged in the pile of clothing until he found it. He held it carefully by the handle, which was not coated. He placed it on the edge of the tub and held his hand out, the one that had a scar in the center from before.

"Stab me again with it to punish me. By all accounts, it should still be an unhealed wound anyway, so…" He kneeled by the tub with his hand offered as a sacrifice. I was tempted to grab the knife and stab him somewhere else, but a new wound on him would be difficult to explain to my family.

"Why would you let me use this on you? You said of all things, this was something you didn't want me to do anymore."

"I'd rather suffer a flesh wound than endure your anger. If you do this, you might forgive me, and we can move on."

I started getting hard as I thought of stabbing him and twisting the knife until he screamed. I picked up the blade and turned it around in my fingers.

"Can I fuck you after?" I asked.

His eyes went to my full erection, very poorly hidden by the clear water.

"Yes."

"Then get your clothes off."

He did so with remarkable speed, and my desire only grew. He wanted my dick in him so badly he was rushing to be punished. To be cut and hurt by me simply so he could have the reward at the end.

I felt something then, something that terrified me a bit.

I was starting to wonder if he was in this for more than simply a good-tasting meal. What if he actually did want me? Love me?

Kidnapped

My hand burned anew, like it had the first time he'd stabbed me. I washed it over the sink, unable to think of anything else to do. I would need Arimathea to bring me some of those vitamins she'd suggested last time.

I wrapped my hand in the hotel handcloth and walked to the bedroom where Jimena had finished dressing. He picked at the damp wrap around his arm but hadn't removed it because he was adamant about not letting me see the wound.

A sharp knock came on the door, and Uncle Wade's voice followed it.

"You boys decent? I have your mom out here. She wants to help you change the bandage on your arm."

I was not. I'd showered but hadn't dressed. I pushed past the pain and focused on pulling on some boxers and shorts, getting them on just as the door opened. I sat and tried to fold my arms in a manner that would conceal the fact my hand wound was fresh instead of over a week old. But in my rush to dress, the cloth came undone, and when I rewrapped it, fresh blood showed on it, completely visible as Wade and Marissa entered.

Her eyes went directly to me, as if she had a special radar for detecting fresh wounds.

"You're bleeding." She was cradling my hand before I could blink. I glanced at Jimena, uncertain if he would find her attention toward me something to be jealous of since she was here to fix his bandage, not mine.

"Guess he didn't listen to all that advice you've been giving," Jimena said. "It reopened when he was helping me shower."

"I'll help you clean and bandage it. Then, I'll do yours, Jimena." She tugged on my arm so I would get up and follow her to the bathroom. "Wade?"

"I put your kit in the bathroom, Madam," Uncle Wade said, sounding far too proud that he was helping. I felt as if I'd missed some vital bonding moment that had occurred in my absence.

She put my hand under the running water, then dosed it in alcohol.

"Did you want me to help?" Jimena asked, loitering in the doorway.

"Sit on the bed. Shoo!" She pushed him away and shut the door. I glanced over in time to see her also lock it. She inspected my hand carefully before she started to wrap it in gauze. "He hurts you, doesn't he?"

She didn't look at me when she said it.

"I believe we've had this discussion before," I said, my voice firm.

"Yes." Now she looked at me, her eyes as stern as my tone had been. "In this exact same circumstance as well. Tell me, Nic, how many times will I find myself cleaning the wounds my son inflicts upon you?"

"You overstep," I warned. "It is not your place to judge, and if you insist, then I'd rather you not help at all."

Her expression softened slightly. "I only speak because I do not think you deserve it, and I fear—"

"Fear for yourself, not me." I pulled my hand away, the gauze not yet fastened in place. I unlocked the door and stepped out. "Your turn."

I grabbed my phone and left the room, not realizing I'd forgotten a shirt and the room key until I'd already stepped outside on the shared balcony at the end of the hall. I sank into one of the chairs arranged around a few tables that overlooked the pool below.

I texted Arimathea to bring me a few things, then closed my eyes and lightly napped while I waited.

"Is this going to be a common thing?" Arimathea asked. I opened my eyes to see her cardigan-wearing self standing there, a small bag sitting on the table in front of me. "Calcium and iron supplement, plus more deferasirox."

I opened the bag and dumped out the bottle but realized I couldn't open the twist tops with one hand. She slammed a water bottle down and began opening them for me.

"Just so you know, I'm not going to keep doing this. Being a caretaker isn't my thing." She cracked the seal on the bottle of water last, then sat across from me. "I did look into the name Jimena gave me. Dolly Walters. She did go missing. Never found."

"Is that your way of saying you're appreciative of the deal we made?" I popped several of the pills into my mouth and drank the water.

"I suppose, although I'm not sure you should be. Are you certain you don't want to change the terms of our deal? Wouldn't you be better off if he's dead?"

"You think I did all this so he could die?"

"He poisoned you with lead. Twice. He murdered three demons. You can't be so ignorant as to think he won't someday kill you."

I couldn't tell her he already had, and no amount of denial kept the thought away that teaching him how to kill a demon was the worst mistake I'd ever made. I knew my death would come at his hands, but the pity in Arimathea's eyes as I realized she knew it too was nearly too much to bear.

"You do know," she said, "and you stay anyway. Well, when it happens, I'll avenge you."

"No."

Her laugh was a sharp bark. "This isn't a deal. You can't stop what I'll do once you're dead. Perhaps you don't cherish your life much, but I think the world will be worse without you in it. So, I'll avenge you when you're gone."

"You'll not kill him. That's part of our original deal."

"Did I say I'd kill him?" She got up and pushed the chair under the table, its legs screeching the entire way. "See you around." She paused and added. "Hopefully." Her body drifted away in a cloud of black smoke that vanished after a few seconds. I stayed outside until I was confident the mix of vitamins I'd put in my empty stomach wasn't going to make me throw up.

I knocked on the hotel room door, and Jimena answered, scowling at me and looking a bit like he wanted to slap me.

"I needed some fresh air." I walked in, needing to bump his shoulder to get past. "Weren't you going to bed early? I thought you were tired."

"I was worried you weren't coming back. What did my mother say to you?"

I passed Uncle Wade's bed and saw him preparing his sleep mask.

"Nothing important," I said. "Looks like we are all turning in early." I flopped down on one of the chairs and closed my eyes.

"Why are you sitting there?"

"I'm sleeping here. I wouldn't want to accidently bump into one of your wounds during the night."

I was certain he disliked this response, but I kept my eyes firmly closed. The aggressive noises he made as he opened drawers and pulled the sheets back were more than enough to confirm his displeasure.

Kidnapper

I opened my eyes but didn't believe what I was looking at. Stephie was standing next to my bed, shrouded in darkness, holding a gun this time. Her incredibly not-dead figure looked coldly at me while my eyes focused on the barrel of the gun, a weapon that seemed far too large for her petite child hands.

"How does it feel to kill an innocent little girl? I'm the first kid you've ever murdered. It's not the same, is it?"

"You're a demon, not innocent."

"Are you really sure of that? Does being a demon mean I'm evil? You don't seem to think Nic is evil."

"You were going to kill me."

"I still am." She fired the gun. My entire body reacted, and I screamed, jumped, and… woke up. I was drenched in sweat. My heart raced. The scream—real only in my dream—stifled me as I gasped for air. The room was dark. Nic slumped in a chair by himself against the wall opposite the bed. My uncle snored lightly under his CPAP. I was alone aside from them but still didn't feel safe. I eyed my suitcase with the lead-coated blanket hidden inside, wanting to cover myself in it.

I wasn't feeling guilty for murdering a kid. I refused to believe that. But it was the first time I'd killed someone in self-defense. And I'd done it three times in a row. I was paranoid more people were going to try to kill me. I'd never been the one hunted before. I didn't like it, and I didn't know how to feel safe again.

When I'd woken in my basement and seen the bulb above me, I had wondered if the people I'd kidnapped had felt like I had that morning. Confused and alone. I knew now that I had been wrong. This is how they'd felt. Powerless, paranoid, and filled with a knowing that they'd never be safe again. Safety and confidence are what I had taken from them, but at least I'd had the decency of ending their life shortly after, so they weren't stuck living in this horrid state for long.

I clicked on the lamp, and its beams chased away all the demons that might've been hidden in the shadows. I sat there a moment, uncertain what to do. Neither of my hotel mates had woken, and I realized if they did wake, I'd have to explain my newfound fear of… well, I wasn't quite certain of what. I certainly wasn't scared of the dark. I clicked the lamp back off to prove it to myself.

I snatched up my room keycard and cellphone, pulled on my pants, and slipped into my sneakers. I gently opened the door, being careful even though logic told me if the lamp hadn't woken them, the light from the hall or sound of the door wouldn't rouse them either.

I stepped into the hall with no actual plans. I simply knew I couldn't sit still, I needed to move, maybe pace in the hall, something. I ended up on the balcony at the end of the hallway. I leaned over the railing and peered down at the empty pool, still aglow with underwater lights. There weren't any party goers at this hour, plus the search party endeavors had likely soured the mood of most vacationers.

"I don't care," Sandy shouted into her cellphone as she walked onto the balcony. I shrunk to the side, hoping to not be noticed. "Pack up your bags and be gone before I come back."

Her eyes went to mine. There was a jolt of shock behind them. I didn't dare begin to guess at why. She dropped the phone from her face and smashed the screen, likely to disconnect the call.

"Sorry," she said. "I'm having a bad night." She glanced around. "Where is your boyfriend?"

"Where is your gaggle of girlfriends?" I couldn't believe the words had come out of me. I really did need sleep. She looked a bit thrown by the question, then huffed and leaned on the railing, an exact copy of what I'd done moments ago.

"I found out one of them has been sleeping with my live-in boyfriend. So, I told her to get out of our hotel room. The room I paid for. And I told him to pack his bags and be gone before I get back." She swayed a bit, leaning over the rail and then back, as if debating a jump. "I guess we are all having shit vacations." She glanced at me. "Someone in your party went missing, right? The little girl?"

"Yeah, yeah, that was my group."

"At least the person who took her was found, right? And he got what he deserved. At least, so says the news."

Did she not know I'd been the one to kill him? It would be nice if the news kept that bit out of the report. Maybe Grandpa had pulled some political favors to keep it that way.

"I should get back," I said. "You came out here for peace, not to see me."

"Yeah, but…" She moved to block the exit. "I could use the distraction. I can't go back to my room until she is gone unless I want to face a murder charge." She barked a laugh that I couldn't share. When I didn't react in a way that told her I understood what she wanted, she continued. "Maybe I could come back to your room. Your boyfriend is there, right?"

"He is, yes."

"Cool." She brushed her fingers through her hair in that unconscious way women do when they are grooming themselves to impress someone.

I pushed the thought down, refusing to let the ugly head of jealousy creep into my thoughts. *Tell her he is sleeping or drunk.* I just needed to say something to let her know she should abandon these efforts.

"Do you guys, like…" She shuffled from foot to foot and gave her eyelashes a quick flutter. "Have an open relationship?"

"You like Nic." Why did I say it? Why did I need to make it undeniable?

She nodded. "I mean, I'll do you too. We can do a threesome. Just something to piss off my boyfriend so I can say, hey, I fucked someone too, you know?"

"Yeah, I know." I thought of how she'd swayed over the railing moments ago. "You know there's another way to get your revenge, right?"

No one would tie me to it. If she fell over that railing, into that pool, no one would suspect murder, not after the recent events in her life.

Kidnapper

I slipped back into the room, leaving the lights off and closing the door as quietly as possible. At least the encounter with Sandy had distracted me enough that I should fall asleep without my fears keeping me awake, or so I hoped. I kicked my shoes off and walked the memorized route to the bed. My eyes adjusted to the darkness as I passed Nic slumbering in the chair. I glanced at his perfect and handsome face, my thoughts dwelling on the fact that I would be enduring the advances of others desiring him my entire life, or his entire life.

Things would be easier if everyone else found him ugly and undesirable. If he was more limited in his dating options, I would feel more secure that he would stay with me forever. I stood there, tussling with the desire. I'd tried to cut him before, and it hadn't stuck. But now I knew the method that would scar him. I went to the bed and wrapped my fingers around the knife.

I stood next to him, turning the knife around in my hand as I imagined all the ways I could cut him. Across his eye, straight down, or an X on his cheek. Perhaps an array of dizzying marks all over like he'd been mauled by a bear.

I rubbed my crotch as I thought of it, becoming painfully hard as I imagined the blood pouring from his face. I'd keep the wounds fresh and open, making them heal slowly so they'd scar worse.

I leaned closer, my breath stirring his hair that fell across his forehead. I wanted to do it. I needed to do this for us. For the health of our relationship to keep the greedy Sandys and Suzies away.

But no matter how convincing my reasons were, my hand wasn't cutting him. He wouldn't want me to. He didn't want me to cut him with the lead. It made him sick, and if I wanted him to stay with me, I needed to obey that one rule. If no others, I needed to obey him in that one regard, and I knew it. I repeated it to myself, reminding myself of how much it had hurt when he'd left me, but I still wasn't backing away.

"I'm so sorry." I couldn't change. I lifted the knife and his eyes opened, darting from the blade to me, and I froze. In his eyes, I saw the terror I'd felt when I'd awoken from my nightmare, and I realized what I'd done.

Nic was still living the hell of paranoia that I'd only begun to experience. I'd taken his veil of safety and destroyed it, and only now did I realize how terrible that was. I tasted bile at my repulsion regarding what I'd nearly done. How he must feel about me. I stepped back, dropping the knife, and trying to think of a way to explain this that would hide the truth.

I wasn't an idiot. He would never believe that I'd just had a revelation. Not after so many broken promises.

"I wasn't going to," I said, knowing full well he was aware of my intention. "I'm allowed to think about it, aren't I? I wasn't going to do it. I swear."

I saw the fear give way to something else in his eyes, a resignation, the look of someone giving up. I dropped to my knees.

"I'm on edge. I was hunted last night. That's all. I don't want to hurt you."

"Says the man who wanted nothing more than to hurt me hours ago," Nic said, his words laced in a tone that gave me an idea of what he meant when he'd said my words hurt him. "I thought I could do this. I thought you could change, but you truly can't, can you? If I stay with you, this will be my life. Living in fear of the next moment you will hurt me until you finally kill me."

"No. No, I can, we can do it like last night. I'll only hurt you when I have your permission. This moment, it's a misunderstanding."

"Everyone has been telling me this is unhealthy and that I should leave you." He stood up, and I didn't have the energy to rise and stop him. I knew I couldn't stop him. "I'm tired of being blind to what you are just because I've been an idiot and fallen in love with you."

What? The words got me to my feet, and I reached the hotel door just as he slipped out it.

"Nic, I do understand. I—"

"Your family will still have my protection, but we are done. I'm sorry." He turned and looked at me. His expression confused me. I couldn't understand it, and I hated that I couldn't. So, I guessed. I took the best damn stab at what he was experiencing that I could think of.

"Leaving me, it hurts you. It hurts you more than staying, so don't do it. Stay. Please, stay."

A sneer came across his face, and he grabbed my shirt, yanking me close to him as he spoke into my ear.

"It doesn't hurt you though, does it? It doesn't hurt you like it does me. You don't love me like I love you. You lust for me, you desire me, but you don't know what love is." He pushed me away as he released me. "The next time we see each other, one of us will die. So, do not come looking for me unless that is your intent."

"Nic, no." Those were the only words I could get out before he vanished, turning into black mist that dissipated into nothing. "I do love you. This does... hurt."

I fell to my knees again. I sat there for a long while, eventually realizing I'd left my damn keycard and cellphone in the hotel room, and I'd need to wake Uncle Wade in order to get back inside.

CHAPTER sixteen

Kidnapper

I sat at the breakfast table, barely aware of my surroundings and the conversations around me. A hand clasped my shoulder and squeezed. The contact broke me from my misery, and I turned my head to look at my brother.

"I'm sorry he left you," Paul said. "And he's an ass for doing it at a time like this. After everything you've been through over the last few days."

"Do you think I'm not at fault for this?" I scooted my chair away. It made a loud screech on the floor, and everyone at the table paused to stare at us. "I fucked it up. I'm…" I buried my face in my hands, wishing I could claw my face off. I was so annoyed at everyone, at everything, and I'd never turned to self-harm before, but having done it twice yesterday, it was becoming a habit. I had to admit the pain was a nice distraction from the internal anguish Nic had caused.

I dropped my hands and spoke dryly. "He was right to leave."

"He could have still waited another day," my mother said, dropping her fork so she could cross her arms and pout properly.

"You're worried our break-up will affect the outcome of which branch of the family Grandpa favors this year?" I pointed my entire arm, the dramatic one with stitches, at the table that was completely empty aside from a few random cousins I didn't know. "You don't think the family who lost a child this weekend is going to win? No matter what the rest of us do? Don't look at me like that. I'm saying what you're all thinking."

I refocused my efforts on eating, not that I was hungry, but it was something to do to keep me from opening my mouth again.

Trish approached the center of the ballroom and rang a bell to get everyone's attention. Grandpa walked up to stand next to her. Despite the early hour of the day and the fact nearly everyone was dressed in black mourning the death of Stephie, he wore a bright red suit. It was overly flamboyant, and at that moment, I wanted nothing more than to murder him. Right there in front of everyone. Fuck the consequences.

"I want to thank you all for attending my birthday celebration this year," Grandpa began. "Due to the unforeseen events our family has endured the last few days, we will be ending the celebrations early. However, I want to…"

I stopped listening to him. I may have needed to be there, but no amount of prodding could force me to give that man the flattery of my attention. I pulled out my phone and texted Nic for the thirtieth time that morning. He'd likely blocked my number or muted the notifications, but I was still going to keep trying.

The entire room erupted in applause, and my mother pulled on my arm. I let her raise me to my feet.

"We won. He's awarding you because of your heroism." She tugged me forward with her until I was close enough to Grampa that she could shove me the rest of the way. She quickly retreated, leaving me isolated in the center of the room with him.

"I know you aren't my blood, but this weekend you acted with a bravery that makes me proud to have you as a grandson. I'm glad you're part of this family, Jimena. I speak for everyone when I say that, and none of us want to imagine what this reunion would have been like if you hadn't come." He reached for a handshake but turned it into a hug after our hands joined. I heard him utter a sob as he clutched me.

Still trapped in the embrace, I glanced at the gathered family members. There was barely a dry eye in the lot of them. They were proud... appreciative... of my murdering someone.

This was weird, different, and gave me all the worst of ideas. Perhaps the way to winning Nic back wasn't by trying to snuff out who I was but by twisting it into something different. Something people appreciated and found useful.

As soon as I could, I wrestled myself free of the attention and slipped into the hall. I'd need a means to skip the accolades in the future, that was certain. I sagged against the nearest wall and tried to think of a way to relay my idea to Nic.

"I thought you weren't going to kill anymore. That was part of the deal." The woman's voice sent a chill up my spine. I froze and looked at her. The revenge demon.

"Who do you think I killed?" Would Nic come protect me? Was I still under his protection? Fated to only be murdered by him?

"A girl jumped off the public balcony last night. Everyone says suicide, but it stinks of you." She gave me a sniff, making me wonder if she really did have the nose of a bloodhound.

"That girl's boyfriend was cheating on her. She found out. Suicide fits."

"You sure know a lot about it."

"I was on the balcony with her."

She grabbed my shoulder, the same one Paul had grabbed. She squeezed far tighter and slammed me against the wall.

"I didn't kill her."

"You lying prick."

I quickly rambled a confession of the details of our interaction, and with every sentence, her grip on me loosened. "I was pissed off, sure, but I only suggested things. Stirred her up a bit, I didn't actually push her. Look at my arm, my foot. You think I could have pushed an unwilling woman over a waist-high railing?"

She let go and stepped back, her eyes still staring like she was trying to get a sense of how much to believe.

"Where's Nic? I want his opinion."

"He left." I rubbed my wrist. She'd been squeezing the same limb I'd cut, and now the nerves were tingling.

"When will he be back?"

"He *left*-left," I said. "For good. He said the next time we meet, one of us will… we broke up. I don't know how that effects the deal you had with him about me, but… whatever."

We stood silently. The moment was dragging on longer than appropriate, but I didn't know what more she wanted from me.

"Sometimes all people need for closure is the truth. They want to know the final moments their loved ones experienced. They want the answer to the why." She stepped closer. "You give me that, and I can let you keep living."

"Yeah, sure." I just wanted her to go away.

"Give me permission to go in your home."

"You can go in my home." I didn't have it in me to argue with her. I didn't have much choice anyway. Without Nic to heal me, I was deteriorating from my self-inflicted wounds. I couldn't very well defend myself.

"Good dog," she said, giving my head a pat. She stepped away with a sneer on her lips. "Think of this like an upgrade. You're working with a more powerful demon now."

Kidnapped

I stood on my mother's porch as I attempted to rally the internal strength to knock on her door. I was saved from having to do so by the door opening on its own. It only opened a crack. The room within was too dark for me to see inside. A voice crept out, the same that had sung me lullabies as a child and had slowly come to address me with a deadened tone of unfamiliarity.

"What do you want?"

If Jimena's harsh treatment hadn't already beaten me, I might have reacted with anger at her disregard toward her own son.

"I need a place to stay." I shoved my hands into my pockets. "Rather, a place to hide. This is the only place I can think of that he won't find me."

"Who?"

The word came out thoughtlessly. "My boyfriend."

The door shut.

"He's a human," I added. "Please, I just need a place to rest and get my head straight."

I heard locks undone, and the door opened. She looked older than I remembered, by a lot. Her hair was white and gray, mixed in swirls of chaos, crowning her wrinkles.

"I can pay you," I said. "For the sanctuary."

"If he's human, you can go to hell and hide from him."

"Shifting is hard at the moment." I raised my bandaged hand. "I have lead poisoning."

She barked a laugh. "I'm becoming intrigued. You have enough mojo to heal some of my crow's feet?"

That was her vice. The reason she'd let my demon father visit, abuse, and impregnant her for so many years. She'd been addicted to what he could do for her. The deals he could make.

"Yeah, I can do that."

"Come on in." She swung her arm wide and gestured for me to enter. I stepped across the threshold, knowing it was warded and would prevent me from shifting while inside.

"Is your boyfriend the one who poisoned you?"

"Yes."

Another barked laugh as she shut the door. "I think I'd like to meet this guy."

I glanced at her over my shoulder. "He's a serial killer."

That doubled her over in cackling laughter. She might have been my human parent, but in that moment, she looked more bewitched with evil than my father was. Once she'd regained her senses, she tapped my shoulder and walked to the kitchen.

"Come, come, you can tell me all about your lover woes over tea, and I'll tell you which laugh lines I'd like removed."

CHAPTER seventeen

Kidnapper

I pounded on the door fervently. I feared the brother had moved, and an unbelievable wave of relief hit me as he opened the door. I didn't even care about the stern expression on his face as he glowered at me.

"He doesn't live here anymore," Marcanian said. I knew that. I'd been stalking the place for the last seven months, and it was clear Nic was gone.

"I'm aware," I said.

"Let him in," a man's voice said from inside. Marc rolled his eyes and swung the door wide. I stepped through the doorway, knowing if I had any good sense, I would fear entering an apartment infested with demons, but I was here on a mission. It clouded my judgement.

Two men were on the couch, busy filling the air with a dense smoke as they puffed away on things that looked like cigars, but I doubted actually were.

"I've been curious about the human working with the revenge demon," the man said, a man I didn't know. That annoyed me a bit. Something had slipped through my research. "This is him?"

"Yeah," Marc said, his arms crossed. "This is Jimena."

The one-sided introduction didn't elude me. The man took a long puff while his couch companion didn't so much as glance at me.

"I doubt you came here simply to appease my curiosity. What can we do for you, Jimena?"

"I want to know where Nic is." My hands trembled as I said his name. I folded my arms to mimic the stance of Marc, hoping it hid my weakness. I wasn't scared of them, but I was deeply fearful of leaving here without an answer.

"You two aren't a thing anymore," Marc spat. "He doesn't want you to find him."

The man sneered.

"Oh, the forbidden love," he said, and suddenly I placed him. I did know him. He was the man who had shown up at the resort and taken Nic away for a night. The man inhaled deeply. "Ah, the sweet pure rage coming off you. What I would do for a taste."

I clenched my jaw, knowing that despite Nic refusing to see me for the better part of a year, I was still under his protection.

"When Nic wants to… not be found, he goes to his mother's house. She has placed wards on it that prevent demons from locating it or stepping foot on her property."

Marc sucked in air between his teeth, making a sharp hissing sound. "Why would you tell him that?"

Nic's father shrugged. "I'm rooting for him. Who doesn't like a good underdog story?"

My lip twitched as I resisted another impulse to strike him. At least Nic's avoidance of me meant he was also avoiding them. I hated the idea of him being around them. They repulsed me, and that was saying a lot considering my hobbies.

"Thanks." The word came out full of loathing, and I turned to leave, hiding the fact that I could do something they couldn't. I *could* find his mother.

Kidnapped

Did you really think I wouldn't find you?

His hand stroked my cheek, and even with my eyes closed, I knew who it was. His touch was etched in my memory.

But when I opened my eyes, he wasn't there. The room was empty like it always was. The room was small and filled only with the twin-sized bed that didn't even have sheets on it. I didn't know if it was my mother's means of sending a message that I shouldn't get cozy or overstay my welcome, but it always left me a bit uneasy.

Reminded me too much of that damn basement and the barbaric way Jimena had treated me. Maybe it had nothing to do with my mother. Maybe I wanted the room to stay bare so that when I woke, I would remember why I couldn't go back to him.

The him in my dreams was a fantasy.

I sat up and rubbed my forehead as the door pushed open with a gentle rapping.

"There's someone here for you," my mother said, her words not indicative of who it might be.

"Is it him?" The words tumbled out as the scene I'd imagined countless times began to play out. "He's found me?"

She shrugged. "I know he's not a demon. Aside from that, I've no idea. You never described him."

Maybe I should have. It might be good for her to see a photo. Did I have a photo? Sly fuck was good at not leaving a trace of himself. We'd gone to an amusement park and not taken a single photo together. How odd was that? How had it not even occurred to me until now?

"He's not leaving. Go down and get rid of him." She crossed her arms and peered at me. "Or would you rather I call the police? If we say this is domestic, they'll—"

"Don't call the police, fuck!" It wasn't so much I was worried Jimena would go to jail and suffer. It was more that I was worried about how high his death count would rise while incarcerated and what kind of monster he'd be once he was out on parole.

I changed my clothes quickly, hating how much I cared about how I looked. I started fussing with my hair when I realized how ridiculous I was.

We weren't together. I was going down there to tell him to fuck off. I set my jaw and went down the stairs. I didn't even bother to peep through the door. I flung it open and spat the words out before I even allowed myself to identify him.

"Fuck off!" I said. Only then did my eyes adjust to the sunlight and see the young teen standing there. He was probably still in high school, although it was hard to gauge with the medical mask concealing his face and nose.

Why had my mother thought this boy could be my lover? Did she take me for a pedophile?

"I know it's a pandemic, and people are rude as fuck these days, but seriously." He pointed at me as if he was my elder lecturing me. "Uncalled for."

"What do you want?" I bit back the onslaught of smart remarks I wanted to throw at him because he was right. I'd had no reason to be that rude.

"You're Nic?"

"Yes."

The boy raised his phone, and I heard the distinct click as he took a photo. The kid tapped the screen, and the photo whooshed away.

"Easiest fifty bucks, ever," he muttered, spinning on his heel. I stepped across the threshold of the door for the first time in months and grabbed the boy's arm. He wailed like I'd just stung him and nearly flung himself off the porch.

"Six feet, asshole! Social distancing. You aren't even wearing a mask." He gave me that derogatory glare again.

"Why did you take my photo? Who did you send it to?"

"It was an ad. Dude said to go to this house, ask for Nic, and take a pic. Bam, fifty bucks." He pointed to his phone as if to indicate he had already been paid.

Is this how Jimena was searching for me? There was a chance it wasn't him, but the churn in my stomach said otherwise. I retreated into the house and locked the door.

"Well? Was it him?"

I turned to face my mother. "He was a teenager."

"I'm not judging."

"I think Jimena hired him to see if I lived here."

"If that's true, then you should leave."

If I left, then my mother would face Jimena alone. I wasn't certain how that would go, but I couldn't risk him hurting her or using her for leverage to get to me.

"No. Let him come."

But he didn't. Two weeks passed, and he didn't show. Was this a new ploy? Turn me into a paranoid wreck? His games were driving me insane.

I was about to purchase a pre-paid phone so I could call him to ask what the hell he was playing at when my mother knocked on the bathroom door. I was spacing off in the shower, dwelling on poor life choices.

"There's another person here for you," she said. "He's an adult man this time. Gives off a real creepy vibe. It might be him."

"Don't let him inside." I turned the water off, realized I had soap in my hair, and turned it back on.

"I don't let anyone in," she huffed. "Talk to him outside on the porch."

I left my hair wet and dried the rest of me only enough to not leave footprints as I rushed down the steps. I wore only a shirt and shorts that I'd scraped off the bedroom floor. I hadn't spotted any underwear and so went without. In my wrinkled shirt, dripping hair, and bare feet, I yanked open the door.

He stood on the edge of the porch, hands in his pockets, a blue surgical mask worn improperly on his chin rather than covering his nose. His lips parted as if to say something, but my mouth engulfed his before he could. I'd completely lost my senses at the sight of him. I kissed him deeply, sucking his soul through his throat as I tasted that longing he always had for me. I ran my damp fingers through his shaggy hair and curled my toes on the chilled concrete of my mother's porch.

He'd finally come for me. I hadn't realized how much I'd missed him. I released his mouth only to trail my tongue down his jawline to his neck. I pulled him into me so I could breathe him deeply at the nape of his neck, feasting on his soul at the source.

It wasn't enough. He didn't want me enough. I slipped my hand down his pants and fondled his dick. He gasped and hiccupped at my touch. I squeezed it, pressing hard, and his entire body stiffened as he came in my hand. I tasted his ecstasy through his soul and growled. He panted against my shoulder and muttered my name.

My senses inched back, like cold fingers prodding my body. I let go of him and retreated to the socially enforced six feet. I stuck my soiled hand in my pocket and luckily found a napkin in it. I balled it in my hand to clean myself, wondering if I'd put on dirty shorts instead of clean.

"What are you doing here?" I asked.

His eyes fluttered, and he sagged against the porch pillar. His face was flushed as his chest heaved. He took the crumpled mask off his face.

"I need a minute," he said. "I wasn't expecting this kind of greeting."

I was starting to realize how dumb I'd been. What if he'd had a dagger in his pocket? He could have stabbed me when I embraced him. He could have brought others with him. I hadn't even shut the house door behind me. I turned and did so now.

"Well, you only have two minutes to tell me what you want. Then this truce ends and you need to get off the porch." Because if I let him stay longer, I knew I would touch him again.

"Can't a man have a few minutes to recover from being assaulted?" Jimena asked.

"Is that a curtesy you offer people?"

I saw his jaw clench at my words. His defenses going up as he recalled the precarious state of our relationship. Or perhaps he was merely thinking of his last victim. We hadn't seen each other in eight months. I didn't want to know how many lives he'd taken in that time.

"I haven't hurt anyone since you left me," he said, as if he could tell what I was thinking. "I've been working with that revenge demon you sent. I've recounted every victim's last moments to her and their identities. It's actually why I'm here. She's been telling the families, the loved ones of those I killed, she… Well, she makes up some story about how I'm getting what I deserved, or that I've turned over a new leaf, and I'm making amends for what I've done. Whichever version seems the most likely to put their minds at ease. And it's got me thinking that I want it to be true. I don't want her to just be telling them some tale they want to hear. I want to actually do good. I know I can't make up for everything I've done, but I can do something."

"You think I'll take you back if you become a good guy?"

"No. I have no delusions of that. You made it quite clear that we are over." His eyes darted away as he said it, both of us ignoring what had occurred between us moments ago. "I want to find people who need my help. Then do the impossible and help them. Like you used to do with your demon powers. Only, instead of feeding on the person making the wish, you would feed on me. I would fuel your power so you can help people." He straightened, getting into his full sale's pitch that had brought him here. "I want to make a deal with a demon. Preferably with you."

"That's why you're here? To make a deal?" He wasn't here to win me back? Something in my gut ached at his words. Did he no longer love me? No, love wasn't the right word. I wasn't sure he was capable of love. Desire, lust, and want were his forte, and it was enough for me. But I didn't want to be used just for my demon powers.

"No other demon will make a deal with me because you claimed me and my family. So, I either need you to make the deal or for you to release me so I can make it with someone else."

"You want to make a deal with another demon?" I shouted the words, my fear of him no longer desiring me, replaced with pure rage that he might turn that affection to another demon. "You think I'd let another demon feed on you?"

"I said I'd prefer it be you, but I didn't know if you'd agree."

"Of course, I won't agree!" I clenched my fists, and I wanted to hit him, knock him off the porch at a minimum, in the hopes it would jar some sense into him. "I don't want to make a deal with you." I settled for grabbing the scruff of his collar and pulling him so close that our noses bumped.

He looked at me with those confused eyes, and I realized he truly had no idea. I could say the words over and over and he would never be capable of comprehending them.

"I love you." I said it, knowing the meaning was lost on him. "I don't want you to be here to make a deal. I want you to come here because you miss me." I let him go, my tone softer. "You're supposed to be my stalker. You're supposed to do whatever it takes to find me and get me back." I gestured at his pockets. "Where are the drugs so you can sedate me, tie me up, and kidnap me? The knife laced with lead?"

"I don't understand." He stared at me blankly. "You said the next time we saw each other, you'd try to kill me."

"I was upset. That was a fight." I slammed him against the pillar he was near, my palm against this chest. "You can do a lot of things to me, Jimena, but you can never, never, give up on us. Do you understand that? You're my stalker. You're supposed to come here and do everything possible to win me back. You should be obsessed with—"

"You think I'm not?" He shoved me back. "I was trying to do the right thing. I thought if I couldn't force you to be with me, at least I could barter with you and have you near me. You have no idea how many scenarios I ran through my mind."

He reached into his front pocket and pulled out a plastic zippy bag.

"Pills to put in your mother's tea in case she let me inside. I figured if I poisoned her, I could blackmail you into coming back and not give you the antidote unless you agreed." He tossed the bag on the floor and pulled out a syringe. "This would paralyze you. I have another with—"

I threw my arms around him and pulled him into a hug. "I don't need to see your entire pharmacy. I'll go with you."

"You will?"

I held him at arm's length, knowing full well I did need to do a full inspection to determine he didn't have something on his person that would kill me but also knowing I would do whatever he wanted, regardless of the risk.

"Don't ever pretend you're over me again."

"Yeah, sure, sorry for pretending to not be your crazy stalker."

"It was honestly the most frightening thing you've ever done."

He rolled his eyes then frowned. "I was serious before. I would like to try to do good in the world."

"A demon and a serial killer doing good works in the world?" I grinned, not entirely against the idea. "Now, you've gone completely insane."

ABOUT THE AUTHOR

Nina Schluntz is a native to rural Nebraska. In her youth, she often wrote short stories to entertain her friends. Those ideas evolved into the novels she creates today.

Her husband continues to ensure her stories maintain a touch of realism as she delves into the science fiction and fantasy realm. Their three cats are always willing to stay up late to provide inspiration, whether it is a howl from the stray born in the backyard or an encouraging bite from the so called "calming kitten."

You can find Nina on Goodreads, Facebook, Twitter and her blog mizner13.wordpress.com.

OTHER BOOKS BY NINA R SCHLUNTZ

Surrogate for a Vampire

Mr. Perfect

Nosy Neighbors

Not a Big Deal

Kale's Paroxysm

INFLUENCE of a GOD (Gods of Earth Series Book 1)

PROPHET of a GOD (Gods of Earth Series Book 2

MUSE of a GOD (Gods of Earth Series Book 3)

ENEMY of a GOD (Gods of Earth Series Book 4)

SYMBIOTE of a GOD (Gods of Earth Series Book 5)

RESURRECTION of a GOD (Gods of Earth Series Book 6)

Dragons and Healers (Enukara book one)

Immortal Black Dragons (Enukara book two)

The First Generation (Enukara book three)

Elemental Dragon Mages (Enukara book four)

The Second Generation (Enukara book five)

Dragon Devolution (Enukara book six)

Decompose Twilight Books: Abridged Editions (prequal)

Amaranthine: Heart of Decompose (book 1)

Aurum: Screams of Decompose (book 2)

Nacreous: Shades of Decompose (book 3)

Made in the USA
Columbia, SC
20 December 2022

74597864R00159